# Barrister's Last Request

ALEX K. WARREN

authorHOUSE®

*AuthorHouse™*
*1663 Liberty Drive*
*Bloomington, IN 47403*
*www.authorhouse.com*
*Phone: 833-262-8899*



*Published by AuthorHouse 12/10/2021*

*ISBN: 978-1-6655-4704-8 (sc)*
*ISBN: 978-1-6655-4702-4 (hc)*
*ISBN: 978-1-6655-4703-1 (e)*

*Library of Congress Control Number: 2021924821*

*Print information available on the last page.*



*This book is printed on acid-free paper.*

# CHAPTER 1

"Name?" asked the officer.

"Jonathan C. Buckley," the man responded.

"Here are your things."

The officer, no older than forty-five, with a belly rounder than Old Saint Nick himself, handed the man his belongings: a brown buttoned-down shirt, a pair of jeans with holes that no fashion designer would dare lay claim to, a blue band that the man wore around his wrist, and a pair of white running shoes.

"That's it?" the man asked skeptically.

"That's all you came in with," the officer said. "Oh, and these."

The keys to the man's 2012 Hyundai Sonata. The exchange was quick and the officer didn't bother to look up.

"Thanks," the man said.

"Sign here." The officer pushed a clip holding a detainment release paper. He slid a red pen along with it.

The man signed and gathered his belongings. He turned to go, wondering if he really had entered with only these items.

"Mr. Buckley," the officer called after him.

The man turned around, noticing the officer still hadn't looked up from his busywork.

"Yes?"

"Let's hope this is your last visit."

"Can't say I'm planning to come back," the man said. "And please, call me Jon."

The officer, holding a stern look, raised his eyes to Jon for the first time. "Next time it won't be so short a visit."

Jon nodded. "I imagine it won't."

He exited the facility to see his car still intact. "They didn't rip it apart. That's good of them."

He'd already changed into his clothes and finished putting his blue band back on his wrist. Jon had been in jail for the past two weeks on a count more severe than reckless driving. Not only had he hit another car by pulling out into a red light, but he'd waited in his own vehicle while the opposing driver came to see if he was okay.

That was when Jon had cracked open another beer, slowly sipping the foam until the tingling first drops entered his mouth. Not much had changed after the police arrived. Drunk driving wasn't taken lightly in his hometown.

But it was his hometown. Every sheriff's deputy and police officer knew of Jonathan C. Buckley. Most had received the chance to book him on one charge or another. Each time he was brought back to the court, Judge Andreas greeted him the same way.

"Not again, Jon."

"Seems like your people have it out for me," Jon would respond.

"Seems like you have an affinity for lawless behavior."

"Suppose you have me there."

Judge Andreas was known for not being lenient, giving the max amount of time for things as menial as petty theft. But there was something about Jon that made him think twice. A brokenness. A semi-lost cause. A once-purpose-filled man who was now lost to something only he could break.

As he started his car and slowly pulled out into the road, Jon thought about what was next. He didn't work, though he didn't have to. Some time ago, he had done work for the city. The city, so proud and once grateful, granted him weekly royalties for his acts.

He didn't have family, though the whole town of Brevington considered him a friend. Often he'd receive invitations to join family dinners or attend banquets at Brevington's local Civic Center. He declined all of them.

So, with no place to go, he went home: a one-floor home in the inner city, pinched between two others of the same acreage and size.

As Jon pulled into the driveway, his neighbor waved. Charles Barrister. Mr. B, as many called him, was in his late sixties. As a retired principal from Brevington High, he spent much of his time tending his garden, preferring the warmth of summer to the seclusion that most of his friends now embraced.

Mr. Barrister noticed the few scrapes and dents to the Hyundai as Jon exited his car.

"That why you've been gone for so long?" Mr. B said, pointing to the car.

"No," Jon said, ducking back to retrieve a six-pack from his backseat. He held it up for Charles to see. "This pretty much did it."

His neighbor shook his head. "Don't they take away your license when something like that happens?"

Jon shrugged and cracked open a can. "Not for me."

Mr. Barrister couldn't help but grin. "Something has to give, Jon."

"I imagine something does," he said, rounding the car. "But until then..." He finished the can and cracked open another one.

Before he could open his front door, Mr. B called out for him.

"Hey, Jon."

"Yes, Mr. B?"

"How about tossing me one of those?"

Jon smiled as he walked over and handed a can to Mr. B, whom he knew had never been much of an athlete. His neighbor had gone into excruciating detail about why his dad had stopped playing catch with him while he was still a kid.

"Ah, yes," Charles said, "nothing like a nice refresher on a warm summer day."

"I suppose not," Jon said.

"Here, take a seat."

They walked to Mr. B's porch, where two rocking chairs were waiting for them. Jon liked Mr. B enough to stay for a while. Were it anyone else, he wouldn't have taken the time to even acknowledge his name being called.

After Jon had caught up on the latest changes to the neighborhood (Mrs. Saunders getting a new cat, Susie Childs receiving an acceptance letter to Clemson, and Kevin Davies being promoted at the Hyundai factory), they simply watched the sun slowly descend.

The silence settled nicely between the two as passersby waved and the youthful generation nodded toward the two. As night drew on and Jon's beer drew low, Mr. B said something that caught Jon off guard.

"I'm dying, you know."

Jon turned toward his neighbor. "Dying?"

"Yep," Mr. B said. "Lung cancer. Stage four."

Jon wasn't sure what to say. He knew there wasn't much comfort to give when a person knew their fate.

"Don't give me that look," Mr. B said. "Sixty-eight is a pretty good number for me."

"Maybe," Jon said quietly. "But you know that I could—"

"I know, Jon," Mr. B interrupted. There was a softness in his voice. "I know you can. But this time, I think bygones should be bygones."

"You know it's been a while, but it's no trouble to—"

"No, Jon," Charles said sternly. "Not this time."

Jon nodded, appreciating his neighbor's strength. Still, he regretted that Mr. Barrister had made a choice that Jon could easily have changed.

"I suppose it's getting late," Jon said. He picked up the cans and took a step off the porch. "Mr. B, you know it's no trouble."

Charles smiled. "I know, son. But it's my choice. Now go enjoy your night, and don't go worrying about me. You're retired, remember?"

Jon nodded and headed home.

# CHAPTER 2

Four cities surrounded Brevington: Germantown, Durrington, Jameson, and Albion. No city was greater than the other. No place was more meaningful, plentiful, or special. But each citizen had their opinion. Each town had its own reputation.

Germantown was among the first to be established. The city was more farm culture than coffee shop corner. Each family owned land that had been passed down from great-grandfather, to cousin, to aunt, to every lineage on down.

The importance had more to do with the last name than the next generation. If Grandpa died and he had only daughters who were married, the land would be passed on to another relative—be it cousin, or otherwise. The only requirement was the last name.

They were the suppliers for each city. Grocery stores and farmers' markets were maintained and kept alive due to their goods. The last name made the difference. The Pembreck family owned the apple orchards while the Middleton family was the only supplier of green beans.

Family mattered in Germantown. Not only for livestock and produce, but for all the cities alike. Without Germantown, there would be no food.

Durrington held the most astute scholars. Great minds from every family flocked to Durrington for a chance to meet intellectuals from across the world. Yet, they were not merely studious know-it-alls who spent their time reading the latest journal articles.

They were dreamers—though most of them detested the term.

They were responsible for every futuristic invention. Blueprints and innovation flowed from their minds and out through their hands. The city was a tech-savvy world of its own.

They provided efficient energy sources throughout each city and remained immersed in culture. They were learned learners—always feeding their curious minds on life outside their norms.

They were almost as nice and kind as the people of Jameson.

Jameson was best-known for...well, its name. Hard-working, coal-mining, construction-toting men and women who never strayed too far from afterwork refreshments of whiskey.

Kind at heart, these families focused on labor. They never strayed away from a building needing to be built or a barn in need of paint. They were the travelers who, like the Durrington city dwellers, made their way from city to city for the betterment of others.

The children from each Jameson household learned by doing, not by schooling. Business conducted by Mom was first explained to the daughter before the contract was signed. Father first explained the purpose of a hammer and nail to his son before any foundation was laid.

Their kids were responsible for the knowledge passed on, and every once in a while, a preteen would be seen enjoying the occasional drink after a job well done. Most other cities frowned at this, but how could they argue when they couldn't fix their cars?

Jameson produced calloused hands and hearty hearts. And not one man or woman from Jameson could say they knew a stranger. They were down-to-earth people who were well-liked by all cities.

Unfortunately, that wasn't the same for the people of Albion.

Albion was the roughest, most crime-ridden city the world had ever seen. No man or woman knew his or her father, mostly because they were either in prison or had died on the street. It was the city of heartache. A cruel reminder that life wasn't fair.

No one visited Albion. It was the only place where crime seemed legal and few outsiders could find a way to make it through the night, let alone navigate the dreary roads during the day.

Many tried to flee, yet few escaped its grasp. Gang violence wasn't a thing because few people gathered together. Paranoia left the citizens scattered—each person fending for themself.

There was no governor. No leader. No power to control the chaos that was Albion. Each daring representative from another city who tried to change the city's ways was quickly chewed up and spit out.

God have mercy on their souls.

Brevington, the last city to be established, was a breath of fresh air. Not a home to any special talent, Brevington was the city of peace and love. Neighbor knew neighbor, and all were invited to visit the city and enjoy their stay.

Judgment didn't exist.

Not because the people of Brevington were above it, but because each citizen was grateful. Without the people of Germantown, they would have no food. Without the people of Durrington, there would be no electricity. And without the men and women of Jameson, every building, park, and indoor plumbing system would fall apart.

They loved all and welcomed all, sparing no expense in the bars and taverns for each family member from Jameson, feeding their affinity for down-to-earth liquor.

When families traveled from Durrington, the people of Brevington provided funding and capital from charitable organizations, showing the city's investment in Durrington and the knowledge they passed on.

Bull riding and horse shows were held in the nearest football stadium as Brevington invited the best of the best from Germantown. The shows were always sold out (not due to Germantown families but, rather, because of families from each city coming to see the events), as family names were highlighted points of pride upon returning to their city.

Brevington was a "give back" city that cared for its neighbors.

Briefly, Brevington's residents had tried to do the same for the people of Albion, but to no avail. There was something about Albion that changed a man. It didn't matter how many people escaped the city; a bit of Albion always remained.

That was why each city had jails and prisons. Petty crimes were committed by the people of each city, but the people of Albion gave necessity to these barred homes of hopeful reform.

Many believed Jonathan C. Buckley was from Albion. Tales were spun on his behalf, yet few knew the truth. Brevington needed him, but everyone feared he might leave for Albion after what had taken place years ago.

# CHAPTER 3

Jon mindlessly watched television as he drifted slowly to his past. The acts he had committed for the city came to mind. The saving grace he had once been for Brevington. Each act more miraculous than the last. Each demonstration he committed for the betterment of his home.

And he thought about Mr. Barrister.

"Why doesn't he want my help?"

Jon shook his head and cracked open another beer. Each sip allowed him space from his thoughts. Each drink dulled his senses until his mind finally settled.

He'd never had much of a taste for the yellow liquid in his past. Younger years showed a man eager to help. Eager to prove himself to the world. And once he had done that, and more, he had started to change.

His deeds were now noticed, but his soul felt used. He loved the thought of helping others. Mrs. Bragonia's son, Jesse, was alive because of him. Mr. Hampton no longer used substances—a life on the street now vanquished because of Jon.

He brought change to every life he touched and hope to those who heard of his miraculous ventures.

He took another sip. Emotions fading. Mind dulling a bit more.

Peace was all he wanted now. Loneliness and isolation brought that which he desired most. No more requests, though his overflowing mailbox showed otherwise. No more expectations, though each royalty check indicated that he was still needed.

"They're better without me," he said, tossing an empty can toward the trash. "I'm better without them."

To an outsider, it would seem that Mr. Buckley was down in the dumps. Wallowing in a pool of self-pity. A man no longer able to face the demands of society.

He knew differently.

The performance that was now put into question. The change he caused now reduced to a magic act. He hated the thought and cracked open another can before the memory could catch hold of his mind.

He was watching basketball. The Brevington Knights versus the Durrington Elites. An aged Sosa Barnett stood before his former home crowd. Cheers were heard all around, as Durrington's once-best player had returned. As the city's greatest basketball player shot around, the solemn face of Sosa showed no hint of missing what had once been.

For a moment, Jon could see a familiar resemblance. An understanding thought telepathically crossed from the basketball player to the humbled man.

"A show," Jon said to the television. "Make sure to put on a good show."

He crumpled up his can and tossed it perfectly at the screen's reflection of Barnett's face as the player forced a smile for the crowd.

# CHAPTER 4

Judge Elias Andreas returned home. He was happy that his long day of court was now over, though a pressing headache consumed him as he plopped onto his recliner. His wife, Emilia, greeted him with a gentle kiss on the forehead. She was in her early thirties while Elias was pushing fifty. The city wanted to frown but didn't. No one wanted to cross the judge.

"Long day?" she asked.

Elias sighed. "No longer than usual."

Emilia smiled, happy to see her husband. Sympathetic to his duties. Grateful that after twenty-three years, her husband still took the job so seriously.

"Come." She held out her hand. "Dinner is waiting."

Elias looked up and smiled faintly. His eyes betrayed him, as the tiredness crept over his face. "All right," he said, receiving her hand. "Let's see what's on the menu for tonight."

As he sat down for dinner, Emilia brought him an aspirin and a glass of cold water.

"The meal was tricky enough," she said, placing food on his plate. "I'd hate to see you not enjoy it."

Elias took the pill and downed it with half the glass. "Would be a shame to do so."

After ten years of marriage and a short time of tumultuous career stress, the Andreas family had no children. Elias, adamant that his upbringing would only foresee him being a horrible father, never thought twice about the matter. Emilia, though satisfied with her choice as a partner, did.

She sliced into her meal and lifted the broccoli to her lips before slowly placing it back down.

"How long have we had this house?" she asked.

Elias had already started chewing on his food. "Going on ten years this May," he said.

Emilia let out a hum. "That seems right." She looked around. "Ten years has not changed its beauty, nor fully filled its spaces."

"I suppose not," Elias said between chews. He gave the house a once-over, looking from the paintings in the living room to the lavish stairway leading up to their bedroom.

Emilia, now chewing on the broccoli, slowly swallowed. She picked around the barely-touched meal.

"Sometimes, when I walk around this house, it slips my mind how many rooms we have." She eyed the empty hallway. "How many rooms are there again?"

Elias felt there might be something more to this conversation, but he didn't know what. "*Cherie*," he said dearly. "You know exactly how many rooms are occupying this home."

"Please, darling," Emilia said gently. "I lose track sometimes. How many rooms was it again?"

"Four rooms, my sweet."

"Ah, four rooms," Emilia said. Her voice was relieved, as if the mysterious number seemed a hindrance to her mind. "Four rooms, and little you and me."

"As God himself would have it." Elias smiled.

He suddenly looked around as if he had forgotten something. *Is it her birthday? Did I forget our anniversary?*

His mind tried piecing together what might be missing. Years of marriage seemed to have shown him that though he knew his wife, he could still never read her mind.

"God and the galaxy of beautiful existence," Emilia sighed. "For all to enjoy, and each home to be full of life."

"Yes," Elias said with curiosity. "As he planned all along."

She looked longingly at her husband. "We have so much to give, don't we? And yet, can't we give a little more?"

Emilia had risen from her chair and was slowly making her way to Elias. Her husband held a smile, piecing together the once-scrambled puzzle.

"Soon, my *Cherie,*" he said, now on his feet, holding out his hands to his beautiful wife. "Soon, you just may have what you want."

# CHAPTER 5

Emilia had slipped off to bed while Elias remained downstairs. Contemplating what was to come. Knowing the promise he had just made to his wife. A secret kept him awake as he stared blankly ahead.

A secret that no one but Elias knew.

Truthfully, he had always wanted children. His upbringing had been rough—an alcoholic father who beat him constantly after Elias's mother had left the family. But it had only inspired him to do more. To be a better father to a son he hadn't yet birthed.

Sometimes he dreamed of having a daughter too. A beautiful girl who gracefully waltzed around the heavy burden of his world. She looked like his wife as a youth, a smile lighting up the room. A breath of fresh air, alleviating him from his career-driven duties.

And then he would awaken. A warm feeling once felt, now disappeared.

His heart desired such a life. It didn't help that he had been afforded a career so financially freeing that he knew both children would be afforded the very best. He'd use these funds to hire tutors for both daughter and son, giving them passage to every great city around them and beyond.

His son becoming affluent in the language that the people of Durrington so often spoke.

His daughter allowed safe haven in both Germantown and Jameson, for he knew she would be happier amongst the people, just like Emilia.

But this couldn't happen. Not with him. Not from him. He had learned long ago, during a routine check-up at the doctor's office when Dr. Stackhouse had so briefly broken down the disheartening news.

"There's no explanation for it, judge," Dr. Stackhouse had said. "The cause of the matter is simply existence. I'm sorry, but you must look on the bright side."

"What might that be?" Elias had asked.

"Adoption allows many men to become fathers." Dr. Stackhouse had walked to his side. "You can still give Emilia what she desires."

"Emilia and I," Elias had sighed. "We both wanted this. How can I tell her that I'm not able? That I can't give her the one thing all men should be able to give their wives?"

Dr. Stackhouse had patted his shoulder. "You are a good man, Judge Andreas. Adoption might not have been the plan, but you know as well as I that life doesn't go as planned. We always fall short of having everything we desire."

Elias had nodded as he got down from the gurney. The day had brought great pain and a deeper shame. He would never share any of this with Emilia.

# CHAPTER 6

Charles Barrister sat at his kitchen table. Medical bills were spread out before him. He felt as if a weight were pressed against his heart. He had not married or had any children, and now more than ever, he wished he had.

Alone in his kitchen, he felt isolated from the very world he loved.

His heart hadn't been content since retirement. But he knew better than anyone the energy needed to keep a school running. He knew he didn't have it in him to continue another year.

Yet retirement wasn't all bad. Given the chance to see the true beauty that was Brevington, he took many walks through the city. Waving to neighbors. Making small talk with local business owners.

A coffee store he had frequented when working had become the second home he never knew he'd had. Every customer from the store became a friend to Mr. B. Some spoke to him out of kindness. Others reminded him of the work he had accomplished.

"My son still talks about you," Mrs. Sanders had once said. "He thought you might expel him for the prank he committed against your faculty."

Mr. B had smiled. "It took everything to convince them not to. But I knew he was a good boy." He took a sip of coffee, inviting Mrs. Sanders to take a seat. "That's what makes learning such an amazing feat."

"How so?" she asked.

"Each child is wired differently." He held up his hand, pointing to his index finger. "Like a fingerprint, no two are identical. I took great pride in getting to know, and soon trust, that each kid passing through the grade system had a desire for better. For a life not many of us are afforded."

A tear came to Mrs. Sanders's eye as a smile broke through despite her efforts to hide it. "You speak as if you have children of your own."

Charles looked down at his coffee cup, a faint smile barely showing. "They were my children, Mrs. Sanders. All of them."

They chatted for the next hour. Mrs. Sanders told of her boy's latest venture after high school. Mr. Barrister spoke about retired life and what it was like. They would have these conversations many more times in passing.

He never knew his work had such an impact on the lives of those who passed through Brevington High. But each parent, each student, went out of their way to let him know what he had done for them.

Thus, Mr. B became famous in the sight of his city. Brevington was his home. And as he sat at his kitchen table, he couldn't help but feel like his home would soon be taken from him. His children would see him no more.

# CHAPTER 7

Fully immersed in the effects of alcohol, Jon thought it time to head to bed. Before he turned off the television, an emergency broadcast crossed the screen. A disheveled reporter appeared. Her hands trembled as she held the microphone and her eyes wildly checked from side to side, as if she were unsure of her safety.

"At ten twenty-three tonight, four boys were found dead in the city of Albion. A thorough autopsy revealed bullets in each victim."

Jon was already on his feet, but he couldn't seem to make them move toward his bed. His eyes were locked on the screen.

"Police have reported that no boy was over the age of eight. A true devastation for the city at large, well-known for its violence and mayhem as another brutal—"

Jon clicked off the television, mumbling a few words under his breath. He knew that even if he could have been there, nothing would change the chaotic nature of mankind. And though he knew he couldn't have prevented this accident, he still found his heart troubled by the brutality that took place in the city of Albion.

# CHAPTER 8

Four months passed. Charles's deterioration began with the daily use of an inhaler, which became a breathing apparatus. Then he lay bedridden in the hospital. Jon sat by his side. A skeleton of a man now lay in bed.

"When I was young, such scenes kept me away from the hospital while my loved ones suffered," Mr. B managed to rasp. "Yet here you are."

Jon nodded. "Here I am."

A smile arose from his neighbor. "You've always been a good friend, Jon."

"I've been a person who cares," Jon answered. "Just so happens that you live close and I've gotten to know you enough that I'm here today."

"And yesterday," Charles rasped out. "And the day before. The week before that. The months before that."

Jon laughed. "Makes you wonder if I really have anything better to do."

A stern look crossed his neighbor's face. "You have plenty."

"Not so much."

"Jon," Mr. B said faintly. "You have chosen where you are now. But there are many out there who still need you."

Jon sighed. "There are many out there yearning for a magic trick. It's not the same."

Mr. B looked up at the ceiling. Silence fell between the two of them. Jon didn't bother to fill the void. It was Charles who spoke.

"It's not my place to ask for a promise from you," he said. "But know that my passing is my passing. My choice. Don't think for a second that I haven't thought about asking for your help."

"If the thought came, then why not?" Jon asked.

"Because this is my time, Jon. My life." Mr. Barrister looked on. "Who am I to cheat death?"

"A wise man," Jon said.

"Or a fool," his neighbor answered. "Regardless, I know how much you have sacrificed to be here with me. I'm thankful. Grateful, really, to have a friend so caring and attentive."

"It's nothing," Jon said, his eyes now facing the window.

"Then if it is nothing, will you do one last thing for me?" Mr. B asked.

"Name it," Jon said.

"Help one last person, Jon. Just one. The city still owes you for the way they paraded you around. But one dying soul that lives beyond our reach is crying out for a savior."

"I'm no savior," Jon said.

"I know, but you are the closest person to the one who is." Mr. Barrister coughed. He lost his breath and struggled to regain it as Jon waited patiently.

"Jon?" Charles asked.

"Yes," Jon answered.

"Please, bring me the water over there."

Jon arose, checking first to make sure there was enough water. Once satisfied with the amount, he brought it over to his friend.

Mr. B took a long sip and gave the water back to Jon.

He raised his hand, index finger pointing to the ceiling. "Just one, Jon. That's all I ask."

Jon wanted to plead his case, but upon seeing his friend in such pain, such helplessness, he simply nodded. "Okay, Mr. B. One last one."

Mr. B smiled and lay back on his pillow.

Two hours later, Charles seized up, eventually breathing out. It was his last breath before passing.

# CHAPTER 9

Samson "Sosa" Barnett sat at the end of his bed. Tears still streaked down his face. Pain gripped his heart as he went through the messages on his phone.

"He's been shot."

"Ambulance is on the way."

"I'm heading to the hospital."

"Please hurry, Sammy."

Sammy. His wife loved calling the all-star basketball player by that name, though he never knew why. No one he knew called him Sammy. Not even his mother. But he adored his wife, and he loved that she had gone out of her way to come up with a name that would forever remind him of their love.

This night, however, it was a cry for help. His son, Monty Barnett, had been kidnapped. And though they lived in the safe, innovative city of Durrington, the kidnapper managed to not only take Monty but also his friends while they were having a sleepover.

The friend's family was close with the Barnetts. Samson didn't think twice about it. It was a weeknight but he felt guilty about not being able to stay in with his son. There was a livelihood to be made, an important game that his team, his organization, was not willing to let him miss.

Guilt ran thick throughout his body, like the blood in his veins. *I should've stayed home. It was only a regular-season game. Monty needed me.*

He knew that if he had been home, his son would be home too. No one would have been put in danger. The kidnapper had planned a ransom only for the sake of the name associated with "Sosa."

According to police, the kidnapping had gone awry as the man had planned to hide safely in Albion.

"Albion," Samson said. "Of all the godforsaken places."

As the kidnapper crossed over from Durrington to Albion, a shootout—unrelated to him, or those whom he held captive—took place. The man was wounded. A gunshot to the shoulder. When the shootout was over, he checked the backseat.

None of the kids moved. They had all been fatally wounded.

Thinking it better to deal with a wound on his own than to be found with three children and the dead son of Sosa Barnett in his backseat, the kidnapper quickly pulled out each body, laying them one by one on the street.

In his panic to flee the scene, he never thought twice about the DNA he had left behind. Police found him an hour later, blood still spilling from his shoulder. DNA tests done afterward would show that he was the one who had kidnapped the four kids.

Sosa received ten missed calls and five missed text messages.

His wife didn't come home, choosing to stay at the morgue as long as she could until her sister picked her up.

"Better she stay with me for a few nights," her sister said.

Samson didn't argue.

He didn't know why this had happened. Why his seven-year-old son had been murdered. All he knew was that he was in pain. And though he was a person accustomed to the pain of an athlete, he had never before suffered such a permanent injury like this.

# CHAPTER 10

Jon awoke the next day, his head too heavy to lift from the pillow. Thoughts swirled through his mind.

*Just one, Jon. That's all I ask.*

There was no one he wanted to help. No person left in his life whom he cared for enough to offer the gift he had been given. Mr. B was the last remaining soul Jon knew to be a friend. His family was gone, having died in a tragic car accident when Jon was only nine years old.

The neighborhood he had grown up in left him friendless and on his own.

That was how he had been for the past decade. Alone. People vying for his help, requesting that he come at once. But that was what he was to them: the help. A dying child made one last request to his parents.

"Can you call for Jon?"

A paralyzed veteran returning home from a war many countries away wrote a letter. The first two letters: Dear Jon.

Rushed to and fro, Jon scrambled like a mad man, tending to every request, helping every man or woman in need. It didn't take long for the city to realize the diamond hiding in their backyard. It wasn't hard to see that his efforts in helping others had landed him the role of the mascot for people lacking any special talent other than loving those they needed most.

This was their out. Their claim amongst all the other cities.

"Come see the Miracle Man!" the newspapers read.

He was the main attraction. A fortune-teller. A circus of one as Durrington, Germantown, and Jameson crossed the borders to see what Jon could do.

One day he found himself at city hall. Thousands had gathered in front of him for reasons he couldn't comprehend. T-shirts with his face on the front. On the back was the word "Believe". Jon wasn't quite sure he could believe this.

Before the first autograph could be signed, Jon left, heading back to his car.

"Jon!" the mayor cried out. "You can't leave now! All these people have come to see you!"

"No," Jon said, turning back. "They've come to see a show."

"Well," the mayor said, bouncing from one foot to the other. "It doesn't matter what they think. You know what you do, Jon. Show them what you can do!"

"I can do what I please," Jon said. "And right now, I want to get as far away from this place as I can."

He opened the door and, sliding into the seat, lowered the window. The mayor, baffled, didn't move.

"Don't give out my address. Don't call. If there's someone in need of help, you treat them like they would in any other city." Jon started the car. "These gifts are not mine to claim. They are not yours, either."

# CHAPTER 11

It was four in the morning. Samson, giving up on sleep, went downstairs and poured himself a bourbon. It was the first alcoholic beverage he'd had in five years. He used to party, having the time of his life after every win. It drove his wife crazy, but he knew what was expected. He would return the way he left.

If he left his home sober, he would return the same.

"If you feel the need to celebrate, I'm not going to stop you," his wife Shirley would always say. "You work hard and you deserve to let loose sometimes. But you won't be coming back here all puffy-eyed, drowning in the scent of alcohol. I don't deserve that. Neither does Monty."

*Neither does Monty.*

The very thought of his son brought a fresh wound to his heart. Sosa took a bigger sip. The pain let up a bit. He had left his phone on the bed and put his house phone on silent. The outpouring of hurt seemed to come from every angle.

Friends reached out to give their condolences. Fans put together Instagram posts of the family whenever they had been seen in public. It was too much for Samson. Sosa had to be brave and grieve in silence.

He cried out at home. Alone. Tears flowed steadily down his face.

He could hear his son's voice. No truth in it. But his voice all the same. He imagined Monty hugging him as he always did when Sosa left for work.

"I love you, Dad! Score one for me!"

But now Samson heard something different. The same excitement. The same loving smile. But the words were different.

*I love you, Dad. But can't you stay here with me?*

Samson took a longer sip. Followed by another, until he had finished his glass. He poured another. This time, he walked away from the bottle and toward the family photos. Shirley had made it a point for the family to have a picture taken each year.

Samson could see his son grow, from the day he was born, until two months prior. Monty always seemed to be beaming. The expression was infectious, causing even his parents to smile after the sixth photo attempt was made.

And though Samson wanted to turn away, he couldn't. He couldn't leave his child. His only son. Alone. With no one to protect him. Even if it was a photo. Even if the son he knew was in a morgue fifteen miles away.

He felt his heart pounding. Steadily. Loudly. Painfully.

He finished his drink, then headed back to pour another. But it had been five years since he had last drunk alcohol. He didn't have the same balance. He struggled to take more than a step before he fell, face down, on the kitchen floor.

He didn't move.

He heard the crunch of his nose and the shattering glass. It would be a mess, but he didn't care.

*I deserve this.*

He laid there until he fell asleep. Dreams dashed back and forth as every family vacation, every basketball game Monty attended, every moment the family spent at home seemed to weave itself in and out in cinematic form.

He awoke later to the screams of his maid, Cecilia.

# CHAPTER 12

Another day had come and gone. It was Tuesday, a day that Judge Andreas despised because every case seemed to pile on top of each other.

He had gone through ten sentencings by the end of the day: three people let out on bail, four traffic fines, two petty theft claimers (resulting in jail time for the two female jewelry thieves), and one innocent case of dog theft.

Elias wanted nothing more than to go home and recline on his couch. After he had announced his final sentencing, there would be no one to stop him. He would kiss wife "hello" and slump down, far from society.

Upon retiring to his office, Judge Andreas changed into his well-worn suit. He wasn't flashy (paying over five hundred dollars for clothes seemed absurd to him). Once he finished changing, he headed for the exit.

His car was parked in the back of the courthouse. It saved him from any media or unwanted attention, allowing him to leave quickly. By his car stood a stout woman no older than seventy, but wrinkle-free, as if her grey, strained hair was the only indicator of aging. She wore a flowing purple sundress with matching heels.

"Oh, great," Elias muttered.

He didn't know who this could be. She was beautiful, an elderly elite who dressed as if she had fifty more years left to give.

"Judge Andreas?" the woman asked.

"Sadly, that is me." He set down his suitcase. "Normally I meet with people inside the courthouse. In a well-populated area. By the front desk. Not by my car."

Elias could see that the woman wasn't amused.

"Well," he said. "Spit it out."

"You've wrongfully charged my son," she said, stepping closer to the judge. "But I won't hold that against you."

Elias had met many angry pursuers of justice. Most of them felt that he had judged incorrectly. All of them were not very friendly.

He quickly checked to make sure she wasn't hiding a weapon. From what he could see, she had only her purse. It was a handbag that he assumed couldn't carry a gun. But he still didn't want to take his chances.

"I'm not armed," the woman said sternly. "Leave it to a judge to be afraid of losing his life while sentencing others to give up their own."

"Fair point," he said, a bit more relaxed. "But I abide by the law. If your son committed a crime, it is no more my fault than that of the victim he violated."

The woman raised her voice. "My son didn't violate anyone!"

"Ma'am, it's a figure of speech," he said calmly. "I don't know your son because, quite frankly, I don't know you."

"Mary Madison," she said with contempt. "My son is Jesse Madison."

Elias took a moment to think. "Yes," he said, piecing it together. "Burglary on West Fifth Street?"

She nodded.

"Ms. Madison, there was—"

"Mrs!"

Elias sighed. "Mrs. Madison, there was video evidence of your son holding up the cashier at gunpoint. In court, he even admitted to committing the crime!"

"I know that!" She snapped her fingers. "I already told you I'm not holding that against you!"

"Then why are you here, Mrs. Madison?"

"Because you thought it right to give my son ten years for a petty theft!" She stepped closer. "Ten years! He left the scene and didn't take a single dollar!"

"Mrs. Madison, a crime is a crime. And that is exactly what your son has committed." He sighed and took a step closer. "I imagine you think me an awful human being for doing my job, but there is more to this than you know."

"I doubt that," she said with disgust.

Elias took another step closer, lowering his voice. "Look, I shouldn't be telling you this, but I trust that this will stay between you and me."

He eyed the woman, waiting for her agreement. She nodded skeptically.

"Have you been to any of my other cases? I imagine you haven't because your son was held in contempt only once. And that wasn't for more than a day."

He picked up his suitcase and hit the button to unlock his car. "I have a reputation around here. Do you know what that is?"

Mrs. Madison shook her head.

"It's for giving my assailants the max penalty for any crime they've committed. Especially those who have given an admittance of guilt."

"You despicable excuse for a—"

Elias held up his hand to silence the woman. "Now, you only hear of the sentencing. But this is Brevington, Mrs. Madison. There are no high-security prisons here. No major jails of worrisome violence committed by inmates."

He slid the suitcase into his backseat.

"The only folks you see in jail are former neighbors, who probably committed no greater crimes than your son. But we have no murderers in this city. No rape victims. No problems with violence. So tell me, Mrs. Madison, what worries you so much for your son?"

She thought for a moment about what the judge had said. It was true. Brevington was a peaceful city filled with peaceful people. Crimes were minimal and so punishment was maxed. Of those who served their time and re-entered society, none of them committed another crime.

None of them came out scarred from their experience.

"It..." Mrs. Madison thought for a second. "It just doesn't seem right."

Elias shut the back door of his black 2012 Ford Fusion.

"Causing a threat isn't right, Mrs. Madison. And neither is stealing. Even if you're bad at it. This is Brevington. Not Albion."

"Then why are you treating him like he's from there?" Mrs. Madison asked.

He turned to face the woman. He noticed that her shoulders were slouched. Her forehead was relaxed. She wasn't angry and he could tell. She just wanted an answer.

"Because if we don't, Mrs. Madison, what's happening over there will happen here. I'm sure that at one point you looked up to Jonathan C. Buckley—as we all did. But if what happens in Albion starts happening here, I don't believe even he could save us."

"Don't be so sure, Judge." Mrs. Madison handed her phone to Elias.

There was a picture of Jonathan and an editorial next to it. But Elias didn't have to read the editorial to know what was going on. The title said it all: "Buckley Goes to Albion!"

# CHAPTER 13

Durrington. Tech-savvy. Innovative. An all-around juggernaut that produced a better quality of life. However, it wasn't just for themselves. Their city, the citizens who made up Durrington, were needed for their neighboring cities to thrive.

Technology improved waterways and dispelled air pollution. The windmills in Germantown would not have worked properly without Durrington's greatest minds coming up with the blueprint. The equipment in Jameson would not be as effective if not for the careful construction and mass production that came from Durrington.

The city held all and wanted all—for the benefit of others. But there was a side of Durrington most travelers didn't see. Rumors and gossip that never seemed to spread outside city limits.

Something was taking place that would change the lives of both the current and future residents.

Some claimed time-travel. Others put forth the possibility that teleportation portals were being tested to improve travel. Some claimed more mischievous creations were taking place.

Breeding between mountain lions and house cats. Murmurings of technological black-out devices that could kill the power for whole neighborhoods. Weather-manipulating contraptions—it would explain why they'd had rain for the past week while other cities experienced only sunshine and some clouds.

Durrington had its secrets, many of which could never be guessed. Most of which were created by overimagination and exaggerating tourists.

Despite the city's good intentions, the citizens of Durrington knew that something else was taking place in their backyard.

# CHAPTER 14

A month had passed since her son was found dead. Samson's wife, Shirley, had returned to the house. Her sister watched as Shirley gently stepped out of the car.

"Are you going to be okay?" she asked.

Shirley smiled faintly. "He's in here." She pointed to her heart. "I'd rather be holding him, but he's still in here."

"Okay, you just give me a call when you get settled in," her sister said. "And sis?"

Shirley had started walking away but turned around. "Yes?"

"As much as you're hurting, I can only assume that Sosa's hurting the same, if not more." She smiled. "He doesn't have someone in his life like you have me."

"I know," Shirley said. "But he's strong, sis."

"He might be," her sister said. "But he lost his only son. A part of himself that extends deep. It's beyond gender and DNA, honey."

Shirley knew what her sister meant. They both knew that Samson had always wanted a son. And when Monty was alive, Sosa had made it known to the world that his son meant everything to him. He had what he had always dreamed of having, only to wake up to a nightmare.

"I'm just saying, sis. Don't lose sight of what you guys have."

"I'll try not to," Shirley said. "And if I do, I'll know who to call."

Her sister stepped out of the car and squeezed her tight. She was hurting for Shirley and wanting to take away her pain. But she couldn't. She could only be there for her. She could only hope things would get better. That they would get past this trying time.

Shirley headed up the walkway. Everything appeared as it used to, but she lost her breath for a moment. Her eyes could see the house, but her heart felt the loss. It was a deep grief that the mind couldn't comprehend. Though the house looked the same, something was missing. Her heart would not let her forget her son.

*We'll get through this together. We'll be happy, just like Monty wanted.*

She had hoped for hope. She didn't know where it would come from. She didn't know why it would be here. But she hoped for it. She realized something different when she opened the door. Her eyes couldn't believe it.

# CHAPTER 15

His Hyundai made it a block into Albion before he shut it off. The streets were spattered with trash. Shops and stores were dark though it was midday. Jon looked down the street. He had never been to Albion before because he had never desired to visit the city.

*Just one, Jon.*

Mr. Barrister's voice rang loud in Jon's mind. Despite his great effort to ignore it, Jon couldn't block out Charles's dying request. He could only try to find that one person. A person helpless enough to cause Jon to come out of retirement.

It was strange to him. He hadn't helped a soul in years. He didn't have the desire to help anyone in Brevington because he knew how that would turn out. Durrington helped itself out. Jameson drank away its problems, and Germantown held such a tight-knit group of citizens that they helped each other with their problems.

Albion was helpless. A land of chaos and death wreaked as the deserted streets made it seem like a ghost town. Several hundred people lived in this city, though the last census had been done two years prior.

*They could all be dead. Or more than half by now.*

Yet he had been led here. Partially by a familiar presence. Another part had led him here too. A part of him that hoped to fail. To not make it back to Brevington. He could never explain it, this part of him that wanted nothing to do with life. This part of him that always led him to drink. He had tried to explain this to Mr. B when he was alive.

"A part of me died that day," Jon had said a year ago.

Mr. B simply smiled. "Hopefully, an unnecessary part of you."

"Is there such a thing?"

"Of course," Mr. B said. "The ego."

"Not sure that's possible." Jon leaned back on the porch chair. "Thought the ego was consciousness—the soul."

"The ego is the ego, son." Mr. B spat out a sunflower seed. "Don't let those textbooks tell you otherwise."

"Whatever it is, it's gone now," Jon said. "It feels like I'm missing something."

"That, Mr. Buckley, is purpose," Mr. B said. "But it was self-guided, self-serving purpose. It dies with the ego."

They sat in silence while Jon thought this over.

"You're a good man, Jon." Mr. B straightened and stood up from his chair. "It's time you let your guide, guide you. Let it in again, Jon. And watch the spirit grow."

# CHAPTER 16

Wade Temple grabbed the morning paper, then headed back inside his house to finish the pancakes his wife had made him. It was six in the morning. He hadn't expected to get the paper until the usual time, which happened to be right when he left for work.

The thump against his front door—the paperboy's accurately hard throw—used to let him know when the paper had arrived. But there hadn't been a paperboy for years.

Durrington's "Paper OnDemand" was an efficient street sweeper that also delivered the paper. This made it easier for journalists and newspaper companies to complete their work the night before, and allowed editors to work early into the morning. The self-functioning machine not only printed the paper but rolled it up nicely too.

A soft-shooter, similar to what one would see at a basketball game, shot out the paper instead of t-shirts. Calculating the distance from the street to the doorstep. Never once causing a disturbance or sudden scare to any resident.

But Wade had gotten used to its sound. As mayor, he needed the news. Yet he was old-fashioned. He preferred the paper compared to hearing people babble on in hysteria.

"The world is frantic enough," he'd always say. "Better to slowly read the coming demise of this planet."

So, when the whizzing, whirring sound came down the street, Wade's ears perked up. The news was coming.

*But why so early?*

His wife, having been up since four in the morning after falling asleep early the day before, was cooking breakfast. Now that Wade was up, he thought he'd take a few more minutes to read his paper in peace rather than at his office.

"I can't believe it!" he exclaimed to his wife.

"What's that?"

"The paper," he said. "They delivered it early."

His wife, Elise, sighed. "That is an amazing feat, isn't it? You do know you can read all of those articles online, right?"

Wade waved a hand. "And hear the opinion of some bombastic reporter trying to earn her keep? I don't think so. Nowadays it's nothing but rumors and scandals."

"It does sell," his wife agreed. "But they can't *all* be lying."

"Maybe not," he agreed. "But most of them are, and I can't say I blame them." He held up the paper. "But this is different."

Elise brought over biscuits and sausage to go with his meal, then made a plate for herself, enjoying the few hours she had to spend with her husband.

"What could possibly make that historic thing different?" she asked.

Wade smiled. "I'm glad you asked."

"I'm not," Elise sighed.

"For one, no left- or right-winged radical gets published in the newspaper. Only hard facts. Data that has been 'seized and squeezed,' as my old man used to say."

He pointed to the headline of the paper. "Also, there's no click-bait."

"Because it's a paper," Elise said.

"That, and because every lead editor knows they would get fired in a heartbeat if there was. They'd have to redact the article," Wade said. "If they redact an article, they lose credibility. That's one thing they can't afford to do because if they lose credibility, they lose their audience."

"Which is bad for business." Elise winked. "I get the business model, honey. What I don't get is why you'd rather wait a whole day for real news than cipher through decent news the night before." She poured herself a cup of coffee. "You are the mayor, after all."

"And that's exactly why I need to read the truth." He had speared a sausage off the plate. "It gives me credibility with the people when they know their mayor is getting the news right when they are. Makes me seem human."

"And it covers your tracks." Elise laughed.

"How so?" he asked, finishing the last of the sausage.

"Think about it, honey," Elise said. "You don't have to preemptively act on the bad news. Instead, you get to wake up when everyone else does and prepare for news you're privy to the night before."

Wade shrugged. "I don't see the problem with that. It makes me like everyone else."

"No, honey, it makes you lazy," Elise said.

"Yeah, well, I suppose you have a point." He finished his orange juice before spreading out the paper. "Now, if you don't mind, I'd like to enjoy this lovely…"

An article stood out. Wade couldn't believe it.

"What's the matter, dear?" Elise asked.

Wade was speechless. He reread the article headline over and over to make sure he wasn't seeing things.

"Wade?"

He looked up. "It's Jon," he said.

"What about him?" Elise asked.

# CHAPTER 17

Trash was sprawled all over the kitchen. The Barnett household reeked something fierce as Shirley walked into the home.

*What in the world happened here?*

Pillows in the living room were facing every which way and a scrambled signal showed on the television. She didn't bother picking up things, not just because they had a maid but mostly because she didn't want to fix anything until she had an explanation.

"Sammy?" she called out. "Where are you?"

No answer. She waded through the mess, reaching the stairway that led to their bedroom. She quickly realized the bedroom was even worse. Dressers were flung open. Clothes covered the floor.

The master bathroom was a wreck. But apart from the whole place seeming to have been ransacked, she noticed the mirror.

It was broken.

Shattered pieces lay all over the counter. Her makeup lay on the floor. She couldn't figure out what had taken place.

*Were we robbed? Did Sammy lose his mind? Where in the world is the maid?*

Shirley headed back downstairs. She had to find Sammy. Her heart was racing as she frantically searched the house for her husband.

*No one is here.*

She was heading to the garage when she suddenly thought of where her husband might have been. Opening the sliding door to the back patio, she remembered the pool. It was Monty's favorite part of the house. She remembered her husband promising Monty that he would take him swimming after the game.

"Oh, Sammy," she said softly.

Her eyes, once again, couldn't believe what they were seeing.

# CHAPTER 18

He stepped out of the car, not bothering to check for traffic. He knew that few cars would come. Few people in the city risked losing something of such value. Everyone else scavenged the streets for what was left. It seemed apocalyptic. Few people outside of Albion understood what was going on.

But Jon knew better. He had met people from the city. Helped to have them arrested, too, as they would make their escape from Albion into Brevington. And although the mayor wanted them arrested, Jonathan never felt it was the right thing to do.

People fleeing Albion were searching for help. Despair and tragedy had taken place long before many of them were born. Those who were able to flee the city were in their early to late twenties. Technically adults, but to Jon they were still kids.

He knew if there was one person to help, they would be here.

He drank the night before and heavily the morning of. What he was doing wasn't practical, and despite what he had done in the past, he knew he wasn't invincible.

Suddenly he heard a sound coming from the alleyway, not ten feet in front of him. He walked toward it. It was still early in the day, so he could see, only no one was there.

"See, Jon," he said to himself. "Spooking yourself for no reason."

He turned around. Not a second later, something heavy made contact with the back of his head. He fell forward. He didn't bother moving as he began to black out.

# CHAPTER 19

"Where are you going?" the woman yelled.

Elias didn't bother answering. He was already in his car, heading down the road.

"Why, Jon?" he asked himself. "That many drinks wouldn't even convince me to make such a dumb decision."

He sped back to his home. Emilia, hearing her husband open the door, rushed down to greet him.

"Elias," she said. "What are you doing back so soon?"

He brushed by her, heading up the stairs. "I need to make a call."

"No, wait," Emilia said.

Elias looked back at his wife. Her face showed panic. "What?" he asked.

"I left the phone down here," she said, pointing to the house phone on the couch. "I was watching a few shows and forgot it when I went upstairs."

Elias held up his cell. "I was going up for privacy. I'll be back down in a minute. I'll tell you what's going on then."

"Wait," Emilia said. "Why not just make it down here? Upstairs is still a mess from this morning."

Elias, sliding his phone back in his pocket, took a step down the stairs. "You've been here all day," he said. "And it's almost five in the afternoon."

Judge Andreas wasn't a hard man, but very logical. Not once in their many years of marriage had he asked his wife to lift a finger, yet she saw fit to always have the house cleaned and the kitchen straightened up.

The only time the bedroom was left a mess was on Saturday, when they both agreed to stay in bed a little longer.

"If the upstairs is a mess, then you must have been busy," Elias said.

"I was," Emilia said. "With some cleaning outside the house. You know how it is outside, Elias." She smiled as if she could feel the sun's embrace. "It's so warm and nice. We never have weather like this."

"That's true." Elias held a skeptical look. "But you were upstairs, my *Cherie.* You were heading down when I came in. And the outside of the house looks the same as when I left..."

Emilia began to talk, but Elias sensed something was off. There was a reason she hadn't cleaned the room, and though he didn't know why, he felt there was something upstairs she was keeping from him.

He'd always had the ability to sense when things were wrong. Yet today, on the day when everything seemed to slip under his radar, he knew he didn't have any more time to waste. He headed upstairs and opened the bedroom door.

He sighed at the sight in front of him. "Great," he said. He could hear Emilia racing up the stairs.

He shook his head. "Another mess to clean up."

# CHAPTER 20

Samson awoke to the splash of water on his face. He blinked wildly. The bottle of bourbon he had tucked under his arm fell against the concrete. It rolled toward the pool as he tried to get up from the pool chair. He couldn't.

His muscles ached from sleeping in such an awkward position, and his legs felt bruised, as the sun had beaten down on them for a length of time he couldn't determine. What he did remember was that he had a wife. He knew that because she was standing in front of him.

"Samson Carter Barnett," she said sternly. "What the hell is all this?"

She pointed toward the house and then to the area surrounding the pool. Trash had found its way to the pool deck along with the chaos inside the house. Samson tried to focus but the alcohol still coursed through his veins.

"Shirley," he rasped out. "I didn't know you were coming back. I thought..."

Shirley snapped her fingers. "You thought what? That I wouldn't come back?"

Samson shook his head. "I didn't know." It took all of his effort to sit up. "You stopped texting and calling and...I don't know. I just thought I was making it worse."

"I called..." She tried to remember the last time she had called. "Last week?"

Samson smiled faintly. "You called a month and two days ago at six-fifty-two at night." He laid his head back on the chair. "I know because that was the last time we spoke."

"Maybe," she said, "but you couldn't possibly think I'd leave after all of this."

She sat beside him on the chair. "That's not what I want, and that's not what Monty would want, either."

"I know," Samson said. His expression hardened. Reaching over, he picked up the rolling bottle of bourbon and popped the cork.

"Because Monty would have wanted me home instead of at the game."

# CHAPTER 21

It didn't take long for Jon to wake up. His eyes, however, slowly adjusted to the light. His hands were restrained, along with his legs, to the chair he sat in. Once he opened his eyes, he was able to look around. It was an abandoned warehouse. Rows of empty shelves. A small space was made for him in the corner.

"Not the oddest thing I've awoken to," he said. "But definitely not convenient."

"Do you know what is convenient?"

The voice came from behind him. Jon didn't move or say a word. He was content to stay where he was. He didn't like the setup, but he figured there must be a reason for his capture.

"The silent type, I see," the voice said. "You are Jonathan C. Buckley, are you not?"

Jon nodded. "It'd be awfully embarrassing if you got the wrong guy."

"Embarrassing, indeed," the voice said.

Jon heard steps coming toward him. He slouched his shoulders.

"Look, I'm sure there's something you want from me," Jon said. "So how about you name it and we get this over with?"

Behind him, someone laughed—a different voice this time.

"Oh, Jon," the voice said. "If only it were that easy."

"I assure you, it is."

"Not exactly." The voice stepped in front of Jon, revealing the man behind it in the dimly lit warehouse. He seemed familiar to Jon, but he couldn't place a name.

"It's been a long time coming, old friend."

"You say that like I know you," Jon said. "I assure you, I don't."

"Oh, but you do," the man said. "Kieran L. Motley."

"Kieran?" Jon asked. "Can't say I'd forget a name like that."

"You have, because it never meant much to you, now did it?" The man stepped aside. "Forgive the drab environment. I promise you, this is not my usual hangout. But you know, when in Rome..."

He spun around slowly, revealing the rest of the warehouse.

"Okay, Kieran," Jon said. "It makes more sense than you think, taking me to an abandoned warehouse. We are in Albion. But if you know me like you say you do, you'd know I don't have much to offer."

"Dear, dear, Jon," Kieran said. An expression of sadness spread across his face. "You know not your own value. Truly a pity."

"Yeah," Jon said. "Poor me."

Kieran laughed. "You jest, and that's good. A sense of humor is needed in this city."

Jon noticed something about Kieran. "But you're not from this city, are you?"

Kieran clapped his hands. "Surely, you are the Jon I am looking for." His smile spread. "But tell me, what gave it away?"

"Not quite sure that matters," Jon said. "But what does matter is why I'm here. So please, do tell. What's this evil plan of yours?"

"Evil?" Kieran expressed shock. "You shouldn't judge a book by its cover, Jon. You really think I mean to do you harm?"

"The knot on the back of my head would say so."

"Dearest Jon," Kieran said, shaking his head. "You are of value. And I'll admit, wrangling you up after knocking you out wasn't my politest move. But how often does the city of Albion come upon someone as famous as you?"

"Again," Jon said. "You're not from here. So why should that matter?"

"I'm glad you rehashed that point," Kieran said. "Because that is exactly why you are here."

"Sorry," Jon said. "I must be a bit concussed. Why am I here again?"

"For the city, dearest Jon," Kieran said. "You are here to save this city."

"Save Albion?" Jon laughed. "Think I've found the hole in your plan."

Kieran smiled. "You think this city cannot be saved. I disagree. You bring hope with you, Jon. That's for sure. But there's something else you bring that even you don't know of."

Jon sighed. "And what might that be?"

Kieran laughed. "Power, Jon," he said with a crooked smile. "A very large amount of power."

# CHAPTER 22

Elias headed back to his car. Problems were evolving around him that he wasn't equipped to solve. But there was a concern that he needed to address. Something more important than his marriage. Something more important than what he found in his room.

Emilia ran out after him. "Elias!"

He didn't look back. He held out his key, slid it into the car, and opened the door without hesitation. Emilia banged on the passenger door.

There were many things Elias had seen during his time as judge. Most of them came from the accused, who demanded the firing of Elias for his injustice and his tendency toward extended sentences.

Wives slashed his tires because he sent their husbands to jail. A teen even showed up at his door, daring to take a swing at the judge when Elias opened it. The boy swiftly came to realize that Elias had studied martial arts, as the judge pinned the high school football star against the window.

There were a great many scenes he wished to never relive, but very few bothered him as much as what was taking place outside his car. He cracked open the passenger window.

"What do you want, Emilia?" he asked calmly.

"Please, Elias," she said, holding out her hands. "It was a mistake. Please, forgive me and come back inside."

"I'm busy," he said, rolling the window back up. "And I'm not a complete idiot," he said to himself.

He drove off, leaving Emilia standing alone in their front yard. Elias pulled out his phone and started dialing. Someone picked up.

"Elias?" the voice asked.

"Yes, it's me," the judge answered. "Did you hear the news?"

"Early this morning," the voice said. "Been working all day trying to figure out our next steps."

"Not sure there's much we can do but wait," Elias said. "There's a reason he's doing this."

The voice sighed. "I'd like to go get him myself, but I'm not setting foot in that city."

"Probably best, Mayor," Elias said. "That's probably best."

# CHAPTER 23

Three guards were left watching Jon. Kieran had left. Jon took his time, eyeing each guard, as he sat restrained in his chair.

"Has to be more exciting things for you guys to do," he said. "Why has he left you to guard me?"

One guard stepped forward. "I think that's pretty obvious."

Jon smiled. "So that I don't escape?"

The guard nodded.

"How disappointed will he be to know that you'll aid me in doing just that?" Jon asked.

The guard laughed. "I don't think that will happen or be a concern of ours."

Jon shook his head. "You think, but you do not know. And that is your mistake."

"Okay, soothsayer," the guard said. He took a step back and laughed. "Whatever you say."

Jon eyed each guard again, then lowered his head.

"Nega-shalrool de bia, son-phomata." He closed his eyes. "Della-shomph, aldo wala."

The guard looked to his left and right. Another guard, a shorter man to his left, looked at Jon and then to the guard who had stepped forward.

"What's he saying?" the shorter guard asked.

The guard who had stepped forward shrugged. "Beats me. He's probably losing his mind. Just make sure he doesn't make any sudden movements."

Jon raised his head, relaxed. Calmly, he spoke. "Do not fear, for I am with you. Do not be dismayed, for I am your God."

"Great," the shorter guard said. "Now what is he doing?"

"I don't know," snapped the guard who stepped forward. "And I don't care. As long as he doesn't get up or do something stupid, I'm not worried about whatever rabble he spits out."

"I will strengthen you and help you," Jon said. "I will uphold you with my righteous hand."

As he spoke these last words, the ropes restraining him fell off. He still did not move. Instead, he looked from guard to guard, seeing what they might do.

"How the hell..." the shorter guard whispered.

"Go," the main guard said. "Tie him back up."

The shorter guard, unsure of what was to come, hesitantly stepped forward. Before he could step behind Jon, their captive spoke again.

"Those who seek the Lord lack no good thing."

"Shut up," the shorter guard said, raising his gun to strike Jon. As he did, he felt his arms go weak. He wasn't able to raise the gun. Seconds later, he dropped the weapon without meaning to.

"Pick up your rifle," the main guard commanded. "Don't you move an inch, Jon—"

The guard was cut off by the sound of the other two guards dropping their weapons. He looked to both of them, confused as to what they were doing.

"Pick those up!" he shouted. "What the hell is the matter with you guys?"

But as he eyed the other guards, he noticed something. Their eyes were glazed over as if each one of them were blind—the films of their eyes as white as snow. He turned back to the shorter guard who was now sitting at Jon's side.

He raised his own rifle. "All right, tough guy," the main guard said. "Go ahead. Move a muscle. I've been itching to get more target practice."

Jon looked ahead. His forehead relaxed. His demeanor of peace sent a wave of fear through the main guard's body.

"The power Kieran spoke of," Jon said. "He is mistaken."

"Huh?"

"Your leader," Jon said. "He thinks this power comes from me."

Jon stood to his feet. The guard winced, trying to find the trigger with his right index finger. Oddly enough, his finger kept slipping. His grasp on the gun weakened. Without meaning to, he dropped the weapon.

"Don't you mo—"

The words caught in his throat. The guard could no longer speak or move. Paralyzed from the head down, he collapsed.

"I'm not here for you." Jon looked toward the other guards. "I'm not here for any of you. And it appears that the one who guides me also has my back."

He walked forward to the exit door, leaving the guards where they were. None of them would be able to move until Kieran returned.

# CHAPTER 24

"Do you believe there is hope?"

The therapist remained calm, asking the question more to gauge Samson's response than anything else. Shirley sat to Samson's right, holding her husband's hand.

"Hope for what?" Samson asked.

"Hope for normalcy, Mr. Barnett."

"He was my son, doctor." Samson could feel his temper rising. "Kidnapped for no other reason than being my flesh and blood. Murdered in Albion with his closest friends." Samson bit his lip. "I'd like to think normalcy has gone out the window."

"Yes," Dr. Palmarardi said. "It has. With his death, all things whole have left, along with peace. They have been held hostage by the acts of this cruel world. A world we have no say in, other than that which we can retrieve."

"English, doc," Samson said.

"What you have lost is beyond anything you ever knew you had," Dr. Palmarardi said. "But now that you know, truly know, what you have lost, do you believe you have the capability to retrieve it?"

"My son will never come back." Samson let go of his wife's hand. "There's no bringing him back. There's no redoing the past. He's gone!"

Dr. Palmarardi nodded, scribbling a few words on his notepad. "You acknowledge the truth, Mr. Barnett. That is good."

"Doctor," Shirley said. "There is no cure for this kind of pain. And I think we all know that. But moving past it, without doing more self-damage, just seems..."

"Impossible?" the doctor questioned. "Hard, yes. Impossible, no. In your pain, you have forgotten what your son stood for."

"He didn't stand for anything," Samson said. "He was our son."

The doctor nodded. "And did your son not have value?"

"He meant the world to us," Shirley whispered.

"And so he still does," Dr. Palmarardi said. "He still lives within you. You both know that. You can no longer think of life as getting past this. There is no 'past this' to get to."

The doctor stood up, returning his notepad to his desk, and then walked over to both of them.

"Everything you do now, you do for him. For what he would have wanted. For how he would wish you two to live. His spirit lives, Mr. and Mrs. Barnett. It is your job to not let his life become merely a memory of tragedy and death."

# CHAPTER 25

Mayor Temple weighed his options.

*Bring Jon back and convince him he can do good works here. Leave Jon and hope he finds his way back. Convince all other cities to aid us in getting Brevington's savior back.*

Every option seemed tempting. Only one option seemed possible.

He had arrived later that morning to his office and was awaiting a call from Judge Andreas. The mayor hoped that his friend would have a better idea of what they should do. It wasn't until seven at night that the judge arrived.

"Elias!" Mayor Temple stood up from his chair. "Such a day it has been."

The judge shook his hand.

"And such a day it continues to be," the judge said.

He tossed a file onto Temple's desk. A few pages fell out. Wade studied them but didn't have to strain too hard to see what they were.

"Divorce papers?" the mayor asked.

Elias nodded. "Afraid so."

"But why?" The mayor was puzzled. "This seems sudden."

"I felt the same way when I saw the man in my bed," the judge said.

"A man?" The mayor was shocked. "Did you at least even the score?"

Elias waved him off. "There's no time for that, Wade. We have a bigger situation at hand." He held out the newspaper. "How the hell did Jon get to Albion without either of us knowing? And more importantly, why?"

At this, the mayor sat down. "I've heard murmurings but nothing substantial."

"Substantial evidence is overrated."

"Judge," Wade said, "they'd throw you out of court in a heartbeat if they heard you say that." Wade rubbed his forehead. "Bad enough they already accuse you of such things."

"Things like what?" the judge asked.

Wade motioned the slamming of a gavel. "Too much of this." He then pointed at the file. "Not enough of that."

"My God, Wade," Elias said. "You don't really believe all that, do you?"

"Calm down, Elias," Wade said. "I wouldn't have put you in office if I did."

Wade and Elias's friendship extended all the way back to high school. Wade, the smooth-talking athlete, had always managed to get his way. It wasn't the same for Elias. The Andreas family had immigrated from a small country town in Italy, and while many imagined a true Italian being a lookalike for John Travolta's character in the movie Grease, Elias managed just the opposite.

He had been a shy teenager with plenty of acne to go around, and he held more weight around his waist than most of his classmates. Wade was the opposite: a slender, six-foot-four build. Captain of the basketball, football, and track teams. Few could avoid his charm.

Elias, more studious than athletic, tutored the football star. Their friendship grew from there, as Wade introduced Elias to the limelight of high school popularity, while Elias helped Wade get his grades up. This allowed both of them to go to Ivy League colleges.

They returned after graduation. Wade entered political office. Elias chose to lay down the law, first as a police officer—after losing a substantial amount of weight—and then as a detective. It wasn't until they ran into each at the Police Gala that Elias proved to Wade that he was still a great ally. This led to Wade naming Elias judge over the city of Brevington.

"What if he chooses to stay?" Wade asked.

"He won't."

"How do you know?"

"Because, Wade." Elias sat in the chair in front of the mayor's desk. "It's Albion. Despite what might have happened in the past, Brevington is home."

Wade shook his head. "You misjudge him, Elias."

"Wouldn't be the first time I was accused of that."

"No, my friend," Wade said. "Think about it. He has no family here. Yes, he knows the neighbors and coffee shop owners, but the whole city turned its back on him when he renounced his duties."

"His calling," the judge corrected. "And I suppose that hefty sum of money remains as an apology?"

"Every week," Wade said. "On the dot. Like clockwork."

Elias rubbed his temple. "I still don't know why you did that."

"Because we were wrong, Elias." Wade poured himself a drink. "He wasn't a circus freak to be paraded around town. He's a human being, like you and me."

"And that 'human being' has visited our jail system plenty a time," Elias said. "He's a criminal. A reckless drunk who continually chooses to drink and drive, yet he gets away with it while the rest of the city watches."

Wade smiled. "I wonder why that is."

"You know full well that if I had my choice..." Elias tried to calm himself. His anger was still rising. "The very injustice they accuse me of is because of him, Wade."

"Maybe," the mayor said. He had made his friend a drink, which he handed to Elias as they both sat back down. "But you must remember, my friend, you are doing the right thing. Jon might have gone his own way, but that doesn't mean we can forget that we started him down this path."

"Every man has a choice," Elias said. He took a sip of the bourbon. "Every man chooses how he wants his life to go."

Wade shook his head. "You're blinded, my friend." The mayor stood up and faced the window. "I've thought about it, Elias. All these years and it still remains the strongest memory."

"What's that?" Elias asked.

"The day we put that man out there for all to see." Wade set down his glass and turned to face his friend. "You should have seen his face, Elias. The pain. The dead gaze left me unnerved for many a day."

"It's just one man, Wade."

"No!" Wade slammed the desk. "He's more than a man, and he means more to the city than you know."

Elias remained silent, unnerved by his friend's outburst. He was still brewing in anger as he thought about all the times he had dismissed Jon.

Wade regained his composure, then turned back to look out the window. "We're getting old, friend."

"Speak for yourself," Elias joked. "I still have my hair."

Wade laughed. "Yes, I suppose that's true. I lost mine quite some time ago."

"And never shut up about it." Elias smiled.

"That too," Wade said. His smile faded. "We have to let him go, Elias."

His words caught the judge by surprise. "Why?"

"Because, Elias," Wade said, still facing the window. "If we bring him back, we are no better than our past. We would be making the same mistake twice, just under different circumstances."

Elias put down his glass. "And if he doesn't return?"

Wade looked down and sighed. "Then Brevington will have lost a true savior."

# CHAPTER 26

It was a silent car ride. Pain filled the air. Anger fueled the tension between Shirley and Sosa. Neither wanted to speak, yet they both had a lot that needed to be said. Shirley spoke first.

"Dr. Palmarardi has a point."

"Does he?" Samson asked. "Because it sounds like he's never lost anything important. As if getting over a lost life is as easy as changing jobs."

A few seconds of silence passed. Samson could feel the tension between them. He never wanted to see a therapist, but his wife did. He didn't want to stop grieving, but his wife thought it was time to move on.

"All these useless phrases," Samson said. "Get past it. Get over it. Move on." He stopped at the light and turned to Shirley. "Tell me, and be honest, Shirley—when has anyone ever gotten over anything?"

The intensity with which he'd started the day had faded. Though he was still angry, he didn't want to be. He didn't want to blame his wife for taking him to the therapist. He didn't want to keep blaming himself for Monty's death. Of all the things, he wanted the pain to stop. Shirley could tell from his expression.

"We never do, Sammy," she said softly. "We use what we've lost to make each day more meaningful." She squeezed his shoulder. "We're going through something so confusing. So out of our control that we are breaking ourselves down trying to figure it out."

Samson wanted to speak, but the pain welled up in his throat. He knew she was right. He knew everything had taken place so suddenly, so abruptly, just when things were getting good. Just when the family was coming together.

"It's not fair, Shirley," he whispered. "I sound like a kid, I know. But really, it's just not fair. We've worked so hard for this. This lifestyle. This love."

Shirley smiled. "Especially the love."

Samson laughed. "Do you remember how scared you were the day we were married?"

Shirley began to blush. "Stop," she said. "I'm still trying to forget about my crazy days."

Samson laughed. "You weren't crazy. I make a living traveling all over the world to play basketball." His smile widened. "It would be crazy if you weren't a little jealous."

"You're so full of it," she said, playfully hitting his arm.

Samson smiled. The light turned green. He began driving down the street. They were a block from their home.

"You say you were crazy, but I remember it differently," Samson said.

"Oh," Shirley said sarcastically. "And how is that?"

Samson took a hand off the wheel and reached out to hold hers. Shirley received it.

"You showed me that you loved me." He squeezed her hand. "You showed me that no matter where I was, or how I was feeling, you would always be there. I've never had that in my life."

They reached the driveway. Samson pulled in, stopping short of the garage.

"You're the reason I wanted to be a good father," Samson said. "You're the reason I didn't lose my way or become like my teammates, divorced and paying child support."

Shirley smiled though the mixture of pain and love that consumed her.

"Monty was proud of you, Sammy." She wiped a tear from her eye. "Always bragging to his friends about how great his dad was. Always wanting to go on the court while you were shooting around, just to show the world that you were his dad, and he was your son."

Samson thought back to those times. Monty would run into his arms no matter how old he was. Samson felt his love. He knew his son loved him more than anything else in the world.

At this, Samson broke down crying. Uncontrollably. Unashamed of whoever might see. The pain he held, and the love he would always have for his son, overwhelmed him.

"Why'd he have to go, Shirley?" he said, crying into his wife's arms. "Why did I lose my son?"

They sat in the driveway, crying in each other's arms. Aching from the pain of losing what had brought them so much happiness.

# CHAPTER 27

Kieran arrived. The warehouse lights were off. The guards chatted amongst themselves. Kieran didn't pay it much mind. He was interested only in speaking to Jon. He would have stayed if more pressing matters hadn't called him away.

He still had to run a company, Motley Incorporated, and that meant soothing shareholders. That meant taking calls and answering emails. It wasn't easy being CEO, founder, and majority shareholder. Add kidnapper to the list of titles and he had more than a full plate.

Yet while he handled business affairs, he couldn't help but think about what Jon had said.

*He knows I'm not from Albion, so where does he think I'm from?*

Kieran dressed just like his guards. He had simply been the first to speak. Maybe a leadership presence—clearly mentioning his name and the partial reason for Jon's capture—gave it away. He was part of the "gang", as he liked to think of it.

Yet he wasn't. And Jon knew the truth. But Kieran couldn't tell Jon why he was there. That Kieran was from Durrington. That he had captured Jon to make other "shareholders" happy, though they weren't the business sort. They were scientists. Inventors. People who wanted more and had it in them to go to any length to take what they needed.

"No," Kieran said to himself. "That will have to wait until this is done."

He was fascinated with Jon and his power. How he had been able to save a city of so many afflictions was beyond Kieran's understanding.

"Surely, if he can help so many people in Brevington, he'll be able to help our cause drastically, and efficiently."

This was his pitch to the scientists and inventors. It was a cult-like following, yet none of them sought to be the leader. Each of them was more curious about the unknown. Each of them was more concerned about how they could improve life—or take it.

"He'll give us what we need," Kieran said to them. "And if he refuses, we will extract that power from him."

Kieran smiled as he walked through the warehouse. However, when he noticed the chair, and the fact that a body no longer occupied it, anger took over. He faced the main guard.

"Look, it happened like this. He—"

Before the guard could finish, he fell to the ground. Not by magic. Not by words. Not by sheer force of will. But by a bullet that had escaped from Kieran's pistol. The guard lay motionless on the ground, a puddle of blood forming around his head.

# CHAPTER 28

It was a no-brainer for Jon. He had to find a liquor store, and fast. He had almost forgotten what it felt like to be led by the spirit. The peace that came with it. The wisdom. But just as the comfort of an all-knowing, all-seeing force had come, it had just as quickly left, leaving Jon feeling weak, afraid, and more vulnerable than he had when he'd first arrived in Albion.

Around the corner from the warehouse, and a block south, he found one. An open liquor store that appeared to have seen better days.

The floor was covered with crumpled chips and smashed jars of items he'd forgotten most liquor stores carried.

No cashier was at the counter. No employee in sight. It had not occurred to him that even though the city was a violence-ridden wasteland, stores like this would be the first to go. No owner dared face off with Albion customers.

"Talk about your local dump," he said, looking around. "Now, where is it?"

He walked the aisles, looking for a familiar taste. Hoping that what he was used to drinking would be right in front of him. He'd never had a taste for hard liquor, but to get rid of this feeling, this desperate anxiousness that held captive his mind, body, and soul, he was willing to try anything that worked.

On the shelf in front of him, Jon found a bottle of whiskey. Still full. Not tampered with or opened. He popped the cork and gagged when the sour aroma reached his nose.

"Not much of a choice," he said, eyeing the bottle. "But, oh well. Bottoms up."

He took a big swig, more than he wanted. His hand trembled as the thick liquid hit his taste buds. He coughed as if smoking his first cigarette, then spat out the taste that was left in his mouth.

It seemed like a mistake, choosing this bottle, until he felt a familiar warmth. The alcohol was working. Easing his tension. Relieving his anxiety. His hand no longer trembled and his mind regained focus. He knew this wasn't good. To tear his body apart with such poison. But the past few years had taught him little else.

It was a quick fix. And more importantly, he didn't have to pray. He took another swig from the bottle and walked around the store. The food had been ransacked. Piles of wrappers were left in freezers. The frozen goods were all gone.

He looked over to his left, where candy had once been. Nothing.

"It's not like I'm on a diet," he said to the store. "Show me something."

He kept walking toward the end of the aisle. Usually, there would be nothing but car fresheners and cheap gloves. Maybe a winter hat or two. But as he reached the end of the aisle, Jon noticed a smaller freezer. In it, he noticed, were ice cream bars.

Jon smiled. "Now that's what I'm talking about."

He reached in and pulled one out to see if it had been opened. It hadn't. He set down the whiskey bottle to peel back the wrapper, then devoured the ice cream bar as if he hadn't eaten in days. Once finished, he reached for another one, finishing it just as quickly.

He knew better than to get a third. His stomach was already rumbling from the dairy now settling in. He looked around again, making sure there wasn't anything else he would need.

When he felt satisfied with his search, Jon headed out the door, then stopped short of the curb. He looked left and right, waiting. He knew that no cars were coming, but he didn't know where to go.

"All right, big guy," he said. "Where to next?"

# CHAPTER 29

Wade filed away a couple of papers, while Elias sat in front of his desk. There were city documents the mayor had to approve and sign for. Elias, with the rest of his night being free, simply waited for his friend. Wade could feel the judge's eyes on him.

"Don't look so entertained," the mayor said without looking up. "By all means, I know this is as exciting for you as it is for me."

Elias sighed. "Is this really all you do?"

"Like your job is so different?"

"At least I get some action out of it," Elias said. "Crying parents. Hateful stares. A jailer or two trying to rough up a guard, only to be put in his place."

Wade raised a brow. "And you think that's better than this?"

"Of course it is," Elias said. "There's no fun in this. No thought. No quick decisions to be made on a moralistic scale."

"You're right," Wade said sarcastically. "All I'm doing is deciding whether raising the taxes will be better for the city while thirty-eight business owners are vying for a place in our already-packed community."

The mayor raised a paper to the light. "Oh, look at that," he said mockingly. "Another complaint about city taxes. Surely all one hundred and sixty-four of these can't matter. Not to a city. Not to a taxpayer who's threatening to destroy the businesses here because they are the ones responsible for the tax increase."

Elias yawned. "Important? Maybe. But boring and inconsequentially mundane? Definitely, yes."

"My old friend, if it weren't for these taxpaying citizens, you wouldn't get paid." Wade set down the paper, which he signed and then set aside. "And if it weren't for my approval or rejection, this city would go up in flames."

"Better to leave that to the firemen," Elias said.

Wade sighed. "Then who would pay them?"

"I don't know, Wade," Elias said in frustration. "Aren't there pension funds for such situations?"

"Yes, Elias," Wade said. "There are. But even those are drying up."

The mayor pushed the remaining stacks of paper to the side. "That's what happens when you have a city that isn't self-sustaining. Whatever is left goes to Durrington, or Jameson, or—god forbid—Germantown. We have little to rely on..."

"Because of Jon?" Elias asked.

The mayor sighed. "I'm afraid so, old friend."

# CHAPTER 30

Tears streamed down her face. Emilia wept at the end of her bed. She had made a mistake and she knew her husband wasn't coming home. She had ruined a good thing, but she wasn't remorseful.

Sad, yes. But not remorseful.

Her life would be different. Elias had taken her hand in marriage. They had promised to be there for each other. Promised to always remain in love. Yet she had broken that promise. And Elias had also broken his. The promise of a child had been a lie. A recent lie. A lie in which Emilia knew he couldn't fulfill his part of the bargain.

But this knowledge came to her in a special way. By a special person. This wasn't the first time she had made a mistake. It was only the first time she had been caught.

The well-known doctor of Brevington, Gregory Stackhouse, had also been Emilia's lover at one time. Single and with no family of his own, he had promised her something he knew the judge could not.

"He just needs time," Emilia said. "When he has more time, he'll want to settle down."

The ease with which she talked about her husband, while sharing another bed, amazed her. It happened so frequently that it seemed almost therapeutic. Yet, she knew she would never leave Elias.

"He hasn't told you?" Stackhouse asked. He leaned up from the pillow. "Emilia, Elias can't have children. Not now. Not ever."

"Oh," Emilia said, surprised by the news. "Then he'll want to adopt, of course."

Gregory laughed. "Emilia, I don't know what to say."

"What is it?" Emilia asked.

Gregory plopped back on his pillow. "I've mentioned the idea to your husband. That's not what he wants." He turned over on his side to face her. "He was set on the idea of having biological children. I think that was a deal-breaker for him."

"Well," Emilia said, waving her hand. "No worries, then. I suppose children are just out of the question."

Gregory held her hand. "Emilia, you don't really believe that, do you?"

Emilia turned over. She didn't speak the rest of the night. That one moment, that one night, ended up being their last. She never saw the doctor again. Elias never found out. Yet Gregory's question stayed on her mind. She thought that with each new lover, there was a chance to complete her family. She had it all planned out.

She would meet with a young lover. He would impregnate her. She would go to the doctor—someone other than Dr. Stackhouse—and confirm that she was pregnant. After the confirmation, she would cook a nice Italian meal, surprise Elias with the news, and they would raise a child, that wasn't his, together.

But her plan had failed. "You've gotten sloppy," she said to herself. "You were so close."

The tears dried as she thought up a new plan. She knew she would have to leave. Elias was the judge, after all. The court would be in his favor because he ran the court. She knew she wouldn't get half of anything from him.

*But where can I go?*

It didn't take long. Her old college friend lived in Durrington—a safe distance away from the news and soon-to-be scandal of said judge's wife found with another man. She packed a suitcase and headed toward her car in the garage.

While on the road, she made a call.

"Shirley, it's Emilia! How are you?"

# CHAPTER 31

Kieran had the remaining guards clean up the mess.

"I can't believe it," he said to the corpse. "You had one job: Don't let Jonathan Buckley escape. And you couldn't do even that."

The remaining guards hauled away the body. The shorter guard, Sam Cowell, approached Kieran.

"No kids. No family," Sam said. "Clean kill. Nothing to worry about. We'll have him taken care of."

Kieran held up a finger. "It's silly to mention this, but if I remember correctly, you were standing guard, too." He turned to Sam. The shorter guard gulped. "And though Jon is a spry fellow, despite being in his late thirties, I have a hard time believing he could take down all of you."

Sam took a step back. "He's different, boss."

Kieran felt his anger rising. "I know he's different!"

Kieran hadn't realized he had yelled this, thinking he'd been fairly calm about the situation. The other guards turned to see what had happened. He smiled, waving them off to continue what they were doing.

"Sorry," Kieran said. "My apologies, Sam, for my temper. But yes. I know that Jon is different. That is why we captured him." Now that he was calm, he began to pace. "What I don't understand is how he escaped. And since the head guard, Toby, is no longer with us, I would like you to explain what happened."

"Well," Sam began, scratching his head. "He started speaking this gibberish. I asked Toby what he thought Jon was saying. Toby said he was losing his mind."

"Gibberish?" Kieran thought about this. "Jon doesn't speak gibberish. What did it sound like?"

"Sir?"

"Try repeating what he said," Kieran commanded.

"Um, I guess it was kind of like…shaaaaay-mala, tehhh-gaah, or something like that." Sam shrugged. "It's no language I've ever heard of."

"That's because it's not a language," Kieran said. "At least not a decipherable one."

He tapped his temple, contemplating what it could be. The answer hit him like a brick.

"Tongues!" Kieran raised his hands. "Jon was speaking in tongues!"

"Tongues, sir?" Sam asked.

"Go on," Kieran said, dismissing his excitement. "What else did he do?"

Sam rubbed his eyes. "He started quoting something at us. I don't know, maybe Shakespeare. And the restraints fell off. So I went over to tie him back up."

Sam rubbed the back of his head. A jolt of pain rose up his spine.

"And then what, Sam?" Kieran demanded.

"And then it all just went black," Sam said. "When I came to, I saw Toby on the ground. The rest of the guards had this misty look to their eyes."

"Like they were blind?" Kieran asked, excitedly.

"Yeah, exactly like that."

Kieran smiled. "Thank you, Sam. I think that will be all for today."

"No problem, boss," Sam said. He started walking to the other guards but stopped. "Hey, boss?"

"Yes, Sam."

"Shouldn't we go after him?" Sam asked. "I mean, if he's out in the city, there's no telling where he'll end up."

"You're right, Sam." Kieran took a step closer. "But it's getting dark. Bad enough being in Albion. Do you really want to find out what happens here at night?"

# CHAPTER 32

Jon watched as the sun went down. The streets were clear and he couldn't see any movement. Yet it wasn't quiet. Scuttling and muffled sounds came from each direction. He couldn't see anyone but he felt as if someone were there. He knew this was a bad sign. He knew this wasn't a rodent problem.

He walked slowly, taking in his surroundings, making sure to not stay in the light, but also to not stray too far from it. He had to see where he was going, but he didn't need to be seen.

He listened intently and heard footsteps coming from an alley. They froze in their tracks as he observed a couple exiting what appeared to have been a grocery store. He could feel their panic. They were an older couple. Their eyes showed brightly, like those of a cat.

*They've adapted. And so quickly. How is that possible?*

The four cities had been built a couple hundred years ago. Jon knew human evolution didn't work that fast. An eerie feeling rose up his neck. He could tell there was more to the city than mere violence and chaos.

The scuttled sounds and muffled voices made it seem like the city was always moving. Was somehow alive. And though an eerie feeling arose, there was something else. Something that overcame him at that moment.

Empathy.

He wanted to get down on one knee and cry. He could feel the city. The panic of the couple who had left the vacant grocery store. The pain of the boys who had been gunned down months ago. He could feel it all.

"No," he said, forcing himself to keep walking. "Not now."

Briefly, he felt faint, as if the weight of the city were pulling him down. His mind fled from one thought to another.

*Hide.*

*Run.*

*Steal.*

*You're not safe here.*

Each thought held truth. Each statement kept the remaining citizens of Albion alive.

"It makes sense now," Jon muttered. "No one leaves Albion the same."

He thought back to the young man he had helped put away in Brevington. The man was young, in his early twenties, when Jon met him. He felt remorse for him. Sympathy for what he had come through just to be locked away.

"You can't trust them, Jon," Mayor Temple used to say. "The city changes all of them. They're not quite like the rest of us."

Jon tried reasoning with the mayor until the man, Lucas Joyner, attacked one of the guards. Jon turned to see the event. So did the mayor.

"No!" Jon shouted. "Stop!"

The guard struggled with the man, which was a feat in itself. The guard was six-foot-seven. Lucas Joyner was only five-foot-five. Yet the man brought the guard down.

"Guards!" the mayor shouted.

In seconds, five guards appeared around the corner. Each grabbed a part of Lucas. Each tried with all their strength to pull him off the fallen guard. By the time they did, the guard was dead. Part of his ear lay by his head. His neck had been ripped apart by Lucas.

Jon looked from the fallen guard to the man from Albion. The man held a different expression. Before, he had been sullen. Now he showed a smile. Lucas was clean-shaven when they'd brought him in. Now blood was dripping down his mouth. Skin from the guard's face stuck to Lucas's chin.

The man's smile widened when his eyes met Jon's.

"Take him away!" the mayor commanded. "And make sure to keep him in isolation! We can't have this happen again."

The mayor studied the fallen guard, whose face was covered in blood.

"And clean up this mess," he said, holding a tissue over his mouth. "If the news finds out about this, people will go crazy. And for god's sake, someone get that ear out of my hallway!"

Lucas was taken away. The mayor patted Jon on the back.

"Like I said, Jon." The mayor calmed himself and pointed to the man. "They're a different breed."

Jon focused on the guard. "They just haven't seen the light."

The mayor, finished with the situation at hand, stepped over the deceased guard. A medical team rushed down the hall.

"Some people don't want to see the light, Jon." The mayor ushered the medical team to the fallen guard. "And those are the most dangerous people. But so it is in the city of Albion. We have to let bygones be bygones."

Mayor Temple went back down the hall and stepped out the doors of the city jail. Jon remained behind. He watched as the medical staff lifted the guard and zipped him up in body-bag. The gurney was stained with blood.

A custodian came by and mopped up what he could. He sprayed the floors with chemicals to clean the area and mask the smell.

Jon watched it all—everything until it was just him. The hallway was silent.

The memory left as soon as it had come. Jon looked around as if waking from a dream. He noticed something had changed. He didn't feel the city anymore. He didn't feel the need to run or hide. Instead, he felt an overwhelming sense of peace.

He acknowledged the feeling with a nod.

"I may not belong here, but I'm not alone." He patted his chest. "Thank you for still being by my side."

# CHAPTER 33

"This is a bad idea."

Samson fluffed the pillows on his living room couch. The trash had been picked up long ago, right when Shirley moved back in.

"And you never liked her. So why is she staying here?"

"Sammy," Shirley said gently. "She has nowhere else to go."

"Don't you think she should have thought that through before sleeping around?" Samson sighed. "Speaking of Judge Andreas, I've never much liked him, either. Which makes this even worse."

"Oh, hush," Shirley said. "It will be for just a couple of weeks. Nothing will come of it, and she'll be out of our hair."

"Let's hope so," Samson said, realizing he had just received a text. "I'll be right back," he said to his wife.

She nodded and he headed upstairs. His phone began to ring and he answered it.

"Why the hell are you calling me?" he demanded.

"Come on, Sosa," Emilia said. "This will be fun, don't you think?"

# CHAPTER 34

Elias arrived just after midnight. A drink or two seemed necessary, and Mayor Temple was more than happy to oblige him. He had more than a few drinks, taking one shot after another, before getting a ride home. He made it up the stairs and sat at the edge of the bed—sitting where Emilia had sat before she left.

"Emilia," he said softly. "Of all people, why you?"

He didn't bother getting undressed. Instead, he fell back, not wanting to move. Not wanting to think. But the alcohol was flowing, so his mind went to and fro. One thought entered as the other exited.

He thought back to childhood. Growing up with his father. The fear he felt. The sporadic anger his dad showed. He thought about how much easier it would have been if his dad had truly been an angry, shrewd man. But he wasn't.

Some nights, Elias would come home to presents. Christmas would be far away. His birthday, long past. But gifts, nonetheless, appeared.

"Go ahead, son," his father said one night. "Open it up."

Young Elias, not knowing what he had done to deserve this, opened the gift. He tore off the wrapping paper, his eyes widening as the game system he desired lay in front of him. His eyes watered.

"Thank you, Dad!"

He remembered his dad smiling, patting him on the head, and then leaving. He also remembered the following day, when his dad was waiting for him to get off the bus. He had just come home from school. Young Elias could see his dad pacing back and forth on the porch.

"Hi, Dad," Elias said, unaware of what was going on. "Why are you outside?"

"Why am I outside?" His dad laughed. "Why do you think, son? Couldn't be because I was looking for a clean plate. No, it couldn't be that."

The frantic pacing continued. The bus driver drove away. Elias knew his mother, who was a nurse, was still working the last five hours of her twelve-hour shift. It was just him and his dad.

"I'm sorry, Dad," he said. "I'll go wash the dishes."

"No, no, son," his dad said, calming himself. Elias could hear him taking deep breaths. "It's all right. I've gone ahead and taken care of that."

He opened the front door for his son. "Now you go along and play with your new system. Would hate for your day to end on that note."

Elias, still afraid, quickly walked inside. He walked down the hallway until he arrived at his room. He couldn't believe what he saw. The gaming system his dad had just bought was strung from the door, wire to wire. The physical hard drive had been crushed to pieces all over his bedroom floor.

Elias picked up the pieces, hoping it was something else. Hoping his dad hadn't destroyed the gift he had given Elias. But he knew what his dad had done. He began to cry. Elias dropped the pieces and covered his eyes as the tears fell to the floor.

Seconds later, he could hear his dad's footsteps. His father stood in the doorway, looking from his son to the destroyed gaming system. No one said anything. It wasn't until Elias turned to see his father that he spoke.

"Why, Dad?" Elias asked. "I could've done the dishes."

"But you didn't!" his dad shouted. "Now did you?"

"No." Elias lowered his head.

"Exactly! You didn't!" His father, more frantic than before, began kicking the pieces all over the room. "You think this is my fault? That I'm the bad guy because you didn't do the dishes? No!"

His voice rose. Elias hurried into the corner of his room. He knew better than to get in his dad's way. Fear had taken over. His only thought was to survive.

"You didn't do the dishes! So this is what happens!" His dad pointed at what was left of the game system. He then turned toward his son. "Now go get my belt."

"But, Dad?" Elias spoke between choked-up tears. "Isn't this punishment enough?"

"Enough?" his dad asked. "You think you deserve less? You think you're getting off that easy?"

Elias shook his head.

"Good. Now go get my belt!" his dad yelled.

Elias headed toward the door. As he reached the hallway, he felt his hair being yanked back. There was yelling. He could feel each blow from his dad. He remembered falling to the floor, curling into a ball until it was over.

When it was, he laid there. Crying. Hurting. Afraid, yet quietly hoping his dad would leave if he didn't make a sound. From his room. From the house. From his life. But he never did.

The memory stung as Elias, still lying on the same bed where his wife had slept with another man, raised a hand to his cheek. The physical bruise that his dad left wasn't there. But the memory still stuck in his mind.

It wasn't until later in life that he realized his dad was mentally ill. But his mom knew. She knew before marrying him. She knew while picking up extra shifts so that she didn't have to deal with his sporadic outbursts.

"Don't worry, Eli," she would say. "He's just having a bad day. We all have bad days, right?"

The abuse continued until he left for college. And even though Elias had escaped his household, he never escaped the feeling. He always felt as if he had done something wrong. And in so doing, he made sure to never break the rules. To do everything right the first time so that he wouldn't be punished for it later—whether it was a bad grade or being late to work.

He became a stickler for doing right.

"So, how did I get this wrong?" he asked himself. "How could she leave me?"

Elias crawled farther onto the bed. He curled up into a ball, as he had done when he was a kid. He faced each returning memory of his father and the beatings he had taken. Each memory flashed before his eyes. Each blow enforced the fact that he was the one who had messed up.

For the first time in ten years, the judge began to cry.

# CHAPTER 35

Shirley waited outside. Samson hid in his room. He knew this was a bad idea. He knew this was the worst possible time for the two of them to have company. But Shirley was insistent. And his guilt over Monty's death made it hard for him to say "no."

Shirley waved as Emilia pulled into the driveway. Her smile brightened. Her mind, however, wondered if this was a mistake.

"Shirls!" Emilia squealed as she exited the car. "Thank you so much for this!"

"Emilia!" Shirley did her best to sound excited. "So glad to see you! What's it been? Five years?"

"Feels more like ten!" Emilia laughed. "But really, Shirls, it's been too long!"

They embraced. Samson watched the reunion from his room. He didn't want to go downstairs. He didn't want to be anywhere near Emilia or her drama. He wanted to get away. He wanted to drive as far away as he could.

"It's safer in Albion," he said to himself.

Emilia brought her suitcase. Shirley watched in amazement.

"Girl, you brought only one suitcase?" She opened the door for Emilia to enter. "Please tell me you need to get some shopping done."

Emilia laughed excitedly. "That is exactly what I need," she said.

Sosa took in a deep breath. Still hiding in the bedroom, he knew he would have to make his way down. Not to be impolite. Not to be a good host. He knew he had to go downstairs because he needed to know things were okay.

As Emilia set down the suitcase, she noticed the family photos hanging on the wall. She'd never had the chance to meet Monty.

"He had your smile," she said to Shirley. "And your great hair."

Emilia eyed Sosa, who was slowly walking down the stairs.

"Thank you," Sosa said.

"It's so horrible." Emilia turned to Shirley. "I couldn't believe it when I heard the news."

"Neither could we," Sosa said coolly.

He hated that she was here. He hated her more now that she brought up his son.

"In Albion, of all places," Shirley said. She invited Emilia to sit with her on the couch. "The whole thing was just awful. Is *still* awful."

Samson laid his hands on his wife's shoulders and kissed her head.

"But we're working through it," he said. "Everything happens for a reason."

Emilia stared intently at Sosa. "It does," she said. "It really does."

# CHAPTER 36

The four o'clock alarm went off. Elias reached for his phone, forgetting it had dropped out of his pocket the night before. He inched toward the end of the bed. His head throbbed and his eyes felt as if they would fall out if he blinked too hard.

The alarm grew louder. Elias realized this hangover was the worst he'd ever had. He reached farther and farther until he eventually fell off the bed. The phone was now by his side. He swiped at it and the alarm turned off.

He didn't feel like getting up. Work would be a pain. The court seemed so far away. His hope of having normalcy back in his life seemed impossible. But he had to get up.

"She can't win, Elias," he said. "You can't let her betrayal ruin your day."

As he thought of jail and the court sessions awaiting him that day, he remembered Jon. He remembered they still didn't know what to do. Wade had made it obvious that the city of Brevington needed him. And Elias agreed. But he didn't agree for the city's sake.

A part of him knew that Jon was special. Not just a nice guy. Not just a good friend. Not even a popular ally. No, Elias knew that Jonathan C. Buckley was capable of doing the miraculous. He knew that the people he helped were forever grateful. That he would never be forgotten by the city or the cities surrounding it.

But after the miracles stopped flowing, and after years of sending him to jail, Elias couldn't help but notice something peculiar: He had never once asked for Jon's help. He had suggested—or technically threatened—that Jon's next court visit would land him serious jail time.

But he had never acquiesced to Jon's special powers. He had doubts about what the man could do. Elias didn't believe in magic or religion. But he had a problem. A problem more severe, growing daily as he ignored it. However, since the situation with his wife, and with the painful memories of his childhood coming back, he knew what had to be done.

He dialed for his secretary.

"Samantha," he said, clearing his throat. "Yes, it's Judge Andreas. Yes, I know it's early. I assure you it was not my hope to awaken you at such a time. But I'm not feeling well. I'll need to call in for today."

He hung up, knowing she would make the necessary excuses, allowing him a full day to do what needed to be done. Struggling to find the strength to move, he got up, then stumbled downstairs to make coffee. As he finished the first cup and poured another, a thought came to mind.

He dialed another number. "Wade?"

All Elias could hear was a loud groan.

"Yes, I know." Elias popped two aspirin into his mouth, washing it down with the fresh cup of coffee. "Too many drinks."

"Elias," Wade mumbled. "I've had a good many drinks in my lifetime. Last night has topped them all."

"I'd say. But do you remember what you told me yesterday?"

"No, no, please don't make me take this shot?"

"No, about Jonathan." Elias took another sip of coffee. "You were signing documents. Said the city would collapse if we didn't get Jon back."

"Not sure I used that phrasing," the mayor said. "But, yes."

"Well, Wade," Elias said confidently. "I may need him, too."

He heard another loud groan from Wade.

"What?" Elias asked.

Wade sighed. "We're going to get Jon back, aren't we?"

"Yes, Mr. Mayor. We are."

# CHAPTER 37

The store was his best choice. He had never enjoyed camping, but Jon knew better than to head back to Brevington. There was work to do. And he wouldn't leave until it was done. Unluckily for him, Albion had no five-star hotels. He would have to rough it out in the city, which to him felt more dangerous than roughing it out in nature.

"Okay, Jon," he said to himself. "If I were abandoned in a grocery store, where is the last place I would look?"

He went to an office in the back of the store. The door was open. It looked as if no one had been there in years. After closing the door, he flipped on the light. Immediately, he regretted his decision.

Dead rats were sprawled all over the floor. Most of them seemed to have been stepped on. Others of them had clearly starved. Their rodent bodies were starved to the very bone. Jon had heard a story about rats—that they grew cannibalistic if pushed to the limits of starvation. It was clear this wasn't the case.

He grabbed a broom and swept the dead rodents to the side. Once he had cleared enough space for him to rest, he turned off the light.

"Dead rats. Maggot guts all over." He laid down and tried to get some rest. "Hell of a place, this city."

# CHAPTER 38

"What if we tell the army?"

"Wade," Elias said. "The army isn't going to help us."

"How do you know?" Wade asked. "I am the mayor, after all."

"Yes," Elias said. "But you're forgetting one thing."

"What's that?"

"Jon went there willingly." Elias rubbed his temple. "And it's the army."

"I know that, Elias." They were in the mayor's office. Wade paced back and forth. "My God, Elias. Why, of all places, did he go there? How the hell are we supposed to get to him and convince him to come back?"

Elias shrugged. "Beats me. But it has to be done."

"I know that!" Wade snapped. He sat down. "Sorry. It's just so infuriating. We must've really pissed him off. Who else would do something like this?"

"Pissed him off, paraded him around the city. Whatever it was, it doesn't matter now," Elias said. "I take it you don't have any bodyguards willing to help us?"

"Elias, it's Brevington." Wade held out his hands. "The city hasn't needed guards for quite some time."

"What about at the jail?"

"What about it?"

"The guards there," Elias said. "Maybe they could help."

"Yes, Elias. I'll gather up the only remaining guards who are watching convicted felons in our only jail and get them to aid us in a rescue mission, where the person being rescued doesn't actually want to come back."

"Well, when you put it that way..." Elias said.

"My good friend," Wade said. "This is a conundrum that we have created."

"We?" Elias protested.

"Yes. We the city. We the leaders of this fine establishment. We have caused him to clearly lose his mind." Wade poured himself a drink. "I fear it is we who will have to make the brave attempt to get him back."

"Wade?"

"Yes, Elias?"

"Is that bourbon?"

"Well, yes."

"Wade," Elias said. "It's only seven in the morning."

"I'm expected to go to the city of Albion with an old judge and a bad back." The mayor took another swig of bourbon. "Did you think this would start without me getting drunk?"

# CHAPTER 39

"Where to first?" Emilia asked.

"The Durrington Hotel?" Samson suggested.

Shirley hit Samson on the shoulder. "Real funny, Sammy. I say we go to the mall. Come on, sis," she said, holding out her hand to Emilia. "We need to get you a wardrobe."

"I thought you'd never ask," Emilia said.

She allowed Shirley to help her up.

"Let me get my purse and we can go," Shirley said.

"Oh great," Samson said. His sarcasm oozed easily this morning. "Make sure to get me a belt, honey."

"A belt?" Shirley asked. "Don't you have enough of them upstairs?"

"Yes, but not one strong enough to strangle myself." He hopped off the couch. "The other ones would just break under my weight."

Emilia smirked. "Maybe we can drop you by the gym, then?"

Samson ignored the remark. Knowing he had to get ready for the game tonight. Knowing the last game he played had been the night of his son's death. The team, management, and fans understood that he would not be back for a while.

Other players who had similar fates befall their family sometimes came back. Using the loss as motivation for the next win. Hoping to rally the fans behind them. But this was often a ploy for an increased fan base. Audience spikes brought bonus opportunities. Some players—especially the lesser-known ones—ate it up.

Sosa Barnett didn't care if the fans loved him or hated him. He had lost his only son. He would come back when he felt like it.

"Have to head out of here soon anyway," he said to Emilia. "Do me a favor?"

"Anything, Sosa," she said seductively. She knew Shirley was out of earshot. They were alone in the living room. "How can I make this more... pleasant?"

"First," he whispered firmly. "You can drop all of that. Bad enough you come here with your drama. It only makes matters worse that we're going through something. And second, move out. Get your own place. Hell, sleep over with your mom. *That* would make this pleasant."

"Oh, Sosa," she said, taking a step closer. "What she doesn't know might drive this whole marriage over the edge. But trust me, I've seen what the other side looks like." She brushed past him. "You can't imagine the opportunities that have opened up."

"You're right," he said, moving in the opposite direction. "I can't. Nor do I want to. But I'm sure *that* is hard for you to imagine." He smiled. "Not having a family, and all."

# CHAPTER 40

Kieran waited until it was fully light before leaving the warehouse. He wanted to see everything. He wanted to be aware of his surroundings. He wanted to find Jon.

"Wake up!" he yelled.

The guards, lying on their makeshift cots, awoke. It didn't take long for them to get up. And though they didn't have to listen to Kieran, they got up anyway. There was a peculiarity to this working relationship.

The guards stared out as a rag-tag group of young adults. Outcasts who had abandoned their homes. Mischief-makers who had tested the boundaries of society.

Lucile Hayes stood a proper five-foot-five, yet she had the looks of a supermodel. At first glance, she seemed a poor choice for the group. But one glance was all she'd need.

She wasn't a weapons kind of gal. Instead, she knew her way around the human body. Trained in martial arts and raised in the roughest parts of Germantown, she had grown up learning to fight. Needing to fight. Knowing that if she didn't, she would continue being picked on because of her family. There was a group of families, known as "townies", who didn't own any land. In Germantown, that was frowned upon and they were treated like peasants.

Her family belonged to that group.

She learned to seduce those willing to get close enough and to pummel those who didn't. Her long blonde hair and short stature caught many off-guard. However, one run-in with Ms. Hayes was enough to never ask for more.

Thompson Lewiston never needed much growing up. An elitist from Durrington, Lewiston was a product of his family's success. Smart and sophisticated, he was their prodigy. Durrington's up-and-coming genius couldn't wait to see the world. And because he couldn't wait, he left.

Stealing moments at a time to visit other cities, he was one of the first to have visited Albion and made it back alive. Yet, he didn't just visit the city. He had plans. He had a vision for the city. Most people proclaimed the city to be a waste, but he saw potential. And so the city became his project. He created a blueprint and settled on a particular spot of land. He created the plans for the warehouse and what it would hold.

He was smart enough to know that he'd have to hide the warehouse in plain sight. One look at the place and you'd think the building had always been there. Few knew that he had set up this hideout long before he knew Kieran. But he didn't do it by himself. His friend, Stephan Shelby, made Thompson's vision come to life.

Stephan Shelby was a six-foot-eight giant of a man. Born in Jameson, he was used to roughhousing on a more violent scale. Many from his city were not afraid of the people of Albion. They just never saw the pointing in visiting. Shelby was the first to take the city, and its citizens, head-on.

He had a temper and sometimes drove out to the city in the middle of the night, hoping to cross paths with someone clueless enough to try his strength. Though he always looked for a fight, he had talent like no one else in his city. Some claimed he could build an entire town with nothing but sand and a hammer.

With Lewiston being from Durrington, and with Shelby being from Jameson, it was quite peculiar as to how they met.

Lewiston, an astute scholar at the time, held a lecture that was open to the public. Shelby, observing the city of Durrington and hearing about said lecture, decided to see what all of the fuss was.

The meeting started rough and ended worse. Shelby debated Lewiston, claiming the lecturer lacked the basic knowledge of infrastructure and building zones. Lewiston denounced Shelby's ideology on the matter, claiming his "Jameson-like ways" caused Shelby to "not have a fully-functioning understanding of anything that didn't pertain to whiskey and horses." The debacle lasted for two hours. Both were winded at the end. Both realized that, in a way, they each had understandable points.

Seeing that the crowd had disappeared quite some time ago, Lewiston approached Shelby.

"What do you know of Albion?" Lewiston asked.

"Outside of their wasteland and lack of foundation, not much," Shelby said.

"What if I told you that could be changed?"

"Then I'd call you a damned fool," Shelby said. "But I'm not above hearing a fool's last request."

Lewiston smiled. "And I'm not above showing my plans to a buffoon."

Lewiston revealed his plans to Shelby. Shelby, never seeing a plan so thoroughly thought out, was quickly on board.

The start of the plan would take some time and required both men to meet in Albion with any time they could spare. That was when they met Sam Cowell.

Sam, the shorter of the three, had grown up on the streets of Albion. Not having much to lose, and seeing two easy marks, he tried to pickpocket the two while quickly walking by.

Upon successfully retrieving both men's wallets, he took off. Though he was short, he wasn't the fastest person Lewiston or Shelby had met. So ensued the chase.

Lewiston caught up to Cowell. Shelby was right behind him. Cowell, not one to get caught so easily, darted into an alleyway. He knew a few miscreants would be there. He knew they would slow down the two men.

Upon seeing said miscreants, Lewiston stopped.

Shelby, however, did not. Lowering his shoulder, he plowed through two knife-wielding men, making a beeline for the fence. Cowell had already jumped over.

Lewiston, not being much of a fighter, gently stepped over both men and soon gave chase to the short Albion man. Shelby, acrobatic enough to clear the six-foot fence, made it to the other side. Cowell, running scared for his life, rounded the corner, where he found himself back on a narrow street.

Shelby smiled as he caught up to the shorter man and reached out to grab his collar. He didn't figure the shorter man to be so daring. He didn't know that Cowell would dive through a store window to avoid being captured.

Caught off guard, Shelby quickly jumped over the broken glass, making sure to avoid scraping against the glass. Unfortunately, he wasn't careful enough. Lewiston, arriving late on the scene, took out his handkerchief and wiped off the remaining glass.

Cowell had already exited out the back of the abandoned store and reached another alleyway. As he headed down the dark path, he realized he had made a wrong turn. He had meant to go to the next one.

Shelby, catching up to Cowell, scowled as he held up his hand.

"I imagine this will require stitches," he said. "Who do you think is going to pay for that?"

Cowell shrugged and trembled. "Insurance?"

Shelby shook his head. "No, I think I might leave that up to you." As Shelby was getting ready to strike the man, Lewiston yelled out. "Stop!"

Lewiston rushed over, out of breath, wheezing from all the unexpected cardio. He held out his hand but bent to his knees.

"Wait," he wheezed to Shelby. "We could use him."

"Use him?" Shelby asked. "For what?"

"He knows the city. And I'm sure he'd rather help us than get pummeled by your fist." Lewiston regained his breath, then stood up straight. "Tell me, thief. What is your name?"

"Cowell," he said, still trembling. "Sam Cowell."

The unlikely meeting became a pleasant surprise as the three of them discussed plans for the warehouse. Later, Lewiston recruited Ms. Hayes due to the constant fights and hoping Lucile would stave off unwanted guests when Shelby wasn't around. Not long after, they met Lucile's ex-boyfriend, Toby.

Rumor spread around Durrington of what they were up to. Kieran, not one to disbelieve a rumor, set up a meeting with the group.

"I have a proposal," he said.

They met in the Durrington Library—an astute building that required membership like a fitness center would, except it was reserved for only the best of minds in the city. "It's not an easy thing, what I am proposing. But I assure you, the pay is good and the reward..." He shook his head. "Well, I can't even put into words the reward this will bring."

The offer seemed curious. Each member trusted the others, but no one in the group felt they could trust Kieran. Still, the proposal was of a curious nature, which each of them was drawn to. A nature none of them could escape.

Kieran was able to see that nature. To see through them. They were rebels. Going against society. Wanting to create something of their own.

They came together for this. They would do more, Kieran knew, with his guidance. The group had nothing to lose and everything to gain, so they agreed. And so they became Kieran and the four guards, now minus one Toby Emerson.

# CHAPTER 41

"Today's the day," Kieran said excitedly. "Let's try not to mess this up."

"Or what?" Shelby asked. "You gonna shoot us, too?"

There was tension in the room, though the only person who had known Toby was Lucile, and she wasn't heartbroken over her ex's death. Kieran had demonstrated his lack of patience, and they remembered that they were with Toby when Jon escaped. The threat of dying made the effort not worth it to Shelby.

"He can't," Lewiston said. "He needs us. And I assure you…" He faced Kieran. "You do need us."

"But this wasn't the plan," Shelby complained. He pointed at Kieran. "And he didn't tell us what Jon could do."

The group's excitement resided only in the idea—the idea of developing something special. Something they had carefully planned out. They would have their new city. The steps were there. Everything would be predictable.

But Jonathan C. Buckley, to their surprise, was everything but predictable.

They didn't know his power, his influence and control of a seemingly uncontrollable situation. He was the one who had been captured. He was the one who would help them fulfill their plan. But he didn't. And now the group had second thoughts.

"No," Kieran said impatiently. "I didn't tell you. Do you know why?"

"Because you wanted Toby gone as much as I did?" Lucile remarked.

Lewiston and Shelby shot her a surprised look.

She responded with a shrug. "Can't blame you for shooting him. But it didn't help that you put him in charge."

"He was a brute and a fool," Kieran said. "How he pulled the likes of you, I'll never know. But it's better for him to take the fall than any of you."

"And now that you know his power, how could you possibly think we could capture him again?" Lewiston asked. "This isn't some clever fellow. He has something backing him."

Kieran raised a brow. "Something 'backing' him?"

"Yeah, it was weird," Shelby said. "I don't know how to explain it. It's the vibe he was giving off."

"Please," Kieran scoffed. "He's just a man who knows something we don't."

"The very same man our parents used to tell us about," Lucile said. "The very man who saved so many people in Brevington that they declared him their savior."

"And now we know why," said Lewiston, tapping his chin. He could sense something was off. "But if you knew he had these powers, Kieran, wouldn't it have been in your best interest to warn us?"

Kieran shrugged. "Better to show you what he could do than for you to just take my word for it."

"No," Lewiston deduced. "No, I don't believe so."

"Is that true?" Kieran said, anger rising in his voice. "And what do you believe, Mr. Lewiston?"

Lewiston took a step toward Kieran. "I believe you need us. But not for the reasons we thought. We are not here to outsmart him. To convince him to help us. No, we are here as bait."

"Bait?" Shelby asked.

"You can get your own fresh bait," Lucile spat out. "I'm not dying for anything or anyone."

"Wait now," Lewiston said, holding up a hand. "That's not the type of bait he's looking for. But I will say, Kieran, it's a very clever plan."

"What plan?" Shelby asked. "What bait? What the hell are you talking about, Lewiston?"

Kieran waited as Lewiston put it all together. Having them guard Jon. Killing Toby instead of letting him mess it up.

"You were going to shoot him either way," Lewiston said. "Weren't you?"

Kieran raised his hands. "You got me. Toby had to go."

Lewiston laughed. He had figured it out, and he shook his finger at Kieran.

"You clever devil," Lewiston said. "You have absolutely no idea what Jon can do. And so you let him test whatever power he has against us so you could come back stronger, better able to control and manipulate him."

Kieran smiled. "Such a clever boy."

Before Lewiston could give a remark, Kieran raised his pistol. He aimed it first at Lewiston, then Shelby, and lastly at Lucile.

"You might think I'm nice enough to let bygones be bygones, but I'm afraid it's not that easy." Kieran took a step back. "This isn't simply an investment in your dreams. This is business. My colleagues expect something out of this."

"They must be so proud," Lucile said. "The Great Kieran, delivering a new city, but from the blood of his mangy group of guards."

"I wouldn't say mangy," Kieran remarked. "But as Lewiston said, I need you." He lowered his pistol and put it back into its holster. "I have no reason, nor desire, to kill any of you. And if we are going to see this through, we have to get Jon."

"You know that's impossible," Lewiston said. "And you know he will not be captured again. So tell us, Great Kieran, what is your plan?"

"Oh, Lewiston," Kieran said. "You disappoint me. Here I thought you had it all figured out."

Lewiston shrugged. "I'm only a genius half the time."

"Clearly," Kieran said. "But my plan is simple. Jon is here for a reason, isn't he?"

The group nodded. "Appears so," Shelby added.

"And that reason will keep him here as long as it remains relevant," Kieran said. "We don't need to find Jon, my friends. We need to find out why he is here."

"Yes, because it's as simple as asking a few friendly neighbors why Brevington's savior has come to Albion," Lucile said. "That will go over well."

"Now, Lucile," Kieran said. "Is anything in life that simple? First we have to find Jon without him knowing so. Once we do, we keep tabs. We follow him to wherever he is led, and we wait until his reason for being here is clear."

Shelby raised his hand.

"This isn't a classroom, Stephan," Kieran said. "What is it?"

"This all sounds great," Shelby said. "Really, it does. But tell me, how will we find Jon without the person who knows this city best?"

"What do you…" Kieran looked around. He cursed under his breath. "Where the hell is Sam?"

# CHAPTER 42

Emilia and Shirley left to shop before going to Sosa's game. Samson got everything ready to head out the door. The game was home, so he didn't have to worry about traveling. He just needed a change of clothes for after the game. With his bags placed in the car, he walked out to the driveway. A basketball still sat by the hoop.

He picked it up. Dribbling around a few times. Wanting to shoot, but finding he couldn't. Nothing was physically wrong. He hadn't played in months, yet he wasn't afraid of being rusty.

The game always came to him. Even if he wasn't feeling good. Even if the odds were stacked against him. He could still play. He could still outmaneuver his opponent. But in his driveway, he couldn't find the strength to shoot the ball.

He stood still. No longer dribbling the ball. No longer focused on anything else. He remembered his game-day tradition.

Monty would rebound and pass his father the ball.

"Come on, Dad," Monty would say. "Only eight more!"

Sosa could see the excitement in his son's eyes. It was as if his son felt responsible for Sosa having a good game. There were coaches on the court, but Monty was the coach at home. Monty felt his job was more important.

Sosa would catch the ball, shoot it, and watch it fall through the net. Swoosh! He wouldn't be allowed to leave until he made ten in a row.

"Five more, Dad!" Monty said. "You got this!"

Sosa wanted to smile, but he could tell his son took this seriously. It was Monty's responsibility to make sure his dad played well. It was his responsibility to make sure his dad won the game.

These moments made Sosa proud. Not because Monty was trying to make him better. Not because it reminded Sosa of why he played the game. He was proud because Monty already knew the secret.

Monty knew that it wasn't about cheering him on. Rather, it was about being there to make him better, stronger. To inspire confidence that would otherwise come from a flippant crowd or irritated coach.

"Good job!" Monty shouted. "You made them all!"

It didn't matter how many games Sosa played. How many times they did the same shooting drill. Monty was always surprised when Sosa made all ten. He was surprised that Sosa was the great player everyone claimed him to be.

Monty would witness it before the rest of the world. And Sosa was happy to show his son the truth: His dad was a great basketball player.

But Sosa knew this wasn't enough. He was a great basketball player but lacked the basics of being a good father. He didn't always say good night to his son. He hadn't seen Monty's first steps, heard his first words, or walked him to the bus on his first day of school. Sosa's career had taken a lot of those moments from him. And no matter how many shots he made, he always felt like he was coming up short.

After the last shot, Monty would run up and hug his dad. Sosa would pick him up, showing off his strength. Roaring as if his son had just unleashed the basketball powers from within. Monty would laugh, proud of himself as much as he was of his dad.

And then Sosa would leave.

As Sosa held the ball, and the memory faded, he stared at the hoop. The orange rim seemed a mile wide. His arms itched as if needing to move. To shoot. To do something to make someone proud. To do something to make his son proud.

He began shooting. Shot after shot. Make after make. He rebounded for himself and ran back to the three-point line. Tears streamed down his face, but he kept shooting. Pain, like a dull ache, beat upon his heart.

His son was dead but Sosa could feel his spirit. Monty's presence was on the driveway. Cheering him on. Jumping up and down as each shot went through the hoop. Thirty shots later, Sosa was done. Still clutching the ball. Still standing as he pictured Monty's smile.

He wiped away the tears and headed to the car.

"They were right," Sosa said to himself. "He is still here."

# CHAPTER 43

Wade buttoned up his zipper and patted down his leather jacket. Confidence bolstering. A glass of bourbon still in his hands.

"How do I look?" he asked.

"Like an old gang member who got kicked out of the gang," Elias moaned. "Come on, Wade. Don't you have any normal clothes?"

"These *are* my normal clothes," the mayor said. "Casual wear is not exactly a part of my addendum."

The jeans he wore had holes in them, like the jeans of the kids who went to Durrington High. Biker shades at the tip of his nose. A smile as if he actually were back in high school.

"Wade, I'm not going to lie to you," Elias said, standing up to show his distaste. "If you go anywhere in Albion dressed like that, we will get mugged, beaten, and left for dead, all in a matter of seconds."

Wade took a sip of his drink. "Elias, you act as if that wouldn't happen regardless of what I wore. I'm the mayor of Brevington, for Christ's sake. My face is plastered everywhere, in every city."

"Wade, first you have to know that you're not that famous outside of this city." Elias changed from his suit jacket, putting on a hooded sweatshirt he'd brought from home. "Also, at most, you are known in Durrington, Germantown, and Jameson. I doubt anyone in Albion even watches the news."

Wade looked up as if weighing the validity of Elias's statement. "That just might be true." He shrugged. "All the more reason to wear it."

"Great," Elias said, shaking his head. "I'm going to die next to an old man wearing holey jeans." He slipped on a pair of sweats. "Doesn't get better than this."

# CHAPTER 44

Jon knew it was time to go. Partially because of the dead rats. Even more so because of the rats that were still alive. He heard them skittering around the room. He felt them crawling over his body. There was no better alarm clock than that.

"Okay," he said, sitting up. "This was a bad idea."

He brushed off the few rats that were on him, then picked up his bottle. He needed a drink to shoot his nerves after having rats crawl all over him.

As he popped the cork to take a swig, Jon stopped. Holding the bottle to his lips. Feeling a tug, pulling for him to get up. No one was there. No physical object lifted him. And he would've thought this strange if it had not happened before.

"All right," he said, popping the cork back into the bottle. "Where to now?"

He had brought a backpack from the last store. Tucking the bottle inside, he headed out of the back office. Behind the counter was a clock. Its hands had not moved. Jon didn't have his phone with him, so he didn't know the time.

He could only tell that the sun was out. Guessing it was morning, he headed out to the street. Hoping to get a jumpstart on the day. Hoping he'd run into fewer people this early in the day.

He walked in the direction opposite from the one where he'd come last night. Hoping he wouldn't run into Kieran and the guards. Hoping to find out why he was here, and fast. He didn't like Albion. He didn't hate it, but there was no civilization.

Every turn led to more worry. More fear. More chaos that could not be avoided. Jon was led by the spirit, yet the spirit never let him know what would happen. His being captured was a perfect example.

Had he known that a group of people was looking for him, he never would have checked out the alley. Had he known that Mr. B was going to make this last request, Jon never would have let him die.

He didn't know if the spirit would have intervened to stop Barrister's death, but Jon still would have given it a try. There seemed to be rules for following the spirit. A depressing one was that he literally had to follow it.

He couldn't stand still. He couldn't wait to get directions. He had to keep moving. And in a city where violence occurred daily, and people died often, Jon didn't want to take any chances.

"Not to be too demanding," he said to no one in particular, "but a little heads up next time would be great."

He knew his request would be ignored. It was either that or he would have to ignore the guidance. The latter was not a luxury he could afford. He didn't know where his car was, nor did he know how to leave the city. His phone had the GPS.

But his phone was back at the house.

Down the street, he could see a few people scrambling around. Digging through the trash. One person broke the window to what used to be a bank, then used the glass shard to open a can of food.

This was in broad daylight. The whole city could see what they were doing, if the whole city were paying attention. They were committing such acts nonchalantly. As if society had no boundaries. As if this was how they survived. Jon waited and watched.

He waited for the loud neighbor to yell down from her apartment window. He waited for the owner of any of the half dozen abandoned stores to come out on the street, scaring them away. He waited for the police to round the corner, coming out with guns pointed, arresting anyone who tried to flee.

But as he watched, none of these things happened. No neighbor. No scary owner. No gun-wielding police. There were only these people. Trying to survive. Trying to make it to the next day. Jon was about to leave when he saw something unusual.

Something moved behind a dumpster to his left. Not a rodent. Not an adult. Something else.

He felt the same tug he had felt before. Pulling him to the dumpster. Guiding him to where he had to go. Jon followed, cautiously approaching. He made it within ten feet. The movement behind the dumpster stopped. So did Jon.

He wanted to say it was okay. That he wasn't there to hurt them. The person behind the dumpster was afraid. Jon could sense it, and the spirit made it known. But Jon, not knowing what the person was capable of doing, also was afraid.

He decided to not take another step. Waiting patiently. Hoping desperately that he wouldn't have to go behind the dumpster. But he could feel the spirit tugging. Pulling. Pushing him to go forward.

So he did.

Once he took another step, the person started running down the alleyway. Jon took off after them, though he didn't know why. The alley led to another street. As Jon neared the exit—and the person had turned the corner—he also turned. But no one was there. He heard no footsteps.

"What was that?" he asked. "Where did he go?"

The spirit didn't show him where to go next. Despite wanting to continue the chase, Jon didn't. He wasn't sure if what he had seen was real. He knew it was a person. And he knew the person wasn't going to hurt him.

But there was something about this situation. Something about the guidance he'd received from the spirit. A revelation of who he was supposed to help. A revelation of why he was there.

To get a clearer picture, he started speaking in tongues. Jon sat at the corner of the alleyway, his eyes closed, allowing him to focus. But it didn't last long. The plan was laid out. The victim was revealed.

"My God," he said. "How is this possible?"

# CHAPTER 45

Wade and Elias stepped into the SUV. The vehicle had a slick, black shine. Wade's security detail had just cleaned it.

"Have you ever been to Albion?" Elias asked.

"No," Wade said. "But it's east. A two-hour drive."

"What's the plan for when we get there?" Elias asked.

Wade smiled. "We go with the flow, as the kids would say."

He put the vehicle into gear, then pulled away from his office. Both of them were concerned, though the mayor was a little less nervous because of the bourbon. Elias still couldn't understand why Wade insisted on driving after having had five glasses of the stuff. But he didn't fight him on it. It was the mayor's car. Elias didn't have to worry about damages.

"Say we do find Jon," Elias said. "Won't we need his help more than he needs ours?"

"Yep," Wade said, pulling a flask from his coat pocket. "If Jon is the man we know him to be, he'll make sure we don't die."

"And if he's not?" Elias asked.

Wade raised the flask, showing it to Elias. "Then I'll give him a taste of the good stuff." The mayor smiled. "You said he had a bit of a drinking situation, right?"

Elias couldn't tell if Jon or Wade had the bigger drinking problem at the moment. He simply shrugged. "They've booked him a few times because of it."

"Then how could he deny this?" Wade took a swig. "Smoothest bourbon this side of the country."

He held it out for Elias to take a drink. Elias waved it off.

"You can't tell me you're going into this hellhole sober," Wade said. "You have nerves of steel all of a sudden?"

"No," Elias said, irritation in his voice. "But I think a clear mind is best. Especially for this, seeing that we know very little about the city. With the murders this past week—at least the ones we've heard of—I find caution to be more comforting than a drink."

Wade laughed. "Elias, friend, we'll be dead within moments of reaching the city." He took another drink. "And there's not much more to it than that."

Elias snatched the flask from Wade. "You really have a death wish, don't you? If you need Jon so bad, can't you at least try to act like this is possible?"

Wade shook his head, eyes still on the road. "I need him, you have that right. But don't think for a second that the two of us can take on a whole city."

"Who said anything about taking on a city?" Elias asked. "We're getting in and getting out. We apologize to Jon and tell him how wrong we were. With good graces, he'll forgive us and come back home."

Wade laughed even harder. Elias didn't see what was so funny.

"I'm sorry, old friend, but if you think Jon ran away just to leave us and the city behind, you've missed the bigger picture." Wade looked over and snatched the flask back from Elias. "That man is capable of remarkable feats."

"And why does that matter to us?" Elias asked. "He'll never do such things back in Brevington."

Wade shrugged. "He doesn't have to." The mayor took another drink. "It's what he represents that matters."

"All the more reason for him to come back," Elias said.

"No," Wade said, smiling. "All the more reason for him to prove otherwise. Not to us or the city, but to himself."

"I'm not getting it," Elias said. "What does he have to prove?"

"That he's not a freak," Wade said. "That he's not putting on some magic show meant to entertain the masses."

"You really think that's what this is about?" Elias asked. "A man on a mission to prove he's not a mistake?"

"Elias, your wife left you," Wade said nonchalantly. "No offense to you, or yours, but that has to hurt. Has to make you feel like you've done something wrong, doesn't it?"

"I didn't *do* anything wrong, Wade," Elias spat out. "She's the one who had the affair."

"Oh, I know," Wade said calmly. "But it hurts either way, doesn't it?"

Elias didn't respond.

"It's okay, old friend," Wade said. "You don't have to tell me. I know. Hell, who else would down that many shots if they weren't heartbroken? In fact, I'm betting what we're doing here today has a bit to do with that, too."

"Yes, Wade," Elias said sarcastically. "Saving Jon is like saving my marriage. Maybe you missed your calling as a counselor."

Wade laughed. "Maybe. I can't read your mind, Elias, but I know the feeling. The want and desire to know who you really are."

Elias sighed. "I know who I am, Wade."

The mayor shrugged. "Maybe you do, maybe you don't. With all that you know, there's still a part of you that doubts. It's in all of us, Elias." Wade took another drink from the flask. "I know that I'm the mayor of Brevington. Have a plaque and all to prove it. But you're a fool if you think I never doubt my ability to protect my city."

Elias thought about speaking up but decided it was better not to.

"Each day I walk into that office. Worried. Fearful." He took another drink. "But I read documents I never want to read, and study subjects I never thought mattered much."

Wade turned onto the highway.

"And do you know why? Because I'll do whatever it takes to better the lives of the people of Brevington. I'll make them understand that their mayor cares, even if I mess up here and there." He pointed at Elias. "You're a fine judge, Elias. You know that. I know that. There's no disproving that fact."

Wade held out the flask again. This time Elias accepted it and took a drink.

"What's my tenure as judge have to do with this?" he asked.

"Nothing," Wade said. "And that's the point. The part of you that's confused has nothing to do with work. It's everything outside of work, my friend. Emilia has shaken your foundation." Wade pointed to the windshield. "Out there, you'll see what you're really made of."

Elias thought about this. Saving Jon. Figuring out who he really was. The time seemed to fly by. The next words came from the mayor as he read the sign.

"Welcome to Albion."

# CHAPTER 46

Sam kept running. Away from Kieran and the group. Away from his friends. He didn't know why, but he was. He wanted to turn back. To apologize for leaving. Hoping they might forget the whole thing.

"What the hell am I doing?" he said as he rounded a corner. "Better yet, where can I go where they can't find me?"

The city was Sam's, and Sam belonged to the city. Albion was his home. It would always be his home, as long as he lived. But that didn't mean he didn't want change. The violence. The crime. The heinous acts committed by the citizens of Albion were too much. Change would have to take place. He just didn't know how.

Enter his dysfunctional group. People he never knew existed. People who thought like he did. They wanted the city to change. They believed, just like he did, that Albion could be saved.

And when it seemed impossible, a new solution came. Enter Kieran and his ingenious plan. Yet, Sam left. It wasn't because of Toby's death. He hated Toby. No, it was something else. Someone else whom he thought better for this cleansing mission.

"Jon," he said, exasperated.

He fell to the ground. Legs too tired to move. Chest too heavy to force himself back up. He wasn't in pain but he knew Kieran and the group wouldn't find him here.

"Sentry Lane," Sam said. "They wouldn't dare come here."

The very street was hidden from the sun. Buildings eclipsed any light. It looked like a dark alley that stretched on forever. If the darkness didn't discourage the group from searching, then the smell would.

It reeked of waste and death. People died on Sentry Lane. But not like in other parts of Albion. In other parts, the citizens were given a fighting chance. Light to see where they were going. Like-minded groups who were out only for survival, not murder.

Sentry Lane housed predators. People who were drawn to pain. People who became a part of the city. Death drew these individuals to Sentry Lane. They didn't want to leave the city. They didn't want the chaos and brutality to end. Sam never stayed in this area. But he knew it existed. Citizens told horrific stories of Sentry Lane.

"Just need to get to the next alley," he said to himself. Legs still unwilling to move. "If I could only get up."

An eerie quiet covered the street. No rustling. No scattering. No movement whatsoever. It was unlike the rest of Albion, which seemed alive. This street was still. Deathly quiet. Sam knew he had to leave or else he'd end up like everyone else who wandered onto Sentry Lane.

He tried pushing himself up only to see movement in front of him. Sam steadied himself, focusing his eyes on a pile of trash.

"Who's there?" he whispered.

He got no response.

Sam got to his feet, eyes darting from left to right, ensuring he could safely make a run for it.

*This was a mistake.*

Managing to move, he turned back the way he had come. He got only a few steps before two hands grasped his shoulder.

"Leaving so soon, Sam Cowell?"

# CHAPTER 47

Shirley and Emilia waited outside the locker room. They were happy for Sosa. Proud of the game he had played. It was his best game this year.

"How long does this usually take?" Emilia asked.

"You witnessed all those reporters crowding into the locker room," Shirley said. "He's contracted for media interviews. He'll have to answer all of their questions before he can even take a shower."

"Can't say I envy that job," Emilia said, covering her nose with a hand. "Trapped in there with sweaty, grown men. It was bad enough when Elias came home and plopped himself on the couch after work. I can only imagine how bad it smells in there."

Shirley laughed. "That's why I wait out here. I'm in no rush to deal with that."

"He really did have a good game, didn't he?" Emilia asked. "Seventy-two points? After being away for so long? I'm sure no one expected that."

"I know I didn't," Shirley said, smiling faintly. "Under different circumstances, this would be BNE-worthy."

Emilia looked confused. "BNE?"

"Best night ever," Shirley said. A smile remained on her face. "Monty came up with it. Every time Sammy had a great game, or broke some record, we would celebrate. Sammy always chose to get ice cream because he knew it was Monty's favorite."

A tear streaked down her face. "It was more for him, you know? Sammy doesn't care for the accolades. He knows how good a ballplayer he is. But for Monty, it meant so much more. It gave him something to look up to."

"Oh, Shirley," Emilia said, embracing her. "I didn't know. But you know what? I'm sure Monty is up there enjoying all the ice cream he wants. Which I'm sure is more than either of you would have allowed on a school night."

Shirley pulled back, laughing. Tears still fell down her cheeks. "No way he could have ice cream this late," she said. "But Emilia, I'd give him all the ice cream that money could buy just to have him back."

"I know, Shirls," Emilia said, holding her shoulders. "I know you would."

An hour passed as they waited for Sosa.

"This might take longer than I thought," Shirley finally said. "How about we wait for him at home?"

Emilia shrugged and smiled. "Sounds good to me."

Shirley spoke to one of the security guards outside of the locker room. He assured her that Sosa would get the message to meet them at home. Shirley nodded. Emilia joined her and they made their way back to the car.

# CHAPTER 48

122-96. The Durrington Lions had won. Sosa remained in the locker room, a towel draped over his head. Reporters pushed by his teammates to interview the all-star. Seventy-two points was a career-high for him.

"Sosa, how did it feel?" one reporter asked.

"Was this game dedicated to Monty?" another questioned.

"Do you think this puts you in the running for Most Valuable Player?" another pried.

"What will it take for you to do this every night?" another reporter shouted.

Samson, no longer wanting to be in the limelight, got up. He walked through the crowd of reporters and headed to the shower. There, he showered alone. His teammates were already gone. His jersey and shorts were fully soaked with water.

He stayed there until a janitor told him that everyone had left for the night.

# CHAPTER 49

Wade parked the SUV by a gas station. He and Elias looked around, hoping they were alone. Wondering how soon it would be before they were spotted. Wade unfastened his seat belt.

"What are you doing?" Elias asked.

"Can't stay in here forever, my friend," Wade said.

He hesitated, shutting the door before getting out.

"Almost forgot something," he said. He grabbed the flask and unscrewed the top. Wade took a large drink from it before offering it to Elias. "A little liquid courage?"

Elias shrugged and accepted the offer. He finished the rest of the bourbon, then handed the empty flask to Wade. The mayor, agitated that his friend had finished the rest of the bourbon, tossed the flask into the backseat.

"All right," he said. "Time to see what Jon has gotten us into."

Elias opened the door and stepped out. He didn't see anyone, but he heard scattering nearby.

"You hear that?" he asked Wade.

"Yeah," Wade said. "What is that?"

"I don't know. Rodents, maybe?"

A shiver went down the mayor's spine. "Makes it seem like the city is alive."

"And not in a good way," Elias said. "Think we should bring a gun?"

"To add to the crime that's already taking place in this city?" Wade asked. "I think not. Plus, what will it look like if Brevington's mayor and judge murdered the rest of the citizens of Albion?"

Elias shrugged. "What would it look like if they found us dead?"

# CHAPTER 50

Kieran split up the group. Shelby and Lewiston would search the south end. He and Lucile would search the north.

"And if they went east or west?" Shelby asked.

"Then we'll search what's left and hope to find them," Kieran said. "I imagine Sam can't be too far. Jon had more time, so our best bet is finding Cowell first."

"But if he knows the city, don't you think he'd know the best place to hide?" Lewiston asked. "I don't doubt your plan, but the work it will take to find Sam far outweighs the work it would take to find Jon."

"And Jon is the person we need most, right?" Lucille jumped in. "So, let's just find him and get this over with."

"Fair point," Kieran said. "Focus on finding Jon. But if you come across Sam, find a way to persuade him back. For the life of me, I don't know why he left."

"You did shoot Toby," Shelby said. "And I'm sure growing up here hasn't boosted Cowell's confidence. Maybe he thought you'd shoot him next."

Kieran thought this over. "It's possible. If you see him, assure him that he is safe. There will be no more shooting."

"Except for the people of Albion?" Lewiston turned to Kieran. "Surely you know that there are crevices in this deeply lost city begging for brute force. As much as I'd like it to not come to that, you and I both know that may not be an option."

"Yes, Lewiston," Kieran said. "I am aware. I'm also aware that rodents are stomped and pests are dealt with. So, if you value your lives, do not hesitate to take the life of anyone who threatens it. Understood?"

The group nodded.

"Good," Kieran said. "Now, let's start looking. We don't have much time before it gets dark."

"And I assure you," Lewiston said. "I will be back here way before that time comes. Strange things happen here at night."

# CHAPTER 51

It was midnight when Samson arrived. The girls were in the living room. Samson plopped down on the couch, mentally and physically drained.

"It's about time," Shirley said, moving over to her husband. "You had a good game, Sammy."

"Best of the year!" Emilia said.

"Thanks, you two," Samson said with a faint smile. "Pretty much left it all on the court."

"I see that," Shirley said, gently massaging his shoulders. "We made dinner after the game. It was getting late, so we ate before you arrived."

"We saved you some," Emilia said cheerfully. "But you better hurry to get a plate. I don't need it, but I might get another. We truly outdid ourselves this time, Shirls."

Shirley laughed. "I'd say. Here, Sammy, I'll make you a plate."

"Thanks, babe," Sosa said. "I'd get up if I knew my knees wouldn't collapse."

Emilia remained on the recliner as Sosa lay back on the couch. He was comfortable where he was. Emilia wished she could move closer. She eyed the basketball star. He sensed her stare and looked over.

"What?" Sosa asked.

"Oh, I'm just wondering," Emilia said. "Have you seen this movie?"

Sosa glanced at the screen. "I don't think so. What is it?"

"A love story," Emilia said. "Truer than any other. As old as the beginning of time."

Shirley sighed and set down the steaming plate. "It's The Great Gatsby," she said. "A classic."

"Doesn't seem old enough to be a classic," Sosa commented. "Seems fairly new, actually."

"It's the remake," Shirley explained. "The original came out many years ago. That might be the one you remember."

"I think I've heard the title before, but I've never seen it." Sosa cut a piece of lasagna and took a bite. "Seems interesting, though."

"It is," Emilia perked up. "I think we've all lived a life like them. Poor to rich. Having something but wanting something else." She stared at Sosa. "And in the end, who knows? We may go out in dramatic fashion, or maybe we'll live happily ever after."

"Let's hope for the latter," Shirley said. "I think we've dealt with enough shootings in this lifetime."

Samson could tell that having Emilia around was helping his wife. Death didn't bother her as much. Their son's passing didn't weigh down Shirley as much as it had in the previous weeks. She was moving around. Going places with her friend and refusing to stay in bed longer than she had to. He only wished he could move on like she had. He only wished his son's death didn't weigh so heavily on his heart.

# CHAPTER 52

Sam jumped forward and wheeled around to see who was behind him. He was shocked that he knew who the person was.

"Sean?" he asked.

"In the flesh," Sean said. "What brings you back here?"

"What brings me back here?" Sam questioned. "What the hell are you doing on Sentry Lane? You know how dangerous it is. You know people die here every day."

"People die in Albion every day, little brother," Sean said. "Doesn't mean I can't adapt."

"Adapt to becoming a killer?" Sam asked.

"Adapt to thriving, little brother." Sean made his way into the light. "You've been gone for a while. You forget how ruthless this city is."

"Not this street." Sam urged Sean to come with him. "You shouldn't have lasted this long. Now we have to go."

Sean shook his head. "Oh, Samuel. How little you have learned." He held out his hands. "These are my only pals. Best buds, if you wish. And they've experienced more than you know. Too many acts of 'unkindness'."

Suddenly, Sam's brother looked around. Sentry Lane was quiet but Sam had a feeling that his brother had heard with more than ears. Sean had become a part of Sentry Lane.

Sam grabbed Sean's hand. "Doesn't matter," he said. "We've both done ruthless things to stay ahead. To stay alive, even. I know you know that's the way Albion is."

Sean smiled. "Is it, little brother? That's about to change, from what I've heard." He pulled his hands away. "A so-called savior is wandering these very streets."

"Jon?" Sam asked. "He might be a spook, but he's no savior."

Sean wagged his finger. "That's where you're wrong, Samuel. The city knows who he is. Had you stayed your hand, you would, too."

A trash can rattled in the distance. Sean looked ahead. He knew the sign and didn't hesitate.

"You're not safe here, little brother." Sean turned Sam around and pushed him. "Go, Samuel. Wish that savior of yours good luck."

Sean backed away into the darkness.

"He'll need it."

# CHAPTER 53

Jon hid behind a dumpster. Not wanting to be seen. Not wanting to give Kieran and his henchmen the upper hand. While he waited, he thought back to what he had seen. To whom he had seen when he had given chase.

"Who was that?" he asked himself.

He couldn't believe someone could manage to survive on their own in this city. He barely survived, and that was with the spirit guiding him. But the proof was before him. Jon knew this person would need help.

"Guide me, God," he whispered. "And show that your way is greater than ours."

He waited. Hoping to feel a tug. Hoping the spirit would stir something in him. He knew it wouldn't. He knew that wasn't how the spirit worked. And so, he waited as long as he could, until a familiar feeling came over him.

An all-encompassing fear jerked to life. A fear that had been there the whole time. The spirit, and alcohol, had suppressed it. But now it was full-blown. He remembered not wanting to be here. In this city. Saving another life.

He remembered wanting to be home. Relaxing on his couch. A beer in hand as he watched the Durrington Lions win another game. But he was in the wild. The true wild. A chaotic despot where everything bad happened.

He clasped his hands together as they began to shake.

"Not here," he begged. "Not now."

Everyone who crossed paths with Jon knew that he exuded an air of confidence. A strong miracle worker who, yes, may have lost his way but was still guarded by a higher power. Most people thought this but they didn't know that alcohol pulsed through his veins.

He was a drunk.

He hadn't always been, but after years of heavy drinking, he had become the very affliction from which he had previously broken people. He knew it. The city knew it. But unlike Jon, the city thought he could snap his fingers and fix the problem.

He'd done so for others in the city. He'd accomplished far greater things for those in worse shape. But the problem was pervasive. Spreading wildly through his body and mind. Affecting every action, move, and decision he made.

He was no longer in control. And if he felt bold enough to believe otherwise, the lack of alcohol would halt him in his tracks. Reeling him back. Trapping him in a prison of fear. Going to Albion didn't make a difference.

He had never wanted to do this sober-minded. The request from Barrister seemed crazy enough, let alone the spirit pushing him to go to Albion. But he hoped to have the strength. He hoped to have the courage to do what was right, believing that a worker of miracles could turn into a spiritual warrior.

He was wrong.

Desperately, he grabbed for his backpack. Hands still shaking. Fear paralyzing him, preventing him from moving forward. Jon fumbled with the zipper until the backpack opened. He reached for the bottle and popped the lid.

He was about to take a drink when he heard a noise. Looking to his left, he saw a group of men approaching. None of them was Kieran. All of them were carrying makeshift weapons.

"Look what we have here," the tallest of them said. "A tourist."

"Oooooh," said the shorter, pudgier one. "I love tourists."

They slowly approached Jon as he put the bottle back into his pack. He eyed each one. There were three of them.

"Let me go first," said the scrawny, average-height one. "I promise to be gentle."

The other two laughed. Cackling sounds, dry and quick. Hoarse, as if they needed water.

"You men sound thirsty," Jon said. "Here, I have water to share."

"Share?" The taller one laughed. "We don't *share* anything around here."

"Would you rather have none?" Jon asked.

The taller one frowned. The shorter, pudgy one elbowed him.

"We have a jokester, boss," he said. "Don't sound like he knows where he is."

"I know exactly where I am," Jon said, taking a step forward. "And I can tell you that if we aren't sharing this water, I'll be on my way."

The taller one, now revealing a gun, winked.

"I'm thinking you're not going anywhere, tourist."

# CHAPTER 54

Wade breathed heavily, waiting for Elias to round the corner. Knowing his friend wasn't an athlete. Hoping the two teens chasing them had let up. While it didn't help that Wade and Elias were outsiders, it was their age that had made them easy targets.

Elias rounded the corner. Wheezing. Collapsing to the ground, barely out of sight of the youths.

"Those kids weren't playing around," Wade said, consoling his friend. "Worse yet, I think they took my wallet."

Elias panted but raised his hands. "Why the hell would they want your wallet, Wade? There's nothing to buy around here."

Wade looked around. "Fair point. Maybe for sentimental value?"

"Yeah," Elias said, "because kids who yell 'we'll slit your freaking throat' seem value-driven to me."

Wade shrugged. "It is genuine leather. I can't blame them for wanting it."

"Wade, I'm not sure we can survive another attack like that." Elias swiped the sweat from his brow. "And those were only children."

"Teenagers," Wade said. "And they're rowdier than the rest. Think of when we were in high school."

"I can't recall screaming threats at any of my teachers."

"No," Wade said. "But you remember the adrenaline. The genuine need for chaos and destruction. That's what is coursing through their veins."

"Oh," Elias gasped. "And here I mistook youthful adrenaline for murder-driven psychopaths."

"That's also a possibility."

"Wade?"

"Yes, Elias?"

"Do we really need Jon?"

Wade thought about the question. "If you want your job, and if I want my city to remain, then yes."

"You do know we won't survive this, right?" Elias said.

"Maybe not," Wade noticed movement in the distance. "But it doesn't mean we can't try."

He recognized that the movement came from two people—the two teens who had chased them.

"I do highly suggest that you give this one more shot," Wade said. "On your feet, judge."

Elias turned to see the teens fast approaching.

"Damn you, Jon," he huffed, getting back to his feet.

# CHAPTER 55

"I don't imagine any of you gents have a towel?"

Jon, tied up to another chair, felt the blood streaming down his chin. "A t-shirt or rag will do just fine."

The taller man slugged Jon again. This time, a popping sound came from one of his fingers.

"My God," the taller man said. "The man's chin is made of steel."

The shorter, pudgier man shrugged. "Told you it'd hurt. Why'd you think I stopped?"

The three of them—each had taken turns beating Jon—stood before him. Jon, with his left eye swollen and his mouth missing two teeth, grinned.

"I thought Albion would be nicer this time of year." He spat out blood. "It's warm. The summer breeze is whistling. And yet here I am. Tied down to another chair."

He knew the worst of the beating was over. None of the three were equipped to deal another blow. Individually, he could have taken them. But they ganged up on him.

"Not so threatening now, are you?" the taller man taunted. "Who has the water now?"

Jon smiled. "Water that can't quench your thirst doesn't have much value, now does it?"

The shorter man took a drink. "Tastes just fine to me."

The taller man grabbed the canteen, taking a drink for himself.

"We must've knocked him something fierce if he thinks this water isn't good."

The three men laughed. Proud of their work. Enjoying the capture of one more tourist. Jon didn't know their plan, but he guessed he wasn't their first captive.

"So, this is the Albion way," Jon said. "I'm guessing I'm not your first victim."

"Nope," the average-height man said. "Jim, Stew, and I get first dibs here."

Jon eyed the taller man. "Jim, I'm guessing?"

The taller man nodded.

"And Stew?" He faced the shorter man, who nodded, too.

"What's your name?" Jon asked.

"Paul," said the average-height man.

"Interesting," Jon said. "Paul is biblical, you know. He led many people to Christ back in the day."

"Christ?" Paul questioned. "Jim, what the hell is he talking about?"

Jim shrugged. So did Stew.

Jon shook his head. "I imagine you guys haven't read the book. But it's important to know what your name means."

"Not a soul told me the meaning of my name." Stew spat and coughed. "Now look at me! Turned out just fine!"

Jon smiled. "That you did. But Paul, I think you'd be interested in knowing a little more. Stories always claimed the name was powerful."

Paul squinted. "I'm listening."

"Good old Paul. He was a leader. He wrote impactful words. Did miracles here and there, too." Jon leaned back in his chair. "And you know what made him so powerful?"

Stew shrugged. So did Jim. Paul seemed skeptical but asked, "No, what?"

"The spirit, my friend," Jon said. "The spirit helped heal the sick, cure the blind, and bring a dead little girl back to life."

"So, he was a magician?" Jim asked.

"No, you idiot," Stew said. "He was a wizard."

"No," Jon intervened. "He was just a man. Like you and me. Doing what the spirit asked. Praised in many cities for the power he showed."

"How'd he get it?" Paul asked. "The spirit or whatever it is."

"That was the easy part." Jon smirked. "He simply requested its presence."

"Like a prayer?" Paul asked.

"Bingo," Jon said. "Hey, it sounds like you have a little bit of the spirit in you, too."

Paul laughed. "Oh yeah? And how would you know?"

"Simple," Jon said. "Did you know what the word prayer meant before I arrived?"

Paul thought about this. He was taken aback by Jon's question. Paul looked from Jim to Stew before answering. "No."

"See," Jon said. "That was the spirit. I wonder what would happen if you invited it in?"

Stew nudged him. "Go ahead, Paul. Do it," he urged.

"Yeah," Jim said. "I want to see what happens."

"All right, all right," Paul said. He turned to Jon. "So, I just ask it to come in?"

"Yep," Jon said. "Just ask it in."

Paul, unsure of what would happen, asked the Holy Spirit to come in. As he did, his arms felt heavy and he slouched over. Stew and Jim became worried.

"What'd you do?" Jim demanded.

"Told you!" Stew said. "He's a wizard!"

"No, Jim and Stew, I just know my place." Jon leaned forward, noticing Paul unsheathing two knives. "I'm guessing your friend does, too."

Before Jim and Stew took notice, Paul had stabbed each in the heart. As Jim and Stew collapsed to the ground, Paul fell asleep. The ropes that held Jon fell off.

# CHAPTER 56

"We'll never find him," Shelby kicked a stone out of his way. "He knows the city like the back of his hand."

"Maybe," said Lewiston. "But I know if we don't find him, we might as well kiss this plan goodbye."

They went in the direction opposite of Kieran and Lucille. Confused. Doing their best to navigate the city. Lewiston hoped they didn't run into trouble. But it was Albion. Trouble was bound to cross their path.

"His plan," Shelby said. "He ever reveal it to you?"

"No," said Lewiston. "But I can guess what it is."

"We all can guess, Lewiston," Shelby said.

"I know Kieran," said Lewiston. "He's not as ingenious as he'd like you to believe."

"He has money and he's not afraid of Albion."

"Are you?" Lewiston asked.

"Am I what?"

"Afraid of this city."

"Not even a little." Shelby looked straight ahead. "I'm kind of hoping for trouble."

"You just don't have any money," Lewiston said. "But I do."

"What's your point?"

"My point is that I have money and you have no fear." Lewiston stopped and turned to face Shelby. "His plan requires things we already have."

"If that's so, why are we following him?"

"Because." Lewiston smiled. "The idea isn't half bad."

"And what's his plan?" Shelby asked.

"Something simple, yet demanding." Lewiston kept walking. "He wants to use Jon as a ploy. A means to kick out the miscreants that bog down this city."

"And you think Jon can do it?"

"I know he can," Lewiston said. "But there's a flaw in his plan."

Shelby thought for a moment. "He can't control Jon."

Lewiston nodded. "But he thinks if we find what Jon is looking for, he can blackmail him."

"I don't know about that," Shelby said. "He might not be scary, but something tells me Jon isn't one to back down from a fight."

"You're right, Shelby. He's not."

"And that's where you think the plan will fail?" Shelby asked.

"Not exactly."

Lewiston eyed the narrow alleyway to his right. He didn't know what was there, but something tugged at him. Wanted him to explore the darkened area. Pushed him to take a step in that direction.

Shelby laid a hand on his shoulder. "Not a good idea." Shelby nodded the other way. "Best to stay in the light."

"Maybe," Lewiston said, agreeing to head back down the street.

He was worried and curious at the same time. There was something about the city. Albion was filled with violence and chaos and the worst citizens that any of the four cities had come to meet, but Lewiston knew there was more to the city. The very atmosphere was tempting. Tendencies he'd never felt before coursed through him. Curiosity grew with each step.

Being a scholar, he'd always wandered toward the unknown. Finding no point in dealing with what was known. Wanting to know what would happen if he pushed the boundaries. He wanted to go where he knew he wasn't supposed to be.

The city played on this tendency. It tempted him toward the unknown.

"You ever get the feeling that no one was ever meant to come here?" he asked. "As if society wasn't mean to exist in this city?"

"More than you know," Shelby scoffed. "I'm guessing you feel it, too?"

Lewiston nodded.

"When I first came to the city, I was lost," Shelby said. "I was trying to get home when I took a wrong turn down the interstate."

Shelby was quiet for a moment.

"I don't know what it was, the curiosity or wanting to get directions. But I got out of the car." He stopped in the street. "It was midday. Not a soul was around. So I got out of the car to find out where I was."

"You didn't see the busted 'Welcome to Albion' sign?" Lewiston asked.

Shelby shrugged. "I didn't, strangely enough. And when I started walking around, I didn't even know I was in Albion."

Lewiston held out his hands to mock his friend. "Decrepit city? Abandoned stores at every corner?"

"I know, Lewiston. But I'd never been here before, remember?" Shelby looked around. "It wasn't until I was attacked that I really knew this wasn't Germantown."

"And you fought them off?" Lewiston asked.

"Not at first," said Shelby. "I asked for help. Told them I was trying to find my way back to Germantown."

"I'm guessing they didn't point you in the right direction," said Lewiston.

Shelby shook his head. "Nope. Instead, they unsheathed some weapons: a wooden bat and a cracked bottle."

"That must've been fun."

"Less fun than you might expect," said Shelby. "It was two guys. One half my size. The other as big as me." Shelby smiled as the memory played through his mind. "I don't know what I was thinking, but I charged back at them."

"Smart move," Lewiston said. "If you have a death wish."

Shelby shrugged. "What can I say? I'm not one to run from a fight. Regardless, I took them out and thought I'd head back to the car."

"So, you hopped in and somehow found your way back home?" Lewiston asked.

Shelby shook his head. "No. I stayed a while longer."

"You stayed?" Lewiston questioned. "Why the hell did you decide to stay?"

"That's the thing," said Shelby. "I have no idea. I wasn't afraid of the city, but I wanted to get home. I realized where I was, but…"

"But the city drew you in," said Lewiston. "Peculiar."

"I'd say." Shelby noticed the sun going down. "There's something about this city, Lewiston. Something not good."

Lewiston huffed. "You can say that again."

"But we're all drawn to it."

"We are," Lewiston commented. "I have an idea as to why."

"Well," Shelby said impatiently. "Spill the beans."

"We're all drawn to Albion because Albion is drawn to us," said Lewiston. "It sounds silly, I know. But the city wants what all of us need."

"What is that?" Shelby asked.

"Life," Lewiston answered. "And to be cured of its affliction."

# CHAPTER 57

It was late. The girls had gone to sleep. Samson, however, had stayed up. Thinking. Wondering. Hoping to escape this pain. Hoping to alleviate it without picking up a bottle. Nothing came to mind. For a moment, he was distracted, worrying about what Emilia would or would not say to Shirley.

But when the night called, his mind stayed alert. Vying for a solution. Calculating equally immoral ways to lessen his hurt. No solution came.

"Still up?" Emilia asked, walking down the stairs.

Samson nodded, purposefully yawning as she reached the bottom step. He was hoping she would get the hint that he was going to bed. Her continued chatter let him know that she did not.

"I have a lot on my mind, too," she said, sitting on the recliner next to him. "Maybe we should share and see where that goes."

"See where what goes?"

"Our thoughts, of course," she answered. "Thoughts of going back to bed or other places..."

Samson shook his head in disgust. He never understood Emilia. And after their brief affair, he never understood himself. He didn't know why she, of all people, had come back into his life.

"You say this like I'm interested," said Sosa. "Yet I'd rather not *share* or let my mind wander. All I want is sleep."

"But you're not tired, Sosa," Emilia said, smiling. "Clearly, there's a solution that will make us both tired."

Sosa stood and headed toward the staircase. "Good night, Emilia."

"Samson, wait!"

Samson, not used to Emilia calling him anything but Sosa, slowed down.

"Another attempt, Emilia?"

"No," she said sheepishly. Her voice had lost its confidence. Sadness mixed with fear seemed to creep through. "I'm not…"

Samson didn't understand. "You're not what?"

"…I'm not doing well, Samson," Emilia admitted.

"I wouldn't imagine," he said, still standing at the staircase. "You cheat on your husband. You come to my home after my family's loss. And now you're attempting to cause more damage."

Emilia smiled weakly as a tear streaked down her face.

"You're right, Samson," she said. "I deserve this. For the first time in my life, I feel like I've lost everything because of my actions."

She hugged a pillow cushion. "Do you know what it's like? To have everything yet feel like you have nothing? To know you're loved yet be unable to find it in you to love yourself?"

The tears continued to flow as Samson took note of her words. For the first time since he'd met her, Emilia was telling the truth. She really wasn't doing well. He took a step down from the staircase.

"I do," he said. "It took losing Monty for me to realize that. And for what?"

He shook his head. Thinking of his lost son. Feeling the pain rise once again as he struggled to force it back down.

"Accolades and broken records," he said quietly. "More money. More deals. More things I don't need."

He sat on the couch. Fatigued. Emotionally drained from the day.

"I think about him," he said, turning to Emilia. "Every day. More than I had when he was here. That's what happens when we lose what we don't deserve."

Emilia wiped her eyes. Hoping the tears would stop. Wishing the pain in her heart would go away.

"You think I'm here to ruin what you and Shirley have," she said. "I'm not."

Samson nodded. "I know. It took me a while to see, but I know."

"I just wish I wasn't me sometimes," she said. "I just wish I didn't always have to get what I want, when I want it."

"And I wish I would've seen what was right in front of me," said Samson.

"Everything I needed was right here. In this house. Waiting for me to come home. Waiting for me to realize that nothing else matters."

"You still have Shirley," Emilia said.

Samson shrugged. "Do I? She's doing great now that you're here. But what happens when you leave? She won't be distracted by your circumstance for long." He sighed deeply. "The pain will return."

Emilia smiled.

Samson noticed. "What's so funny?"

Emilia shrugged. "It's amazing how clueless men are."

"Says the woman who cheated on her husband."

"Even then," Emilia said. "He was clueless. But men choose to see what they want."

"Is that so?"

"It is," Emilia said. "You have no idea how hard today was for her. She cried at the salon while getting her hair done. She cried in the woman's changing room while I was trying on clothes." Emilia shook her head. "She was in tears most of the game, Samson. She pulled it together in the fourth quarter only because she knew she was coming to see you."

Samson didn't know what to say. He was surprised to hear this. Shocked that his wife shed a tear in public. The whole time she was smiling and laughing, she was secretly still hurting. Still feeling the waves of angst come over her, just like they did for him.

"I didn't know," he said softly. "I thought being around you had made it better."

Emilia shook her head. "She's in pain. But she's asked a lot of you. Like this arrangement. She told me how desperate you were to put me up in some old hotel."

"Not old," Samson said. "Probably not five-star. But definitely not old."

Emilia waved him off. "Regardless, she didn't want you to see how much she was hurting. How she needed a shoulder to cry on. So, she asked you to put up with me instead."

"She didn't have to," he said quietly. "I would've found a way..."

"A way to what, Samson? To act as if my very being didn't irk your soul?" Emilia laughed. "She told me before I entered the house not to expect much more than a 'hi' and 'bye' from you."

"I'm surprised that would've have sufficed," Samson said. "But you're right. I was being clueless. I couldn't see that she needed me. I couldn't see how selfless she was being."

He knew then what he had to do. He had to let his wife know it was okay to show her pain. To cry in front of him. To know he was there for her no matter what.

"Thank you, Emilia," he said, squeezing her hand. "I needed to hear this." Samson headed up the stairs. "Have a good night. And try to get some sleep."

Emilia waved and nodded, agreeing to do both. However, once she heard him close the bedroom door, she cried. She would continue crying until the morning, when she finally fell asleep6.

# CHAPTER 58

"I think I'm going to head back."

Wade, winded and about to hurl, held his hands on his neck. He had been a great athlete decades ago, but years of drinking and stress had left him half the man he used to be.

Elias, though in worse shape, spoke up. "Too late now," he said, bent over, sucking in air. "The car is over five blocks away. And I'm betting what's left of it isn't drivable."

Wade smacked his forehead. "My God, Elias. How dumb are we? We should've known. There's no way someone hasn't stripped down the SUV by now."

Elias shrugged. "Guess we really do need Jon now."

Wade, in a fit of frustration, threw his flask through a store window. Elias, surprised at the act, showed a concerned expression.

"In this godforsaken city with no weapons and no booze," Wade yelled. "It can't get worse than this!"

As he spoke, a trashcan rattled behind them. Elias noticed it first. Turning, he observed something odd. Someone was hiding behind it. Waiting. Staring at the two men. Elias took a step closer.

"Wade," Elias nudged. "Look over there."

"Those damn kids again," Wade said in exasperation. "I'm tired of running." The mayor started walking toward the trashcan. He clenched his fists and flailed his arms. "You want a piece of me?" he yelled. "Come on, cowards! I'll show you what a real adult can do!"

At that, the person behind the trashcan moved and fell back onto his hands. Elias realized it wasn't the two kids who had chased them through the city. It was someone else. Someone they had not encountered before.

"Wait, Wade," Elias said, holding up a hand. "I don't think that's them."

"Doesn't matter," Wade spat out. "I'm tired of being chased around this city. If it's a fight they want, then it's a fight they're going to get!"

Wade ran toward the trashcan. The person behind it took off in the opposite direction. Elias felt something familiar but it was unclear. As the boy took off around the corner, Elias noticed that Wade had stopped short of the trashcan.

"Showed him," Wade said.

"That's weird," Elias said, taking a couple of steps forward. "I feel like I know him."

"Who?" Wade asked. "That boy?"

"Yeah," Elias said. "He seems familiar."

"Elias, unless you've started handling our juvenile detention facilities—of which we have none—then I doubt you've crossed paths with him."

The judge remained quiet, thinking of where he had seen the boy before. Wondering why he seemed familiar. But instinct took over. He remembered they were still in Albion and danger still lurked around the corner.

"Let's get moving," Wade said. "Who knows what will hop out next."

Elias agreed, catching up to Wade.

"Which way should we go?" the judge asked.

"A lot of choices with absolutely no guide, my friend," said Wade. "I say we just keep heading forward."

And forward they went. Continuing through the city. Lost and unprepared for what was to come.

# CHAPTER 59

Kieran liked Lucille. It wasn't attraction, but something he admired about her personality: a straightforward, play-no-games mentality that more aptly appealed to his own likeness. He was a genius first and a pursuer second but sometimes he wished to be like her. More action and less thinking. More living and less planning.

"I've not heard much of your story," he said as they wandered the street. "Are you also from Albion?"

"If I were, would we be looking for Sam?" Lucille asked sarcastically.

"No," Kieran said, "I suppose not. But you walk these streets as if nothing bothers you."

"That's because I'm not worried about the people here," Lucille said softly. "I care for the city, but the people have gone to hell. More animal than human. If they're going to do whatever it takes to survive, so will I."

"Wow," Kieran said. "Such a brooding nature. How can you save a city with that glum attitude?"

Lucille turned to face Kieran. She was small but intimidating. Kieran had already witnessed her mettle. He had witnessed a fight she was part of in Albion. Once, she had cut off a man's ear and fed it to him, while bashing in the man's teeth, simply because he had demanded her purse.

Kieran didn't know if it was the man's threat of taking her purse or the fact that the man assumed she had one that had set her off. Either way, Kieran became a fan of her work.

"I don't mean to offend," Kieran said with a smile. "I only wish to know your motives. I have a hard time believing any man can convince you to do something you're against. So, why remain with the group?"

Lucille glared and said nothing for a moment. She turned back to the street.

"You're still the enemy, Kieran," Lucille said. "Make no mistake of that. We might have a common interest, but I've run into your kind many a time."

"My kind?" Kieran said, intrigued. "There are no others like me."

"There are always people like you," Lucille said, still walking down the street. "People who bite off more than they can chew. People who are driven by greed and accolades rather than genuine kindness and humility."

"Well," Kieran said thoughtfully, "you have me there. I am in this for me. But I've never hidden that fact. Still, we have a common interest in wanting to change the city, and I work better knowing the people I'm in bed with."

Lucille laughed. "Should've thought of that before you made this offer."

"Thought of what?" Kieran asked.

"Knowing who you are in bed with," said Lucille. "You still trust us, Kieran. To do your bidding. To help you achieve this great accomplishment. But have you ever thought of the alternative?"

Kieran tapped his chin. "The alternative being you and the rest of the group stabbing me in the back when the mission is done?"

Lucille nodded.

"Oh, many a time, my dear friend. Many a time."

Kieran stopped. So did Lucille. The briefly made eye contact. Briefly, Lucille cared about what Kieran had to say.

He raised his hands. "It's simple. I'm at your mercy. And if the group wants me out, do you really think I could overpower all of you?"

Lucille showed no expression. "Not now, you can't. But I'm guessing you're smarter than that. If it's not control you're after, then only one thing is left."

She didn't have to say it. And neither did Kieran. They both knew what he was after. They both knew Kieran would find a way out of this if he really had to. They were guinea pigs in his experiment. He was willing to sacrifice everything just to prove he was right.

# CHAPTER 60

Sam managed to escape. Still not understanding. Still confused about why his brother would choose a life of violence over change. They had both grown up in Albion. Surviving. Doing what it took to make it to the next day.

But he never thought his brother actually liked it. He never thought this city could actually change him.

"Where to now?" he asked himself.

He had no place to go. No person to trust. He'd thrown that away when he'd left the group. He also knew the city. The citizens were more apt to take a life than to save one. They, too, were doing what it took to survive. Only then did a new name come to mind: Jon.

He didn't know the man and Albion didn't entertain the news. Their city was troubled enough. They didn't much care about what happened anywhere else. So, when Kieran told Sam and the group to capture Jon, he didn't know what the man was capable of.

He didn't know the power he held.

When Jon made his escape, Sam thought it was a pointless endeavor to chase him. Jon, a man able to incapacitate a group with his words, would not have a problem making his way through Albion.

But what confused Sam was how Jon had ended up captured in the first place. When they had first happened upon him in the alley, Jon had seemed unknowing of what was to follow. Clearly, his power wasn't foresight or he might have bested Sam and his group. But he didn't. The capture was easy.

"So, what is he?" Sam asked himself, rounding the corner to another street. "And why does Kieran think he can control him?"

Sam had so many questions and so few answers. But he knew there was only one way out of this. One way to ensure the group's plan would succeed without Kieran. He would have to find Jon first. Worse yet, he would have to persuade the man he had captured to save this city. To rescue him, and his brother, from the chaotic nature of Albion.

# CHAPTER 61

Still fazed by recent events, Jon kept walking. Worrying. Wondering what was to come. He hated the spirit for this. For not knowing. For continuously walking blindly into traps and new messes that he could easily have avoided had he stayed home.

But he wasn't, nor could he return home until the spirit's bidding was done. He could have run for it, hoping to head in the right direction. Hoping to hitchhike his way back home. But the chances of him making it two steps without dying in this city were slim. He knew the spirit was the only reason he was still alive.

He knew he had no choice when it came down to it.

"Where to next?" Jon asked aloud. "I'm sure this is all rather amusing to you, but I'd like to go ahead and get this over with."

He was annoyed and tired. Agitated by the day's feat. Noticing the sun descending, once again, and realizing he had no place to rest. It was then that he felt the spirit tug at him to turn right. A building resembling a church stood before him.

"Typical," he said under his breath.

He entered cautiously, aware that even sacred ground wasn't safe. Not at night. Not in Albion. He checked behind the pews, keeping a watchful eye for any sudden movements. He was alone.

Jon set down his backpack and fished around inside to see what food was left. He managed to secure a candy bar. Jon unpeeled the wrapper and devoured what was left of the chocolate treat. In front of him were two items: a sheet of paper with hymns and a bible. Not being in the singing mood, Jon reached for the bible.

Despite how he felt about the people of Brevington, and his many nights of drinking, Jon never strayed too far from the word. It did, however, make him feel like a hypocrite. He didn't want to hear from God, but he always felt connected to the word. The stories of tragedy and triumph drew him in. He didn't know its power.

He only knew that he could see himself in each story. Job, his favorite of the bible characters, seemed to draw him in each time. A life of tragedy turned triumph. But Jon never focused on the triumph.

The tragedy was realistic.

Death and plagues that were not coerced. Doing what was right only to see the fruit of his labor turn to ash. That was the world Jon lived in. That was the chaos he witnessed each day. The truth of his retirement was less a renouncing of public appearances and more a declaration of his inability to deal with each problem.

Cancer and disease. New strains of the flu. Rape. Murder. Abuse. In Jon's mind, that was what humans had succumbed to. He could heal a child of his wounds and scars, but he couldn't change the parents who abused him.

He could take away sickness. But he couldn't prevent the car accident taking the life of a little girl. On and on, he noticed that he wasn't saving lives. Only extending them. Only renting a few more minutes for each victim.

The people of Brevington didn't see it this way. They saw only the miracle. The magic show that took place on their doorstep. Jon could see the bigger picture. The real problem his city refused to face: His people didn't want change. They only wanted to make it to tomorrow. They only wanted to indulge themselves in a carefree life.

"No more," he said on that day. "No more will help them. No more will I ease the very worries that were meant for change."

As he opened the bible and reread the first chapter of Job, he was reminded of that day. He was reminded that true change didn't come from him but, rather, from God and the spirit.

# CHAPTER 62

"Let's head back," Lewiston said, noticed the setting sun. "It'll be dark here soon."

"We will," said Shelby. "There's still some light, though. There's still time to find Sam or Jon."

Shelby, seemingly entranced by the city, kept walking. Lewiston repeated his suggestion only to get the same result. His friend continued walking.

Lewiston knew better than to try to stop Shelby, but he also knew that night lowered their chances of survival. He was ill-fitted to defend himself if Shelby were taken down.

"Not a good idea," said Lewiston. "The worst parts of this city come out at night. I know you have a vengeance streak to uphold, but I'm not of the same breed or mindset."

"Then go back," Shelby said, "and tell Kieran I'll be there shortly."

Lewiston noticed a wild look in Shelby's eyes. Pupils fully dilated. Lewiston had known his friend longer than anyone else in the group and had seen Shelby take down more Albion citizens than he'd known possible. But that had been in defense. Tonight, Shelby was on the offensive.

And though Shelby had mentioned to Lewiston the reason for his frequent visits when he was younger, Lewiston had never witnessed anything like tonight. He sensed a desire for violence.

"Shelby," Lewiston warned, "you're not yourself. Come on, old friend. There will be chances for violence another time."

"I'm not looking for violence," Shelby said, "but tonight seems urgent.

Sam knows this city better than any of us. Tomorrow, our chances of finding him drop dramatically. Same with the next day."

"That's not true," said Lewiston. "We can narrow down the streets. Eliminate the dead ends Kieran and Lucille have found. Opportunity is still on our side."

"Look." Shelby turned to face his friend. "I'm not heading back. So you can either keep up and shut up or head back."

Lewiston wasn't afraid of Shelby, though he had every reason to be. The basis of their friendship wasn't trust or any feel-good moment. It was logic. Facts that both he and his friend could use. They would always come to a logical conclusion. What Shelby was doing that night seemed ludicrous to his friend. Lewiston wouldn't stand for it.

"There's an eighty-seven percent chance of being attacked tonight," Lewiston said. "A ninety-six percent chance of multiple attackers, and a ninety-nine percent chance you will not have been their first victim."

Shelby smiled. "I guess the odds are not in my favor."

Lewiston shook his head, realizing what he had done. "This isn't a challenge, Shelby. It's life or death. I prefer you to not be part of the latter."

"Trust me, then," Shelby said.

"There's no trust when it comes to anything outside of numbers," Lewiston replied. "I won't follow you. Not in this city. Not with these people."

Lewiston turned as Shelby went on. He stopped before going too far.

"Shelby," he said.

His friend stopped.

"We are greater than our nature and smarter than our desires," said Lewiston. "Always remember that."

Shadows formed as the abandoned buildings blocked the incoming light. Lewiston was smart enough to have memorized the signs as they passed each street. He didn't know if his friend had done the same. What he knew was that the odds were not in Shelby's favor. Lewiston always believed in the odds.

# CHAPTER 63

Jon shut the bible and put it back in its place. He remained quiet, listening for any signs of life in the abandoned church. Nothing. Lying back, he thought of the events that had taken place. The person who had run away from him. The two men who had died. He always erred on the side of life. The spirit seemed opposed to his ideals. The deaths still bothered him.

He thought he was there to help a life, not take one. Not to cause more chaos. He felt for the people of Albion and he had hoped to bring a few back with him to Brevington. But he remembered this wasn't his plan. This wasn't his request.

And though his late friend wanted him to save one last person, it was the spirit that chose the destination. Jon could only trust the spirit and hope for the best. Hope that the spirit would let him keep his life when all was said and done.

# CHAPTER 64

"Great," Wade said. "It'll be night soon and we have no place to go."

Elias spread out his arms. "The city is our home for tonight." He pointed to a couple of buildings. "You get to choose where we stay."

Wade sighed. "You know we are not the only ones taking residence in these buildings, right?"

Elias shrugged. "So, we fight them off."

"Like we did with that kid?"

"Exactly," said Elias. "Just yell a little louder this time. I'm afraid adults don't scare so easily."

Wade laughed. "We are royally screwed, my dear friend."

"Now, Wade," Elias said, "that's no way for a mayor to speak. This is a chaotic city with very chaotic tactics."

"And we are bystanders, not animals," said Wade.

Elias raised a brow. "Aren't we?"

"I'm afraid this city has affected your mental state," Wade said. "Unless you're trying to make a point out of all this nonsense."

"Wade," Elias said, "haven't you had a day when you wished you could say whatever you wanted? To do whatever you wanted, because a levy pitted you against the city, or a city council member disagreed with you before hearing your proposal?"

"Yes," Wade said, "but that doesn't give me a license to kill."

"No," said Elias, "of course it doesn't. But it gives you a license to defend yourself. To take out whatever fear, anger, and rejection you might have felt in the past, and channel that toward your assailant."

"So," Wade said, "you have lost your mind."

Elias shook his head. "I just know that I'm not going to be a victim in this venture. To bow down to the evil that has consumed this city. If it wants a fight, I'm going to fight back."

The judge said this and walked toward the entrance of an abandoned building. He opened the door and held it for his friend.

"Now, are we going to get a good night's rest, or are you sleeping on the street?"

# CHAPTER 65

Night quickly turned to day. Jon noticed the sun shining through the windows. He wanted to go back to sleep. To pretend this was the nightmare and his dream was reality as he inhaled the pine-filled scent of the dusty pews.

"No," he mumbled. "Let me go back to sleep."

But he couldn't. And the spirit wouldn't let him. Its force felt like a man shoving him, waking him from his slumber. There were times when Jon was thankful for the tug of the spirit. And there were times when he wished it didn't exist.

He could ignore it, but that didn't mean it would go away.

What was deeply embellished in the spirit was also deeply embellished in Jon. And though he always had a choice, he wouldn't ignore it as long as he was in Albion. His life depended on it. His very survival depended on what the spirit had to say.

After pulling himself up, Jon brushed off his pants, zipped his backpack, and headed out the door. He rushed only because he could feel the spirit's tug waning. Missing its guidance was like missing the bus. You either got there on time or you waited until the next one. Jon wasn't going to wait. He didn't have time to spare.

# CHAPTER 66

Samson lay next to his wife. Her warmth soothed him. Her presence relaxed him. Monty, basketball, and Emilia swirled around his mind. But he'd deal with that later. Right now, his wife needed him. Right now, the only person who mattered was her.

"Sammy," she said sleepily, feeling him crawl back into bed. "Glad to see you're back."

He kissed her cheek. "Couldn't sleep."

Shirley smiled faintly. "Talking to Emilia is better than Nyquil," she said. "I'm surprised she's still up, too."

"She has a lot on her mind."

"Elias?" Shirley asked.

"The very same," said Samson. "She feels guilty for what she did. For ruining a good thing."

"As she should," said Shirley. "You don't wreck a home and you don't have affairs because you feel less or have a moment of weakness." She turned to face Samson. "You never did, and I know how hard that must have been."

"It was," Samson said, forcing a smile. "But I couldn't risk losing you."

Shirley kissed him. "And I couldn't live without you. Sometimes just seeing you gives me strength."

Samson continued smiling. "About that," he began, "Emilia told me. You're in more pain than you're letting on."

Shirley slowly turned back around. "I'm managing," she said, turning away from her husband. "And Emilia has a big mouth."

Samson laughed. "Babe, you can't hide these things. I know you think I'm mad at you for inviting Emilia to stay..."

Shirley waited for him to continue. "... and?"

"And what? I'm pissed she's still here," he said jokingly. "But I know we're both in pain. I know it's easier getting through it when someone close to you is going through pain, too." He kissed the back of her head. "I'm not a huge fan of her, but I'm glad you have someone to enjoy the day with." Sighing, he lay back on his pillow. "I haven't been as available as I need to be anyway."

Shirley turned to see his eyes and laid her head on his chest. "Don't say that. You're always there for me, Sammy."

"But I need to be there more," Samson said. "I've always been bad at this."

"That," Shirley said, "and shooting free throws."

Samson playfully pushed her away. "I'll have you know I'm shooting over seventy percent from the line."

Shirley shrugged. "I don't know, Sammy. I thought the point of it being a free throw is that it's free. But who knows." She pulled him back in close. "The only thing that matters is that you are here. And that is what you've been. Even when Coach has called. Hell, even when the manager tweeted about you missing another game."

Samson raised a brow. "I thought that was a heartfelt tweet. You really think he was trying to rush me back to the court?"

Shirley shook her head. "Sammy, it's a business, and you're their moneymaker. If you're not out there, he's losing money. Of course that tweet was meant to get you back on the court."

Samson gave her a quizzical look. "He did mention something about 'rescue' being on its way."

"You're his knight in shining armor."

"I'm a basketball player," Samson said, laughing. "I'm only here to play ball."

Shirley pulled him in close and kissed him. "No, Sammy. You're here for much more than that."

Samson took her in his arms. Both of them forgot about the problems that were soon to return the next day. Both of them enjoyed the other as if they were the only two in the world. Hardship had brought trials. Pain had brought them back together.

The night meant more to Samson than he could have imagined. Love, true love, was between his arms. A soul entwined with his own. Never to break. Never to falter. He knew they would get through this. He knew he could never risk losing her again.

# CHAPTER 67

"Did you hear that?" Lucille whispered. "Sounds like footsteps."

She pulled Kieran down with her, hidden by a dumpster. Kieran quietly obeyed. Trusting her instincts. Knowing that if they were to survive, she would be the reason why.

Before them were two men. Both with beards. Both a foot taller than Kieran. One dragged a bat while the other brandished a knife. The sun was down and Kieran never thought to head back.

He wanted to find Sam and he needed to find Jon.

Want and need both distracted him. Had he known how late it was, he would have persuaded Lucille to go back. But there was something peculiar about the city. An attractive curiosity that begged for his attention. An alluring propensity causing both he and Lucille to tempt fate.

She held a finger to her lips. Watching the men stop in the street. Noticing each of them staring in her direction. It was dark but Lucille could see their faces. She could also see their smiles as they slowly walked toward her and Kieran.

# CHAPTER 68

"Since when do abandoned post offices have rats?" Wade asked, kicking one to the side. "And why does it smell like piss?"

"Means there's food around here," said Elias, "and the piss came from the rats. Put two and two together, Mr. Mayor."

Wade followed Elias. Rounding a corner. Moving slowly to the back of the abandoned post office. Elias wished he had chosen a grocery store. His stomach grumbled. They hadn't eaten the whole day.

"Remind me again why we didn't grab something to eat?" Elias asked.

"In Albion?"

"In Brevington, Wade," said Elias. "I'm starving."

"Not going to lie, old friend." Wade stepped around him. "These rats and their odor have created the perfect diet for me." He looked around the abandoned back office. "My God, I could use a drink."

Elias felt something under his shoe. A moist slime came up as he lifted it from the ground. A brownish mixture dripped off it. Wade watched in disgust.

"Make that a double," the mayor said.

"Come on," said Elias, who continued to walk. "There's a manager's office around here somewhere."

As they kept walking, more rats raced by them. More droppings met the soles of their shoes. If Elias's stomach was upset before, it was now worse for a different reason.

"Okay," he said, watching a mound of rats flee in every direction. "There's no godly reason for there to be so many."

"They reproduce faster than rabbits," said Wade. "But I wouldn't expect a judge to know that."

"I wouldn't expect anyone to really care," said Elias.

The mayor shrugged. "The more you know…"

# CHAPTER 69

Lewiston approached the abandoned warehouse. He opened the door and realized that he was the first one back.

"That can't be right," he said to himself. "They should have been back hours ago."

He thought Kieran and Lucille would have booked it at sundown. They were smart, unlike his friend Shelby. They were also in more danger. The city bred contempt and hatred. An affinity for violence and misguided tempers were a part of that. But one thing could make it worse.

The opposite sex walking around at night.

Lewiston wasn't worried about Lucille handling a few men. But what about five or six? Albion's desperate nature made him wonder.

*Was she really safe? Would Kieran even try to help her?*

He knew the answer before asking: Kieran was a genius, but not much of man. He paid others to do his bidding. To dirty their hands instead of his. He wanted no part of the violent nights of which Albion was capable.

Though Lewiston wanted to rush out to save his friend, he didn't. He couldn't. He picked up a chair and threw it across the room. Realizing he had left both Shelby and Lucille in danger. Realizing he was becoming more like Kieran.

# CHAPTER 70

Sweater dripped. His body fatigued. Shelby leaned against a building. Two assailants crossed his path. Two men believing Shelby was a defenseless tourist. He made quick work of them. Jabbing a knife into one. Choking out the other and then stomping him out before the man's cries could be heard.

He was in rare form. Content roaming the city. Seeking a fight wherever one was offered. He knew better, though. To head back. To retreat with the group. But he didn't. Instinct took over. A base nature guided his thoughts.

*Have to find Sam. He'll know where Jon is.*

The thought repeated itself as he meandered down the street. Sometimes hoping for the worst. The city satisfying his craving.

It took only another block until he found his match. One man. A foot taller. Obese and much wider. Shelby smiled.

"That didn't take long," he said.

The man didn't speak. Instead, he charged at Shelby, a wild expression on his face.

Shelby ducked out of the way. Tripping the man as he went past. Watching the giant fall to the ground. The citizens of Albion were violent but also clumsy. They had never met someone like Shelby.

As the man got to his feet, Shelby threw a right hook that landed cleanly on the man's jaw. An audible snap echoed through the air. Yet the man didn't go down. Anyone else would have been bent over in pain. Anyone else would have run away.

But the man didn't. Turning to face Shelby, he threw a jab.

Shelby reacted in time to avoid the punch, then countered with a gut punch. The man stumbled back, clearly upset. But still no sound.

"That all you got?" Shelby taunted. "I've fought bears bigger than you."

He hadn't, but he was feeling good about the matchup. He knew that taking this gallop down would be all the vengeance he would need.

The man looked up and smiled widely. His teeth were missing. It was a clear sign to Shelby that this wasn't the man's first fight.

He came charging at Shelby again, this time stopping short of swinging. Shelby moved to the side. The man did, too. Shelby threw a wild punch. The man, reacting quicker, reeled back and landed a heavy blow to Shelby's chest.

Shelby fell back, breathing heavily. He struggled to catch his breath. The man took the opportunity to grab Shelby by the throat. Watching Shelby squirm, he delivered another heavy blow to Shelby's gut.

Shelby threw up his lunch. The man dropped him to the ground. Without thinking twice, the man struck Shelby with an elbow to the back of the head. Shelby didn't move. Didn't breathe. He died mere seconds after the blow was delivered.

# CHAPTER 71

They ran. The two men turned into four as Lucille realized what was happening. It was a trap. The wind rushed by. Footsteps pounded behind them.

"Go!" Lucille shouted.

Kieran didn't have to be told twice. When Lucille tripped on a can, Kieran thought about turning back. He wanted to help her but he was a block from the warehouse and didn't dare ignore her command.

He rounded the corner as he heard her scream. The door to the warehouse was unlocked. He rushed in and latched the door shut so that no one could follow.

# CHAPTER 72

Sam, oddly enough, lost his way. The night was different from any other. He felt exposed. Hiding away as the rest of the citizens tore each other apart. For the first time, fear took over. But he knew he was a sitting duck if he stayed still, so he kept walking.

As he rounded the next street, he noticed the sign. Spring Street. The abandoned warehouse was only a block away. As he neared the street, he caught sight of something else. A group of men was huddled around a body.

It was motionless. Even if it had been able to move, the men seemed to not let it out of their sight. As he drew closer, he began to recognize the body. The face. The hair. The person on the ground was Lucille.

Sam rushed at the men. Careless of the result. Knowing he had to save her.

"Get away from her," he yelled, "or I'll have all of Sentry Lane come after you!"

The men looked back. Noticing Sam. Hearing his threat and thinking little of it. They knew Sentry Lane. But they didn't know who this man was.

One man nodded to the other. Each turned to face Sam. Each walked toward the fool. Sam, no longer able to turn back, kept running. Kept pushing forward to his demise. Coming closer to what he realized would be the end of his life. But as he came closer, and as the men stepped away from Lucille, something strange happened.

Sam hadn't landed a punch, but the men—who would have killed him—fell back. Faltering without reason. Collapsing to the ground. Sam walked over, waiting to see if they would move. When he was assured that they weren't moving, he ran to his friend's side.

He noticed her wounds. Bruises forming around her eyes. Her clothes were ripped. Her pants were halfway down her legs. From what he could tell, she hadn't been raped. Pummeled to the ground. But still alive.

He checked for a pulse. Her heart was beating steadily. His mind still reeled as he realized that he, too, had survived. He knew he couldn't risk taking her back to the warehouse. Instead, he heaved her over his shoulder. Thankful that she was passed out and couldn't feel the pain. Hoping he could reach an abandoned store that he knew was only a block away.

He was short in stature and not very strong but the adrenaline overwhelmed him. In his current state, he could've lifted a car. His legs took off as he raced away from the scene.

Friend over his shoulder. Confusion still in mind. Sam found the store and kicked the door open. As he headed toward the back, he realized he wasn't alone.

In the corner by the dairy aisle was a woman who sat with her child. Her eyes widened in fear. The little boy huddled in his mom's arms. Sam could tell the boy was no older than two or three. He didn't have time to decide whether or not he could trust them.

"She needs help," Sam said. "She's been hurt."

The woman, unsure of whether to believe him, slowly stood up. She would have raced to the exit had she not heard the screams of a woman only moments earlier. She realized this must have been the woman. The man was her rescuer.

"To the back," she said, leading the way with the boy in her arms. "There is a first-aid kit and the water still runs."

Sam followed her. His shoulders felt heavy and his legs gave way with each step but he didn't let go of Lucille. He wouldn't fail her now. He had already failed the group. He wouldn't fail one of its fallen members. As they neared the back, the woman had Sam lay Lucille on a wooden desk.

"Ice," the woman said. "The swelling will get worse. She could lose her sight if we do not get some quickly."

Sam rushed to the frozen food section, hoping it hadn't been ransacked. As he did, he noticed this wasn't like the other abandoned stores. It still had food. Aisles that seemed untouched. There wasn't much left over, but if he had to guess, the woman and her son were the only ones there.

He found two frozen bags of peas and rushed them back to the woman. Gently, she put one under Lucille's eyes. The other she put on her ribs.

"Broken," the woman said quietly, pointing to Lucille's ribs. "She tried to put up a fight."

"What makes you say that?" Sam asked.

The woman pointed again to Lucille's side. While Sam was gone, the woman had ripped off Lucille's shirt. Small bruises lined one side of her body, while the other side revealed one very large bruise.

"She fought back," the woman said, "making the men angrier."

Sam looked up. "Did you see what happened?"

The woman shook her head. "I only heard her scream."

Tears formed in Sam's eyes. His friend, who most likely was looking for him, had risked her life. Wandering the streets of Albion. Not knowing what the night held. It was a different beast at night. A mixture of chaos and destruction.

He began to blame himself until he realized an unsettling truth: There were others in the group. Surely they wouldn't let her go by herself. Surely someone else should have been with her.

He thought about who it might have been. He knew Lewiston wouldn't have abandoned her. He needed her. Cherished her for more than her looks. There was no way he would have left her side.

Shelby came to mind, but Sam quickly dismissed the thought. He was a fighter. He would've fought off the assailants for the fun of it. Sam knew that if Lucille was in trouble, Shelby would've done his best to bring down the whole damn city before letting it take her.

Then it dawned on him.

"Kieran," he said to himself. "You backstabbing coward."

# CHAPTER 73

Morning approached as Elias began to stretch. The sunlight woke him from his slumber, while Wade remained huddled in the darkest part of the office. Still snoring. Still at peace, but only after clearing the room of any rodents the night before. Elias thought to wake him up but didn't. Instead, he headed out of the office and into the main lobby.

There he knelt and did something he hadn't done since he was a little boy. Not knowing what to say, he simply bowed his head and let the words flow.

"God, it's Elias. I know I have no business praying—now of all times—to you. Or to hope for your help. But I'm here now, and I don't know what to do."

He stopped and looked back, making sure Wade wasn't coming. Once assured, he spoke on.

"I know you sent Jon here. I have no qualms about it. The way we treated him in Brevington..." He sighed. "To say the least, I can understand the scenic change. We've gone after him, but I fear our egos have bitten off too much.

"We're two old men, God. Fat and out of shape. Risking our lives for pride's sake. And though we need him, I realize now that we need you more. Jon can't save us because he's not in charge. You are. As much we'd like to head back to our safe and cozy homes, we know it's not that simple. In some ways, I feel like this wasn't our plan, but yours. Your plan for our life. Your plan to help us see that it's not about us. It's not about Brevington or saving the people there..."

Before he could look up, Elias felt Wade's hand on his shoulder. Getting on his knees beside him, the mayor urged Elias to continue. Elias did.

"You brought us here for you, Lord. Nothing more. Nothing less. So, help us to find Jon. Not to change his mind. But to help him finish the work. In your name we pray, amen."

"Amen," Wade said. "Now please, Elias. Help me up. My knees are more than sore from yesterday."

Elias laughed as he helped up his friend. He took in a deep breath before realizing what they would have to do.

"It's not that big of a city, you know," Elias said, "but it's a different world compared to what we are used to."

Wade nodded. "Sadly, my friend, it is. But, if he really did bring us here and if we are to find Jon, we should have nothing to fear."

Elias nodded as they headed to the door. Neither knew where to go. Though he had prayed, Elias felt overwhelming fear.

"Where should we go?" he asked.

Wade shrugged. "Where the Lord guides, he will provide."

"Does the Lord giveth directions?" Elias prodded.

"No," Wade said, "but I spotted a liquor store around the corner. Come on. Let's see if they have anything left."

# CHAPTER 74

Lewiston was appalled. As Kieran burst through the door, Lewiston felt an emotional tug that yanked at his heart. He waited to see Lucille. But she didn't come. Only Kieran stepped through the door. As he watched the genius planner lock it behind him, Lewiston knew that Lucille wouldn't make it.

"Where is she?" Lewiston asked.

"As if it matters now," Kieran muttered. "She won't be joining us."

"What do you mean 'she won't be joining us'?" Lewiston demanded.

He felt responsible. He knew that even though Kieran was supplying this venture, he was responsible for the group. He was responsible for making sure everything went off without a hitch. That the lives entrusted to him would remain in his hands and not handed over to the city's chaotic nature.

"She was caught by a mangy group of men," said Kieran. "An awful bunch, really. Homelier than nomads in the desert. I would have turned back to help, but two men turned into four, and then into six." He shrugged. "What I was I supposed to do?"

"What were you supposed to do?" Lewiston asked in astonishment. "You were supposed to fight! You were supposed to make sure she escaped. You didn't even have the courage to die with her!"

Kieran raised his hands. "Lewiston, please," he said calmly. "You're not thinking rationally here. Even Lucille shouted for me to go on ahead. Was I supposed to argue with such a logical command?"

Lewiston fumed. Not saying a word. Not able to believe what was being said about his friend.

"She had been caught, and there was nothing I could have done," Kieran said. "If it's any consolation, they had guns."

"I didn't hear gunshots," Lewiston said. "And it seems you came away unscathed."

"Unscathed?" Kieran asked, disgusted by the observation. "I had to watch a member of our group die tonight, Lewiston. Unscathed, my friend, is not the right term for this current situation."

It was then that Kieran had a curious observation of his own. He looked around, noticing that Shelby wasn't with them.

"And what of Shelby?" Kieran asked. "I doubt he went back for a midnight stroll."

"He..." Lewiston began, not knowing how to explain. "He decided it best to keep on with the search."

Kieran showed a confused expression. "Continue the search? At night? In Albion?" He clicked his tongue in disappointment. "Now, Lewiston, my friend, we both know that was a poor decision. Clearly led on by ego and the compelling competitiveness of this city. You didn't talk him out of it?"

Lewiston shook his head. "He wasn't in his right mind. And though he's usually of sound logic, something occurred tonight that I can't quite explain."

Kieran smiled. Knowing Lewiston's thoughts. Saying aloud what they both knew to be true.

"It's the city, Lewiston. The city drives maddening tendencies overboard." Kieran put a hand on Lewiston's shoulder. "We have suffered major losses tonight. Sacrifices, if you will, from those we care for most. We mustn't let such tributes go without retribution. We must see this to the end, for their sakes."

# CHAPTER 75

So many roads. So many street signs. Jonathan, led by the spirit, turned from one neighborhood to the next until he finally entered a new part of the city. This part reminded him of home. The only difference was that the houses back home didn't have broken windows and busted-down doors.

The desolate city from which he came bustled with crime and mischief. This suburban part of the city seemed peaceful. Houses were stacked together like in the metropolitan city Durrington. Yet no business was being done. No inventions were being made.

What could have been never was. And what used to be possible for this city when it was built no longer remained.

"Arsenal Lane," he read aloud. The street sign was still intact. "Have to admit, God, this *is* better."

He continued walking, then realized that the same person he had seen before—the one who had darted away from the dumpster—was there, staring at him. Jonathan stopped, hoping to avoid scaring him away for the second time.

"I'm not here to hurt you," he said.

The person before him did not respond.

"I'm from Brevington," Jonathan said, wondering if he should step forward. The person looked like a deer caught in headlights. "Do you know where that is?"

Still no response. There were fifty or so feet between them. Jonathan knew the person could hear him.

"Look," Jonathan said in frustration, "I don't know who you are, but I have a feeling I can help. This is the second time we've crossed paths."

The boy didn't move. Not wanting to stay, but also not wanting to leave. The man before him seemed trustworthy. The stranger had a presence that made him seem different from anyone else the boy had encountered.

"How do you know me?" the boy asked.

Jonathan was confused. "I never said I did."

"Then why are you following me?" the boy asked. "You're the only who hasn't tried to hurt me."

Jonathan raised his hands. "I'm not following *you*. I'm..." He wasn't sure what to say. He didn't want to spook the boy or seem like he had lost his mind. "...I'm following my gut on this. That I can trust you. That I can help you get out of here because I believe you're one of the good ones."

"I am," the boy said quickly. "But I was told to never trust strangers."

"And I'm sure living in Albion has made that advice true, as far as experience goes," said Jonathan. "But I am not from this city. And I have no intentions of hurting anyone."

The boy stepped back. "It was you, wasn't it?"

Jonathan kept his hands up, confused by the question. "It was me who did what?"

"Killed those two men," said the boy. "You did it."

Jonathan wiped his brow and nodded. "I did," he said. "Only after they captured and tortured me."

The boy, once wanting to run away, remained still. He didn't know the man before them but there was a peaceful presence about him. Still, the man had also confirmed that he was a killer. Jonathan could see the confusion on the boy's face and he took a step back.

"These are confusing times, kid. Trust me, I know. I don't want to be here. On this street. In this city. But I made a promise to a friend."

"What promise?" the boy asked.

"A promise to save one more life," said Jonathan. "And right now, you seem like you could use some saving."

The boy hesitated. Wanting to ask more questions. Wanting to ensure this wasn't a trap. But the city had changed him. Made him more cautious. Made him more doubtful of those around him, especially those who offered to help. Survival coursed through his veins. Running, though exhausting, seemed to be the only option.

"How can I trust you?" the boy asked.

Jonathan shrugged. "Truth is, you can't. Nor do you want to." He sighed heavily. "I'm not a good man and I've done a great disservice to the people I've cared about. To turn your back on me wouldn't surprise me. And I can't force you to trust me."

He took a step closer to the boy. The boy remained still.

"The only question I'll ask is this." Jonathan bent down and rested on his heels. "Do you want to stay in Albion or do you want to get out of this city?"

The boy, not hesitant to know what he wanted, didn't respond. Instead, he thought the question over. If there was one lesson he had learned from being in Albion, it was that most wants came with a catch. Most people who promised one thing ended up doing the other. He didn't want to be made the fool.

"I don't know you," he said, "and I can't trust you."

Those were the last words Jon heard before the boy ran off again.

Jon sat back, now resting on the ground, as he watched the boy run away. He wasn't chasing him this time. No, he knew better. This time, he would trust the spirit.

Not because he wanted to. Not because he wouldn't survive without it. But because, for the first time, trusting the spirit seemed right. He spoke his peace. Gave his reasoning for rescue. There was nothing more that he could do.

And though he wanted this manhunt to be over, he knew this was just the beginning. He knew the boy needed saving.

"Since when have you ever made things easy?" he asked, his head up to the sky. "Why it has to be this complicated, I will never know."

He sat there for a while. Not moving. Not praying. Just waiting. He knew he would have to head in one direction or the other for the spirit to guide him. But he didn't want to adhere to the spirit just yet. For once, since he had been in Albion, he wanted to admire the city for what it could be. To take in what many people had once considered their home.

# CHAPTER 76

The morning came with sorrow. Lewiston, beside himself after losing his group, sat in a chair. Calculating the chances Shelby was still alive. Figuring the odds of Sam's return. In two days, he had lost his group. The only person still there was Kieran, who remained in a separate room.

Lewiston knew Kieran was still going to execute his plan. He didn't know how, but Kieran's determination to bring change to Albion by reaching Jonathan first was unstoppable. Though Kieran, too, had suffered the losses, he would find a way. He wouldn't leave until it was done.

Lewiston thought about the consequences Kieran would suffer if he returned to Durrington empty-handed. Unable to change the city. Having to admit to his investors that his plan had failed.

*What were the chances they'd banish him here?*

Left in Albion to fend for his life. No friend or group on his side. The thought brought a smile to Lewiston's face. When he realized Kieran wasn't coming out of his room any time soon, Lewiston had an idea. To be exact, it was less of an idea and more of a choice that left a three percent chance of survival.

He rose from the chair and headed for the door. Lewiston unlatched the heavy lock and stepped into the fresh air. When the door closed behind him, he knew he wouldn't be returning. He also knew death was right around the corner.

But he didn't care. He had lost his group. His closest friends. His family. Ingenious plans didn't matter if there was no one with whom to share the spoils. That was why he felt guilty for Shelby. That was why he felt bad for letting Kieran's idea become the chosen plan.

And Sam. Lewiston didn't know what he could have done to keep Sam in the group but he knew the group needed him. Needed his trust and assurance that Lewiston's plan, not Kieran's, was best.

Lewiston had made the mistake of choosing Kieran over the group. Of believing his own plan was inadequate compared to Kieran's. He couldn't admit it because it was a feeling. And going by feelings was not how he lived his life.

Numbers and data led the way. So, when he gave into Kieran's work and put his aside, Lewiston knew he had failed the group. As everything spiraled out of control, he knew his group's fate was on him.

He walked the empty street, remembering the street signs he used to navigate his way back. He began to retrace his steps.

"I doubt you're out there, Shelby," he said, "but I will find you and I will not fail you again."

# CHAPTER 77

Sam didn't remember falling asleep. He only remembered the bruises. The broken ribs. His friend sprawled out on a desk, barely breathing. As the memories came flooding back from the night before, he stood up, realizing that he had left the woman and the boy to stay with Lucille while he was out in the store.

Rushing back to the office, fearing the worst for his friend, he noticed that Lucille was no longer there. The woman and the boy were still asleep in the corner. Sam left the office and rushed down the hallway.

"Where are you?" he asked quietly. "I've already lost you once. I won't lose you again."

He turned the corner and saw men's and women's restrooms. He headed into the women's restroom, hoping to find her. When he walked in, he didn't see anyone. The only thing he noticed was the lights. He imagined they hadn't turned themselves on, though the woman or the boy could have left them on. Sam hoped the latter thought was wrong.

He headed to the stalls and checked to make sure they were empty. Out of the four, the first three held no sign of life. Slowly, he opened the fourth stall to reveal a knife pointing back at him.

"Sam?" she asked weakly. "Is that you?"

"It is." He sighed with relief. "How are you feeling?"

"Like I was hit by a freight train," Lucille said, sheathing the knife. "How did I get here? The last thing I remember was..."

Her words trailed off as the beating from the night before came to mind. Each kick freshly felt. The consuming realization that her life was about to end imbedded deeply into her mind.

"I was going to die, Sam," she said, a tear trailing down her face. "I was going to die, and that coward Kieran was going to let it happen."

Sam knelt beside her. "You should have, but you didn't."

He breathed deeply, letting out air as if the weight of his conscious crushed his lungs.

"It's my fault, Lucille," he said. "If I hadn't left, you guys wouldn't have been wandering dangerous streets. And you wouldn't have searched for Jon so late at night."

Lucille shook her head. "I wasn't looking for Jon, Sam," she said, reaching out for his hands. "I was looking for you."

"That makes it even worse," he said, "I shouldn't have left."

Lucille raised his face by his chin. Their eyes met. The feeling of forgiveness flowed between them.

"You knew something was wrong," she said, "and you left because you knew you couldn't outreason that coward and Lewiston."

She smiled. Her eyes were kind. They held an understanding that her friend had done what he thought was best. She only wished she could have followed suit.

"You did what you thought was best, and you were right."

"How was I right?" Sam asked. "They still haven't found Jonathan."

Lucille shook her head. "You were right because you knew Kieran wasn't the man he claimed to be. Lewiston knew it too, but he's held up by intellect. He goes by logic, and though that made him a great leader, it also served as his greatest weakness."

"Last night, he revealed his true colors," Sam said. "He left you to die. We have to make this right before it's too late."

Lucille nodded. "We have to find Jon before he does."

# CHAPTER 78

"What in the hell," Wade said, huffing it down Marrow Avenue. "I'm too old to be running around this city like a chicken with its head cut off."

Elias, a few feet behind him, focused all his strength on outmaneuvering the two teens behind them.

"You'd think they'd give up by now," he said. "Why are they still following us?"

They had been running for over three blocks. The two teenaged boys showed no sign of letting up. Both appeared athletic and intimidating at the same time. The two old men were out of options.

"We have to fight, Wade," Elias yelled. "Running will be the death of us!"

"Speak for yourself," Wade hollered. "I'd rather collapse from a heart attack than get pummeled by those punks!"

Elias, fed up with running, stopped to catch his breath. He turned to face the two boys who trailed ten or so feet behind. Elias didn't know how this might go, and he figured the worst was yet to come. But he was tired of running. Tired of being out of control. Hadn't he taken a vow to do good? Hadn't he followed the rules?

His wife leaving. His abusive childhood. All of it came to this point. All of it came to his decision as to whether he would stand and fight, or turn the other way. Running with no end. Worrying about the next problem that was coming around the corner.

Clenching his fists, he waited for the boys. They had also stopped, confused by the old man's tactic.

"We thought you'd never stop," the younger teen said. "Looks like you have a death wish after all."

"Yeah," the other boy said, spitting in front of them.

Both were unruly. Clothes dirtied. Hair greased and matted as if they hadn't washed in years. Elias could see both were missing teeth. And the few teeth they had were sharp and pointed. It reminded him of the Dracula movies he had grown up watching.

"I'm done with this," Elias said. "You either kill me or I kill you. Regardless, we're done with this game."

The elder boy looked to the other. "You hear that, Steve?" he asked.

"Yeah," Steve said. "Sounds like easy dining today."

"If it's food you want, I don't have any," Elias reasoned, hoping to dissuade the two. "There's barely any left in this city anyway."

The older boy grinned. "I think you'll do just fine."

"You cannibalistic, squirmy punks," Wade yelled.

Elias hadn't noticed his friend. Nor did he notice the bat that Wade was now wielding. The judge flashed back to his friend's baseball days. Setting the homerun record at their school. Having the highest batting average of all the boys.

Snapping him out of the flashback was something Elias never expected. As Wade slowly approached the boys, Steve—Elias presumed— made a partial remark. But he wasn't able to finish it as Elias watched his friend swing the bat.

Making critical contact with the younger boy, Wade cracked the younger boy's side with the bat. The boy instantly collapsed.

"Hey!" the older boy yelled. "No one lays a hand on—"

Another swing cut off his words, quicker this time. Elias couldn't believe what he was seeing. The boy's shoulder popped as Wade made perfect contact with his left arm. The older boy also collapsed to the ground, groaning in pain. Steve, who sucked desperately for air, bent over on the ground. Neither of them was in good shape. Neither of them had expected the old man to actually swing.

"Come on, Steve," the older boy said, grabbing his friend.

Steve heaved up his lunch and forced himself to get up and follow the older boy. They scrambled away, running faster than both Wade and Elias. The mayor turned to see his friend's shocked expression.

"What?" Wade asked. "They were going to eat you."

"Eat me?" Elias asked, remembering the threat. "Maybe, but Jesus, Wade."

The mayor twirled the bat between his fingers, then gave a few practice swings as if the boys might come back.

"Can you believe it, old friend?" he asked, grinning. "I still got it."

Elias sighed and wiped the sweat from his face. "Maybe I gave you too much of a pep-talk the other day."

"No, Elias. You told me exactly what I needed to hear." Wade handed Elias the bat. "If it weren't for you, I would've stayed in that old post office."

Elias never thought to ask why Wade had joined him earlier that morning in prayer. He knew his friend wasn't religious. He knew Wade hadn't set foot in church except for during town hall meetings or to congratulate the pastor of a new church planted in the city. Wade might have shaken hands and would say a few words, but he never stayed for the service.

"Isn't it ironic," Elias said, "that after praying to get through this day, you immediately turned to violence?"

"Isn't it more amazing that after running around this godforsaken city, we haven't found a single bottle of whiskey?"

"I never knew you to be such a drinker, Wade," said Elias.

"Well, friend," Wade said, "you've never known me to beat teens with bats before, either. I suppose there's still more to me than you know."

The mayor sat on the sidewalk, breathing heavily, doing his best to regain his strength.

"All I know is that you saved my life. I might have talked a good game, but I doubt there's much these two could have done," Elias said, raising his fist. "We're going to need your athletic expertise if we're ever going to get out of this place."

The judge threw Wade the bat. Wade caught it with ease.

"Well, let's hope there aren't more punks out there needing to be taught a lesson," said Wade, using the bat to help himself up. He wasn't sure what to think. He still felt weak from the prior events. But he knew that something was wrong. That if they ended up making it to Jon, sparing some miracle, he would not make it back to Brevington.

# CHAPTER 79

The next day was grim. Samson, unsure of what to do, sat at the edge of his bed. His fear had come to life, and it had caught him off guard. Trusting the next day would be better. Hoping his secret would not be revealed. The letter sat beside him. In it was a note from his wife. In it was proof that Emilia had confessed to the affair.

He didn't know why Emilia had told Shirley, or what she hoped to get out of it. All he knew was that it didn't matter. He'd lost his son and now his wife. He couldn't find a reason to keep up the façade of being okay, so he headed to his car and left.

The women were already gone, as he figured they would be. The liquor store, only a mile and a half away, called to him. Inside, he purchased two hefty bottles of whiskey. The cashier, recognizing the basketball star, asked for an autograph. Samson left the money on the counter and headed back to his car. Without thinking, he popped the cork to one of them and drank while heading home. He didn't care one bit if he was pulled over.

It was lucky for him that he lived so close as he did eighty down the road. In his backyard, Samson drank until half the bottle was empty. His mind reeled, imagining Shirley's shocked expression. Wondering how she had managed to leave so calmly as to write a note and not even throw something at him.

Shouldn't they have talked about this? Shouldn't she have let him explain that it was a mistake made years ago, when the pressure of his teammates finally got to him and he became a victim of his own success?

No, that would have been childish. That would have been an excuse heard millions of times from lesser men. He knew this was his fault. And so, he continued to drink. He drained the bottle until a quarter was left.

He thought about calling her. Pleading for her forgiveness. Hoping she would hear him out and not trust the words of a home-wrecker. Isn't that what Emilia was? Hadn't her actions caught up to her, causing the judge himself to abandon the only person who could have loved her?

Anger rose with each thought, with each plea he wished to give, and with each promise he had broken. He was officially a failure. Losing his wife and son. Losing himself in the process. The worst part was that his son didn't have a choice. He had died. His wife, however, chose to leave him and his actions.

Samson finished the bottle and tossed it into the pool. He popped the cork to the other and continued drinking. Thinking back to days when he was in the pool and his son, still unable to swim, would run around the sides.

"Monty," he would warn, "you keep running like that and you'll fall in."

With childlike fervor, Monty pushed the limits. Getting closer to the edge. Running faster until his father came close to getting out. Yet as Samson moved toward the edge, his son began to slow down. Finding it less fun when he knew the stakes were not high.

"Don't, Daddy," Monty chided. "Swim back to the middle."

This confused Samson. "And what happens if you fall in?"

Monty would smile and point to his father. "You'll save me," he would say, laughing at such a silly question. "Won't you?"

Samson kept drinking. He wasn't able to save his son. He wasn't able to save his marriage. He wasn't even able to save himself. His past had caught up to him, and he didn't know what to do. He didn't want to do anything without Shirley in his life. He barely had the will to go on after losing his son.

The last bottle, still half full, remained enticing. Its remnants were foul in nature but superior in results. Numbness overcame him as the alcohol pumped through his veins. He could feel it now and relaxed as the day's chaos came to a close.

This was what he wanted. This was what he needed. If he couldn't have his son, then this would have to do. If his wife no longer wanted him, then he would want for nothing else. This would have to do. No friends or family. No God to call on. There was just the bottle and its prescriptive healing. The doctor couldn't have ordered anything more efficient on this day.

The thought took him back to his first year at Durrington University. A full-ride scholarship. In high school, Sosa was the phenom every college scout needed. Freshman year was his year and no one would tell him differently. No one except his injury.

Never had he broken a bone or so much as twisted an ankle. No injury had he suffered until today. The news hit him hard. He had been undercut by Jameson University's seven-foot center, landing awkwardly on the hardwood. The moment flashed by as he woke up in the hospital with a concussion and a torn ACL.

The news had been gut-wrenching but not fatal. He knew he'd get another chance. He knew the only problem was that he would sit out the rest of the year. He would be back on the court the following winter. But when the year ended and winter came again, he played sparingly. The coach, Andrew Atkinson, believed it best to give him some more time.

"Next year, son," the coach said. "We'll get you going then."

But next year came and he played less. It wasn't until senior year, starved for stardom, that he was able to prove himself. To prove he was the greatest player in college history. It was that year when he met Shirley. It was later that year when he was drafted and, now playing professionally, he found out she was pregnant.

From one hospital to the next, he knew he would be there for his son's birth. And as he held little Monty in his hands, he made a promise.

"I won't fail you," he said. "I will never let you go."

Night had come and Samson, unable to move, lay by the pool. He passed out just before he could push himself into the water.

# CHAPTER 80

Jonathan rose as the sun fell. Darkness surrounded him. He wanted to head back to the city but didn't know which way to go. He walked in hopes that the spirit would tug at him, but the only tug he felt came from his stomach. He was hungry. He stopped and opened his backpack to find one candy bar left. He unwrapped it and took a bite. In a matter of seconds, it was gone. Yet, he was still hungry. He knew better than to check the houses for food.

They were not like the abandoned grocery stores in the city. They were empty and eerie. It didn't take the spirit to let him know he shouldn't search them. He turned away and continued walking. Hoping to find his way back. No longer worried about getting lost.

It was then that he felt a familiar tug pulling him in the opposite direction. He stopped to think about it. Could he have come from the other direction, or was the spirit leading him to more trouble?

"You've gotten me out of a lot of situations," he said, looking up at the sky. "But you're wrong this time. The city is that way."

As he pointed in the opposite direction, he heard a sound come from behind him. Quickly, Jon turned to see what it was. Hoping to God that he hadn't been led to another capture. And though he clenched his fist, ready for a fight, he was surprised to see who was there. Smiling, he walked up to the boy.

"You decided to trust me?" Jonathan asked.

"I did." The boy nodded. "Until you started talking to yourself."

"I wish it were that simple," said Jonathan.

"That you were you crazy?"

"No," said Jonathan. "That I was the only one who heard me."

He faced the direction the spirit suggested. Realizing, once again, that the spirit was right. The boy was the life that needed saving.

"Okay, kid," he said. "Which way back to the city?"

The boy pointed and started walking. "This way."

Jonathan followed. He was more aware of his surroundings. Willing to give his life if it meant protecting the boy. It wasn't out of obligation or feeling—he didn't even know who the boy was. Rather, the spirit led him here for a reason. It would be embarrassing to lose him now.

"How'd you get out here anyway?" the boy asked.

"By car," said Jon.

The boy frowned. "You drove here?"

"Yes," Jon tersely responded. "I drove here"

"Who drives a car to Albion?"

"I'm starting to think you were left here for a reason," Jon said, keeping an eye out for any attackers. "That or you're deaf."

"Am not," said the boy, "but if you drove here on purpose, I'm guessing you're not the brightest crayon in the box."

Jonathan shrugged. "Maybe I'm not," he said, unable to disagree.

The boy muttered a few words under his breath. Jon didn't care enough to ask what they were. He only wanted to make it back, though he didn't know why. As crazy as Albion was—and as bad as it had treated him—he knew the city better now. It was familiar to him.

And though he preferred his home to the city, there was a part of Albion that reminded him of home. The only part that made any sense to him. He wasn't a miscreant or scrounger but he didn't exactly fit in. Brevington was a city full of people who never ventured to other cities. They knew of Jameson, Germantown, and Durrington but rarely did anyone leave. Partially because Brevington was safe. Partially because no city needed them. For Jon, it was a conundrum few understood. It was one thing to be exiled from your city. It was another to exile yourself to staying within the city but away from the rest of Brevington.

"Were you born here?" Jon asked.

"Nope," said the boy. "From another city. I was brought here."

"You," Jon said sarcastically, "were brought here?"

Sensing the sarcasm, the boy only nodded. Jon smiled, forgetting how enjoyable it was to frustrate others for a change. After a moment, the boy spoke up.

"It wasn't by choice," he said.

Jonathan frowned. "I imagine not," he said. "But where are the people you came here with?"

The boy remained silent. He added an extra step to speed up his walk, causing Jonathan to take longer strides. Jon had rested most of the day, so he wasn't worried about keeping up. What worried him was the boy's response. The unease of it made him think the boy might need more than rescue.

"Your family," Jon said louder. "Where are they?"

"Not here," the boy mumbled in agitation.

"That's obvious," said Jon. "I'm asking *why* they are not here."

The boy stopped in the street and turned to Jon. "Do you want to get back to the city or not?"

Jon raised his brow, unsure of the boy's threat yet entertained at the same time. However, he wasn't willing to have a boy put him in his place.

"Look, kid. It's a long way out of here, and there are people looking for me who aren't exactly friendly," Jon said. "I just need to know those people looking for me aren't looking for you, too."

"I don't know any people," the boy said, turning to continue toward the city. "I'm by myself here."

"Seems like you've managed on your own," said Jon, "but the people looking for me are not from Albion."

The boy looked at Jon, yet continued to walk. "What do you mean?"

"I mean they aren't from here."

"From Albion?" the boy asked.

"Geez, kid," Jon sighed. "What are you, a broken record? Yes, they are not from Albion. But I'm guessing they were sent here for a reason."

"To capture you?"

Jon breathed deeply. "Afraid it's more complicated than that."

"How so?"

Jonathan didn't look at the boy. Instead, he kept walking. Wishing he had the answer to his question. Hoping they made it out of the city before finding out.

# CHAPTER 81

Sam thanked the woman while her son sat in the corner. He knew it took courage to trust anyone in Albion, let alone a man carrying an injured woman into her space. The woman smiled, trusting that he would look out for the injured woman. Trust, she thought, was the missing ingredient. Sam already knew that to be true for his city.

He headed to the front of the store. Lucille was waiting for him.

"Are you sure you're good to go?" Sam asked. "You were banged up pretty bad last night."

Lucille lifted her shirt. The bruises were gone. As Sam noticed, he looked up, realizing the deep bruise around her eye was gone too. He was at a loss for words, wondering how such healing could've taken place.

"I can't explain it," said Lucille, "but I'm better. And yes, we have to find Jon before it's too late."

Sam nodded and led the way. It was early morning and quiet. No scurrying about. No assailants perusing the street. He headed east and walked past the warehouse. It was four blocks later before they stopped.

"Okay," said Sam. "There's a chance he'll come to this intersection before nightfall."

"That's if he knows where he's going," said Lucille. "He's not from here, remember?"

"Something tells me he's getting guidance," said Sam. "Remember the warehouse? No one can escape four guards using words alone without knowing what they are doing."

"Good point," said Lucille. "So, what are we going to do? Just wait?"

Sam shook his head. "No, but we have a collection point. We'll head farther east and look down each road. He's bound to be either close or heading in our direction."

Lucille held up a finger. "Question," she said. "What do we do when we find him? I kind of doubt he'll be excited to see us."

"You're right," said Sam. "He won't, but he's not beyond reason. All we have to do is tell him the truth."

Lucille laughed. "The truth? As in explaining the capture and how we suddenly realized we've made a mistake? Won't that be a little ironic?"

"Sure it will," said Sam, "but it's the truth."

Lucille was skeptical. "Something tells me you haven't thought this through."

"You're wrong." Sam smiled. "I have. He's not beyond reason because he's not acting out of his own will."

"Are you saying someone else is controlling him?" Lucille asked.

"No, not someone," said Sam. "But something."

"Like the city?" Lucille asked in confusion.

"No," Sam said, a bit of irritation creeping into his voice. "Am I the only one who remembers him speaking and the ropes coming off? Or when he spoke to us and everyone suddenly froze?"

"Well, no, but that doesn't explain why he'd listen to us," said Lucille. "He has the power to do whatever he wants."

"But that's just it! He doesn't have the power. Not really." Sam paced for a moment. "Think about it. If he was able to simply walk out of the warehouse without so much as a hair being touched, why were we able to capture him?"

Lucille shrugged. "Because we caught him off guard?"

"No," said Sam. "Because he couldn't escape. Or, he could have, just not at that moment."

Lucille was worried for her friend. She placed a hand on Sam's shoulder, knowing he wasn't making any sense.

"Are you sure you're okay?" she asked.

Yes!" Sam said, regaining his composure. "Listen. It makes sense. He's not in control of that power. If he were, he would have known something was wrong. Lucille, who goes into a dark alley in Albion? No one! Because of muggers and rapists and killers. That's common sense. But he did because he was drawn to it."

"To us?" Lucille asked.

"No, something bigger," said Sam. "I don't have a lot of time to explain this, but the feeling you get from this city—that eerie, 'something is out to get me' feeling—is the same feeling he has, except the opposite."

"Like a guardian angel?" Lucille suggested.

"Yes!" Sam said. "Like a guardian angel. Trust me, I know it sounds crazy. But it makes sense if you think about it."

"Well, he did come all this way," said Lucille. "And no one visits Albion unless they are looking for trouble."

"Exactly," said Sam. "And what are the chances Kieran would show up a week earlier with a plan to change the city that would involve Jon?"

"I don't know," said Lucille, "but wouldn't that make Kieran some kind of evil genius?"

"Or just evil," said Sam. "It sounds crazy, Lucille, but there are forces at work here that are beyond us. Our group stumbled into each other, but that was only after Lewiston and Shelby decided to take on this idea. But Kieran…"

Lucille didn't have to hear the rest. She knew it was weird enough that Kieran came by himself. No guard to protect him. No way of escape. She remembered him mentioning how he had never been to Albion. He didn't know the layout or the people but he had a plan to change the city.

"Sam," Lucille said. "I'm beginning to think you're right."

Sam grabbed her hand. "I know I am. I also know you weren't on the best of terms with Toby but being killed in cold blood…" He wasn't sure how to say it, but he continued. "That's just wrong. Kieran didn't know him well enough to hate me. He just shot him for letting Jon go."

"I know," Lucille said, looking down. "And it's not like I miss the jerk. But it was still pretty messed up."

Sam nodded. "Something tells me these strange forces are coming together. Fighting over the city. Fighting over who will control the people and their future."

"And if we don't help the right side…" Lucille rushed toward the street. "Come on!"

"Wait," Sam said, rushing after her. "Where are you going?"

"No time," said Lucille. "But I know how Kieran is going to find Jon!"

# CHAPTER 82

The room was cold. The bed was unfamiliar. She couldn't believe it. After all these years, her former friend—the very one her husband hated most—had betrayed her. Had taken advantage of her family.

Shirley sat at the end of the hotel bed. Her phone was turned off. She was alone with her thoughts and her pain. The pain, in truth, wasn't because of the news. Emilia might have told her but Shirley sensed the peculiarity of it all. His hate for Emilia. Emilia's need to be around him. It only made her understand. She could see why Samson didn't want her to stay. She could see why Emilia had reached out to her and not anyone else.

Emilia wasn't looking for someone to console her. She was looking for a marriage to ruin. To show that no one was perfect, least of all Samson. The revelation allowed Shirley to see where everything had gone wrong.

And yet, she felt guilty. Guilty for Samson feeling lonely enough to cheat. Guilty for letting Emilia back into their lives after her Samson had so vehemently voted against it. Thinking this was all her own fault. She snapped out of the trance.

"No," she said aloud. "This was Samson's doing. He chose to sleep with her. He chose to put himself above his family."

Shirley couldn't help but think he was like every other athlete. Every teammate Samson talked about. Every wild night they had without him. Shirley could see why he no longer stayed out late. No longer partied with the rest of the team.

He'd already done the worst. Committed the one act he knew she wouldn't put up with. It was clear that he felt bad about it. Guilty about his affair. And Shirley could see why he soon became faithful and so family-focused toward the end of Monty's life.

"Monty," she whispered. "Monty, I am so sorry."

It was one thing to let her son believe in his father. The perfect dad every kid should have and more. A superhero. A man with no flaws. But she knew if her son were still alive, he would be crushed by this. In a way, she felt as if his spirit was crushed by this.

As she slid to the floor, she began to cry. Tears of mistrust. Tears of pain. Tears damning the man who had made her feel like they would get through this. As if they'd done all they could to give Monty the life he deserved.

Now she was left with no son, a cheating husband, and a broken heart. She didn't know what was worse: the affair or the fact that she still wanted him. Needed him. Hoped he had an excuse. Hoped he had a reason to explain his actions.

Maybe he was drunk. Taken advantage of. He was an athlete, after all. One of the best in the sport, if not the best to ever play it. Maybe he was drugged. Each thought rushed in. Each excuse sounded better. Yet none of them held. The truth pierced through all of it.

She cried throughout the rest of the night. Hopelessly alone. Too afraid to call her sister out of fear that she also might have made a move on her husband. Shirley couldn't trust him. She couldn't trust anyone.

# CHAPTER 83

As the sun rose, with each ray bouncing off the water, Samson woke up. His eyes could see the water but his body felt as if each organ had been rendered useless. He wanted to move, but not get up. To somehow roll into the water, toward a death he would have to neither explain nor be saddened by.

His fans would understand. He had lost his son. His hope for living was gone along with his child. His wife had left him because of his mistakes and no one else was left. They would write a book about him. Create a statue of him. Life, after all, would go on.

And though he tried with all his might, he couldn't move. He couldn't think. Everything hurt within him. Worse still, he remembered the note. The failed promise. The broken vow. If his son's death hadn't hurt before, it hurt even worse now. He had no more tears to give. No sorrow to console him.

His son was gone and he had cheated on his wife. Not recently. Not while his son had passed. But in his past, and by his own choice, Samson had broken up his marriage. Though it had happened years ago, he felt like it had taken place yesterday.

Without opening his eyes, he rocked back and forth. Continually, agonizingly as his stomach, and the alcohol within, rocked with it. Eventually, he gained enough momentum. Eventually, he felt the water's cold embrace as he sank to the bottom of the pool.

# CHAPTER 84

"Shelby!" Lewiston yelled. "Shelby, if you can hear me, say something!"

He retraced his steps. Arrived at the last spot they had been. Shelby, however, wasn't there. No trace or sign of his friend. No living soul to help him find his family. He wanted to scream. To shout Shelby's name as loud as he could. But he knew better. He knew the odds of his friend alive were slim.

He walked cautiously through each street. Aware of any lurkers. Hopeful that he wouldn't be attacked. It was afternoon and the sun's reflection was bright. That made it hard for anyone to sneak around. If an assailant were to come, Lewiston would have enough time to run. He hoped his friend had run. He hoped his friend had survived the night.

When he rounded the corner to the next street, Lewiston stopped to examine where he was. Far from the last place he had seen Shelby. Far from anyone he knew. Anxiousness rose within as he hurried to the next alley.

Hiding behind a dumpster, he tried to catch his breath. To calm himself before he was found. It was then that he heard footsteps. He realized he was not alone.

# CHAPTER 85

The boy led him to the heart of the city, or at least what Jon believed was its heart. Almost a week had passed and he still had little idea of where he was. He didn't pay attention to the street signs as followed blindly—first the spirit, and then the boy. But now that the boy was in charge, Jon didn't second-guess the boy's instincts. For once since Mr. B had passed, Jon was glad to not be alone.

"A few miles more and we'll be by the highway," said the boy. "I hope your plan works."

"Why do you say that?"

"Because," the boy said, "that is where they wait."

"Who's they?" asked Jon.

"I call them the tricksters," said the boy. "The ones who act like they're here to help."

"Oh," said Jon, "thanks for the warning."

He thought back to when he had entered the city. He didn't remember seeing anyone or being offered any help.

"Why were they not there when I came to the city?" he asked.

"Because you kept driving." The boy shrugged. "Most others stop for directions or help."

"Thankfully, I like being lost," Jon muttered. "So we just keep heading forward?"

The boy nodded. "That's the plan."

"Great," said Jon.

A few more steps. A couple more miles. They were in the home stretch. He didn't like traveling on foot but would push through until they reached the end. Were it up to him, Jon would have kept on in his car. Searching each block until the spirit eventually forced him out. But he wasn't going by his intuition. And though he had been captured and beaten twice, the spirit always managed to get him where he needed to be.

"So," said the boy, "what is your plan?"

"Hard to say." Jon scratched his head. "Did your parents ever teach you about God and the Holy Spirit?"

The boy stopped, distressed by the question, regretting, in that moment, that he had trusted the man.

"Yes." The boy was skeptical. "They brought me to church every now and then."

"Good," said Jon. "That will make this less awkward."

"And less believable," the boy said, continuing on.

"Say what you want." Jon tried not to sound defensive. "It brought me to you. Twice. And despite my lack of self-defense training, I'm still alive."

"So am I," said the boy, "and I'm only nine."

"Nine?" Jon was surprised. "You can't only be nine. That doesn't make sense."

"Why?" the boy said defensively. "Because I've survived without anyone's help?"

"No," said Jon. "Because just a few months ago..."

It was then that Jon remembered why this boy looked familiar. The news. The murders. No boy over the age of eight.

"What is your name?" Jon asked.

"Why?" the boy scoffed. "Not like it matters."

"It does." Jon grabbed the boy's arm. "What is your name?"

"Get off of me." The boy tugged back. "I didn't ask yours, so back off."

"You're him." Jon's eyes widened. "Monty."

The boy, not expecting to have been remembered, regained control of his arm and kept walking. He didn't want to talk. He didn't want to remember.

"Don't you know what this means?" Jon caught up to him. "Your parents thought you were dead."

"No," said the boy, "they wanted to believe I was dead."

"That's not true." Jon stood in front of the boy. "And this is impossible! They brought bodies back to the city morgue. All identified."

"Obviously not." The boy stepped around Jon. "Because I'm right here."

Jon thought over the events of the story. The kidnapping. The shooting in Albion. But what never came to mind was something simple. A small piece that seemed insignificant at first but that opened his eyes in the end.

"The highway." Jon pointed far off in the distance. "You said people usually ask for directions or help when they come into the city?"

The boy nodded.

"How do you know this?"

Monty was quiet. He tried to hide the pain but Jon knew there was more to this than kidnapping.

"Monty, I'm trying to help." Jon knelt. "How do you know that's what they do?"

A tear streaked down the boy's face. "Because I waited," Monty said, wiping away the tear. "I waited to see if my parents would come."

"They would have had they not been fed a bunch of lies." Jon rose to his feet, thinking about what had happened that night. Wondering why the world hadn't been told the truth. "Did you see any police or news reporters?"

Monty shook his head. "Some drunks and people who were lost." He kicked a stone off the street. "No one else."

"Monty." Jon put his hands on the boy's shoulders. "No one knew. They reported you dead along with your friends." Another thought came to mind. "Your friends," he said. "Where are they?"

More tears streaked down the boy's face. Jon could tell this wasn't good. He had a feeling Monty was the only one who escaped.

"The person who kidnapped us," Monty began, struggling to say the words. "He…he didn't stop when the tricksters came out. It was like he knew what they were trying to do. So he kept driving. Except he didn't know it was a trap."

"A trap?" Jon asked, surprised. "As in, they knew he was coming?"

Monty shook his head. "There are people who wait, just in case the person keeps driving. They have traps set to blow out the tires. Stopping the car and giving them enough time to break in."

"But this is Albion," Jon reminded himself. "Few come and go. And those who do never come back the same …"

Monty could see the man's eyes, wildly trying to piece things together.

Hoping to figure out what he, the person who had been kidnapped, already knew.

“They weren’t shot, were they?” Jon asked. “They were taken away.”

Monty nodded. Not wanting to say more. Walking away as Jon tried to make sense of it all.

# CHAPTER 86

The maid arrived at the Barnett household ten minutes late. As she entered the house, she called out for anyone there. Hoping to explain her tardiness. Believing it worthwhile to do so, seeing that her son had come to town last night as a surprise. She hadn't seen him in over three years, as he studied in Jameson under a rigorous farmer. An education due, in fact, to the Barnetts' generosity, though she believed it better for him to get an education in Durrington.

She called out again without any response. Believing the house was empty, she went on to her duties. It wasn't until she noticed the empty alcohol cabinet that she thought something might be wrong. A similar incident had taken place months ago. With no one upstairs and no one in the bathrooms, she headed outside.

It didn't take long to see what had happened. It took even less time for her to call the neighbors for help, followed quickly by 911. The neighbor remained after pulling Sosa from the pool. Having been trained in CPR, he started at it, hoping the famed ballplayer was still alive.

When the ambulance arrived, they continued CPR. The time seemed to fly by. The maid, worried out of her wits, tried to reach Sosa's wife. Each time, it went to voicemail. Each try caused her to lose a little hope.

It was soon restored, however, when the medic managed to retain a steady pulse. Sosa was alive. Long live Sosa Barnett.

# CHAPTER 87

Kieran thought of a plan. One that wouldn't require his lost group. One that would require him to be clever in ways he hadn't thought possible. There was no backup. No aid to finish what he started. Just his wit. His mind had always been his greatest ally.

As he unlatched the lock and opened the door, he began to form a new plan. One quite a bit more devious than the last. One that would ensure Lewiston and Cowell would pay. He didn't have time to dilly-dally any longer.

He felt the charge of the city rushing through him. The violence. The chaos. The very foul nature, consuming Albion by the day. And though he didn't want to do this alone, he had no choice.

It made him wonder about humanity and those he called partners. He thought of the investors back in Durrington who were skeptical of his accomplishments and had little faith in his ability. His cunning and charm made this possible—along with his knowledge of the city architecture and his assurance of a group working ahead of him, though not with him just yet. He thought of the power he would gain as he would become the new leader of Albion. And juxtaposed with that, the fear he would command.

"Yes." He roamed the streets. "This city. This brute force of mayhem. It can't be rid of violence. Not yet."

He knew it was better for the remaining cities to still fear Albion. Otherwise, they would take control of it in its weakened, depleted state. Violence gone meant bureaucratic debate over who would rule. They'd probably rename it. Change the meaning of what was into what ought to be. The very thought appalled Kieran, as he wanted to lay claim to this city. This idea. This vision.

He continued walking. No longer afraid of the violence. No longer wondering where one might flank him, bringing certain death in minutes. No, he felt a part of the city. As if he belonged. As if, as its leader, he should get to know what made Albion tick. The thought drove away the fear. Albion's rightful leader was finally home.

# CHAPTER 88

Lewiston noticed her hair first as she peeked around the dumpster. He was still hidden, falling back in shock, as he thought she might be a ghost. The thought didn't seem as preposterous compared to the evil he had witnessed in this city.

"How?" he exclaimed. "Kieran said you were taken—beaten to death—a block away from the abandoned warehouse."

She shrugged. "Kieran isn't what he seems. And I imagine he told you some fanciful reason as to why you should go ahead with his plan."

Lewiston stood only to jump back as the man behind Lucille approached. "Sam." Lewiston blinked quickly. "How did she—"

"It's a long story," Sam said, holding out a hand. Lewiston shook it, glad to see they were alive. Sam looked around as if one more were missing. "Where's Shelby?"

"I fear the worst has happened to our dear friend." Lewiston peeked around the corner to make sure they weren't being followed. "He stayed out through the night, though I warned against doing so. It doesn't matter, though. The fault lies with me."

Lucille was confused. "*Your doing?* Lewiston, this was Kieran's plan. His bidding. He wanted to get Jon by sacrificing us."

Lewiston brushed her words to the side. "You don't understand."

"Then help us." Sam stepped forward. "Help us understand what is going on."

"Kieran meant to tear us apart. That much is certain." Lewiston continued to stare at the ground. "But I started this. The group. All of us being here…it was supposed to be something different. Something…"

"To do with family?" Lucille suggested. "You didn't do this, Lewiston. We all agreed, remember? Kieran didn't force you to say yes, and we didn't have sense enough to say no. We are here, right now, because of our mistakes."

"And as for Shelby," Sam chimed in, "he went his separate way. That was his choice. Not yours. A leader doesn't manipulate others to follow, nor does he force them to do his bidding. He lays out the best strategy in the hopes that others will follow. If they choose otherwise, then that burden no longer weighs upon you."

Lewiston took in what Sam had to say. He knew he had tried to persuade Shelby to retreat. He had even used logic to prove his point. But what Sam said was true. If Shelby wished to follow Lewiston, he would have. He chose differently. And though Lewiston could see the truth, the thought of losing his friend still hurt.

"You're right, Sam. Shelby made his choice." Lewiston straightened up and turned to face Lucille. "Now, how do we stop Kieran?"

# CHAPTER 89

Elias did what he could to bury his friend. With no area to dig up and no shovel, he brought his friend to the nearest store. It was the best he could do. Tears flowed as he mourned his friend. Not wanting to move. Not wanting to let him go. He regretted pushing Wade to come with him. *No one should die in Albion,* he thought. *No one should be buried away from their family.*

The only consolation was that his friend had died doing what he believed to be right. Wade knew the city needed Jon. He also knew Elias needed him. Elias spoke a few words and ended with a heartfelt prayer. Grief weighed on his chest. He didn't feel like finding Jon. Yet he knew he had to finish this. For Wade. For the city of Albion. There was a reason they had come here and Elias wasn't leaving until the job was done.

"I won't let you die in vain," he said, covering the corpse. "I won't let this be for nothing."

He left the same way he had come to the city. Worried and afraid. Hopeless, yet foolish enough to believe he could find Jon. He didn't know which way to go, especially because night had come. He knew he was better off inside one of the abandoned buildings.

Yet he kept walking. Twirling the bat in his hand like his old friend had done. Dismissing the fear that tried to overcome him. He didn't feel brave, nor did he want to test his luck. But he wasn't leaving without Jon. He wasn't leaving until it was finished.

# CHAPTER 90

"There's a time and place for this, gents."

A group of thugs surrounded Kieran. Each brandishing a weapon. Each hungrier than the other for violence. He decided it best not to move.

"I didn't make it all the way here to have my head knocked off," he said.

"It appears you have."

The voice came from outside those surrounding him. It was a gruff and powerful voice. Kieran could tell this was the leader. He just didn't know which man was talking.

"My name is Kieran L. Motley." He turned, looking for the man in charge. "And I have a proposition for you."

"Do you?" said the voice. "It doesn't look like you have much to propose."

Kieran stopped trying to find the man, speaking aloud as if the voice came from the sky.

"Your city," he pointed to a building, "is under attack."

The group of thugs laughed wildly. Wrenchingly. As if their vocal cords no longer functioned correctly.

"Oh, I know it doesn't seem like it. With your menacing weapons and eerily foul ways." Kieran took a step to the side as one of the men moved in closer. "But I assure you, there are those who wish to take the city from you."

"Like you?" The voice echoed and boomed through the alley. Kieran, noticing the darkened clouds, knew he had nothing to lose. Either he would either convince them to join his side or he would perish like the fallen victims of the city.

"Not like me," Kieran snapped. "I wish to see the city flourish. To grow and gain power. Maybe more organized, but more power nonetheless."

"You must not feel the power around you," boomed the voice. "For if you did, you'd know the trouble you are in."

"I know." Kieran scooted to the side as another man came closer. "I have no right to ask for your help, yet here I am. Doing just that. And do you know why?"

He looked around. Eyeing each man. No longer worried about what they might do. No longer caring for the booming voice or its intimidating presence.

"Why?" asked the voice.

"Because I know this city," said Kieran. "Its chaotic means of vengeance. Its violent nature. I know the source of its power. And it is not from any man."

A figure slowly approached, standing a foot taller than Kieran. Features unlike any man. A presence of fear, now in human form. Its gruff voice cut through the air.

"So what powers the city, Kieran L. Motley?"

Kieran gulped. He had hoped this was some sort of Wizard of Oz play in which the man behind the voice was actually smaller and weaker than the rest. His hopes had been dashed in a matter of seconds.

"You believe this is your home," said Kieran shakily. "But there are those who roam these very streets who would say otherwise. They wish to change the city. To domesticate it and those within its walls."

The figure laid a finger on Kieran's chest. Eyes staring into his. Breath worse than any Kieran had smelled before.

"And you don't?"

Kieran shook his head. "No, there would be no point to it. To get rid of the very citizens who make Albion great. Who make Albion *feared*."

The figure observed Kieran, knowing it could not trust him yet also knowing that his words contained truth.

"My brother remains in this city." The figure stepped closer, finally revealing the face of a man. "He wishes to band together a group that will come to his aid."

The man eyed Kieran as the smaller man took a step back.

"Last I heard, you were part of that group." The man stepped closer. "And you lead them, is that not so?"

"I've left them," Kieran said defiantly. "They wish to sanitize this place.

To rid it of its people and its inheritance. I assure you, I am no longer with them."

The man crossed his arms and said loudly, "And what plans do you have for this city?"

Kieran shrugged. "I only wish to see it thrive. To see Albion become the greatest of the five cities. They will bend beneath your power. Not the other way around."

The man moved closer. Eyeing Kieran. Appearing prepared to strike the shorter man. And yet, Kieran remained still.

"Tell us of your plan," the man commanded. "Tell us how you plan to save Albion."

# CHAPTER 91

Sosa's body rested peacefully on the hospital bed. His wife had received the call just as she turned on her cell. Pumping the alcohol from his body caused him to jerk from side to side. The doctor decided it best to sedate him. The drugs would give him time to rest. They would also give Sosa time for his mind to relax.

The sleep was heavy and the dream quite unusual. He saw a man holding his son's hand, about a hundred feet away.

"Monty!" Sosa called out. "I'm here, son! I'm here!"

The boy only looked at his father. The man remained still. They seemed like wax figures, lifeless, but still there. Sosa tried running toward them but he could only run in place. Some invisible boundary prevented him from going any farther. He tried running even harder.

"Monty!" he cried out. "Why won't you come to me?"

It was only then that the man let go of Monty's hand. Monty looked up to the man and was greeted by the shake of his head. Monty kicked at his shoes and then faced his dad. Tears began to form in Sosa's eyes.

"Soon, Dad," Monty said. "I will see you soon."

"No," Sosa whispered. "No, I can't lose you again."

Monty smiled and returned to the man. The man was smiling, too. Sosa assumed he was the kidnapper, taking away his son. Robbing him again of what he had already lost.

"I won't let you take him." Sosa ran harder. "Not again! Not my boy!"

The man, without saying a word, nodded to the father. Kindness in his eyes. An expression of gentleness that led Sosa to doubt his first conclusion. But if he wasn't the robber, why wouldn't give Sosa back his son? The question had barely formed before the man tugged at Monty's arm. Monty, looking into the man's eyes, knew it was time to go. He faced his dad one last time.

"Soon," he repeated with a smile. "Very soon."

Sosa cried out for his son to come back. To not leave him again. To not let him go on without being by his side. Monty was the only person who saw him in a better light. As Sosa continued to shout, his vision began to blur. The two figures slowly faded away.

Shirley watched her husband squirm from one side to the other. Hearing him call out her son's name. Watching helplessly. She knew her husband could see Monty for only one reason. *He's dying,* she thought as tears streamed down her face. *My husband is dying.* The nurse, seeing the woman's expression, came over and gently rubbed her shoulder.

"He'll be all right," she said softly. "It's the last of the alcohol. It holds on tight but once it's gone, he will rest and everything will be back to normal."

Shirley nodded. Choosing to believe the nurse. Not knowing what she would do if she lost Sammy. The hate she had felt disappeared. She could think only of what she had left. She could think only of what Monty would have wanted. And as Sosa finally came back to a peaceful state, she continued hearing his voice. The voice of a desperate father crying out for his only son.

She cried the rest of the night. Happy to still have her husband. Saddened by the effect her son's death was having on Samson. She knew how much Monty meant to him. She knew she could forgive him for what he had done.

# CHAPTER 92

Sam led as Lucille and Lewiston followed. He knew the city but he didn't know Kieran's plan. He hoped the man had left, giving up on trying to change the city. No one could control Albion. And after seeing his brother on Sentry Lane, he knew the truth. Albion was no longer a place but an all-consuming form of evil. And as much as he hoped Kieran had simply made his escape, Sam knew better. He knew the fight had just begun.

"There's only one way he could actually see this thing through." Sam turned to Lucille. "There's a reason he needed our help. He couldn't navigate this city on his own, nor could he carry out the plan without help. He needs something more."

"A stronger force," Lewiston thought aloud. "But how? No one is left in the city but Jon."

"Then Jon is who we need to find," Lucille said. "But we already knew that. Sam, where do you think he could be?"

"There are only two parts to this city." He pointed east. "The suburbs and the actual city. If he's in the suburbs, we need to head east."

"Wait," Lewiston said, holding up a hand. "I don't think he's there."

"By what logic?" Lucille asked.

"This is embarrassing to admit," Lewiston said. "But I just have a feeling."

Lucille and Sam stared, dumbfounded by Lewiston's remark. *He's finally reached his breaking point,* thought Sam. *He's definitely lost his mind,* thought Lucille. Lewiston was supposed to be the logical genius and now he was going off of a feeling. *We're in for it now,* thought Lucille.

"Don't look at me like that," Lewiston demanded. "I don't say this often but sometimes a person simply knows what he knows. And I know that he's not there."

"Because of your feeling?" Lucille teased.

"I have to admit, Lewiston," Sam chided, "a feeling isn't much to go on."

"Isn't it?" Lewiston asked. "This whole city is based on a feeling. A feeling of madness. An effective feeling of evil that consumes each citizen until driven mad. Craving violence and corruption. Chaos being the very least of its worries."

Sam turned to Lucille. "He has a point."

"Then tell us," said Lucille. "Where does your feeling say Jon is?"

Though he had lamented on sound reasoning, Lewiston thought the idea of being able to follow a feeling was preposterous. But what he felt wasn't an emotion. No, it was a tug. A pull that seemed convincing enough to believe he actually knew where Jon might be.

"That way," he pointed. "I think."

# CHAPTER 93

Jonathan sat on the ground as Monty took in his surroundings. They were back in the city. Back to the abandoned buildings. Back to having a target on Jon's back. He didn't mind being targeted. His life, he knew, was no longer in his hands. But he cared for the kid, if not for any other reason than for the fact that he was so young. Jon wasn't a parent, and nor did he have any siblings who had borne children, but he knew the innocence of a child. He knew the nine-year-old may put on a great front, but deep down the boy missed those who still loved him.

"What are you looking for?" Jon asked.

Monty looked back. "The next place."

"Where do you think that will be?"

Monty shrugged. "Hopefully close."

"If you don't mind me asking," Jonathan said, standing, "how exactly do you know? The next place, that is. And what makes you think we need to go to it?"

The boy shrugged again. "I never know where I need to go."

Jon began to smile. "Because of the spirit." He laid a hand on the boy's shoulder. "Face it, kid. That's the only reason you're still alive. The spirit guides you, doesn't it?"

The boy shrugged off Jon's hand. "I don't know what you're talking about. It's just a gut feeling."

"No," Jon chided, "it's not. Trust me. The spirit led me to you. To this city."

"Thought you said your friend did that," said Monty.

"No, he requested that I save one more life." Jon took a step forward. "He never told me to come to Albion. If he had, I would have taken him for a fool and disregarded his request."

The boy paused. "Who was he to you?" he finally asked. "It doesn't seem right to just go off the words of a dying man. That just doesn't make sense."

"There are a lot of things that don't make sense, kid," said Jon. "But he was a friend."

The boy thought for a moment. He didn't understand how this stranger had been led here when Monty's parents remained at home. Jon noticed the boy's puzzled expression.

"You're thinking too hard," he said, pointing to the boy's scrunched-up forehead. "What's on your mind?"

"You're the only one who came to look for me," said the boy. "You came all the way here to this crappy city to find me."

"No one knew you were alive," confided Jon. "I didn't even know you were alive. I told you. Your parents think you're dead. And the rest of the world barely remembers what happened. That's the way the world is."

The boy looked up at Jon. "What do you mean?"

He sighed. "The world sees you for what you mean to it at that moment. At that time. And once you die, the world forgets about you." He looked down at the boy, regretting the last few words. "Except for your parents."

"Is that why you're here?" asked the boy. "Because you think the world doesn't care?"

"I'm here to find you," Jon said. "I didn't know it at first. But that's why I'm here."

He looked around. Seeing the empty city for what it was. Knowing the rest of the world had tried its best to forget about Albion.

"The other four cities," Jon said. "They don't care what happens to Albion. They don't care if it crumbles. If people die. Or if people are taken. They barely care about what actually matters in life."

The boy thought about the man's words. It made sense. No one else had come to rescue him because no one else cared to see if he was alive.

"They see what they want to see until it's too late," said Jon. "I just don't think that's how we're meant to live."

"Neither do I," the boy said, his eyes watering. "I think everyone matters."

"Because they do," Jon said. He faced the boy and bumped him on the shoulder. "You matter. I matter. And this city matters."

The boy wiped his eyes. "So, does that mean you'll save the city, too?"

Confused, Jon gave the boy a look. "No," he said. "Even if it could be saved, I'm not sure how anyone would do it."

"That's easy," said the boy. "One person at a time."

"I guess that makes sense, if these people actually want to be saved," said Jon. "But I don't think they do."

"That's what the rest of the world thinks," said the boy. "And I don't know. The people here are…strange. But that doesn't mean they should be left behind, right?"

Jon thought about this. He wanted Albion to be different. To be in better shape. He didn't want its chaotic nature to continue. But he was just a man. A flawed one at that. He had no idea how he could save a whole city. He had no idea how he could convince everyone in Albion to strive for better.

"This city is rough," said Jon, "I'm sure someone with more influence and power could save it. But not me."

The boy smiled and walked away. Jon followed him. They continued in silence before Monty decided to speak up.

"You say the spirit led you here, right?"

"Yes," said Jon. "Right to you."

"And the spirit wasn't wrong, was it?" the boy asked.

"No, I don't believe it was."

"Can you say the spirit is ever wrong?" asked the boy.

"Maybe not wrong," lamented Jon. "But definitely flawed in its ways."

"But right about everything else," said the boy. "Don't you think?"

"What are you getting at?" Jon asked. "It's tiring enough answering the same question five different ways. Just say what you're trying to say."

"I'm just saying..." The boy shrugged. "If it's right about coming to this city. And it's right about finding me. What do you think the spirit says about saving this city?"

"It would probably say you were crazy," Jon said, smiling at the boy. "And I'm guessing, if it were completely up to the spirit, it would have us do just that."

The boy smiled. "So, what do you think we should do?"

Jon sighed. Disappointed with the boy's logic. Even more discouraged by the spiritual influence taking place inside of him.

"Looks like we're saving a city, kid."

# CHAPTER 94

"He'll ruin everything if we don't stop him," said Kieran, "and I assure you, he has the power to do just that."

"Jonathan Buckley," the man said. "The Christian boy. Brevington's *savior.*" His emphasis on the word brought a chill to Kieran's spine. "He's come for Albion?"

"Yes," said Kieran, "and everything in it."

"Interesting," said the man. His gravelly voice echoed throughout the air. "What gives him power?"

"That I do not know. But I've captured him once. And I—"

"You," the man moved closer, "did nothing. Your team captured him."

"And who commanded them to do so?" Kieran questioned.

The man didn't bother replying.

"Regardless, he escaped," said Kieran. "And he didn't lift a finger to do so."

"How could that be?" the man asked. "Is he armed with the Word?"

Kieran, knowing full well how Jonathan had escaped, couldn't tell the truth. If the man knew of the Word and its power, he would take on Jon himself. Without Kieran's help. Which didn't bode well for the Durrington native. He knew he couldn't let the chance of ruling Albion slip from his grasp again.

"No," he said. "I wasn't there when he escaped but I know he managed to break the bonds. Possibly escaped while the hired help was napping."

The man mulled this over. He knew Kieran was weak. Smarter than any he'd met before, but still weak.

"What was their punishment?" the man asked.

"Death," Kieran said coolly. "I shot Toby. He was the guard in charge. My bullet. My gun. The rest of them knew better than to cross me."

The man rubbed his chin. "Interesting," he said. "Very interesting."

Kieran fought to control his irritation. "What is so interesting about shooting a man?"

"Your guards." The man smiled. "Even after threat of death, they still abandoned you."

"Abandoned. Ran for their lives. I tend not to care either way," said Kieran. "My asset is my mind. I came up with the plan. It would be in poor taste to not have a Plan B."

"So, you needn't my help?" the man asked.

Kieran stepped forward. "You are the only one I need. The only person who can help me save Albion."

The man, amused, observed Kieran. Watching him sway. Watching him pretend to be in control by wanting to join forces.

"And if I find him myself?" the man questioned. "What stops me from killing him?"

Kieran didn't think twice. He knew the group was still out there. Worse yet, he knew Lewiston was still alive. He might have left the warehouse but Kieran knew that Lewiston was smart enough to survive. To know where help may be and shift it to his advantage.

"The group," said Kieran. "They might not seem like much but they hold a mind equal to mind. One willing to sacrifice everything for the sake of taking the city. He, and the rest of those misfits, are more formidable than you might believe."

The man grew tired of the façade. He had determined that the game between two minds was not equal. He may not have known the group that opposed him, but he knew Kieran. The city had already revealed his motives.

"You are but words, Kieran L. Motley. You must know that I see that. What you really wish is to rule. To have power. To take Albion for yourself and destroy anyone who opposes you."

Kieran was speechless. He didn't think the man a fool but he did believe his point was valid. The man needed his help. Without him, Kieran believed the city would fall. Yet the man saw right through him. He was but words, and no amount of them could save him now. The ghoulish form of a man came close to Kieran.

"This city, however, is lacking one thing." The man seemed to hover as he slowly circled Kieran. "Not a leader. Nor a power-hungry mongrel. No, the city needs something more."

"What more could Albion need?" Kieran gulped.

The man smiled as he stopped. He towered over Kieran as he held out his decrepit hands to grip Kieran's shoulders.

"You say this mind of theirs would sacrifice everything to take the city," the man said. "I wonder if you would do the same to save it."

Kieran fought his hardest to break free of the man. But he couldn't. He was unable to move. His feet felt cemented to the ground as the feeling in his arms left him. He was paralyzed, yet still standing. And as the man watched Kieran struggle, he continued to smile, satisfied with his new host.

Kieran yelled in agony as pain pierced each nerve. He could hear the chaos of the night. Every murder since the city had been founded. Every capture since Albion's existence. All of it came flooding in. And what was he to do? He couldn't break free from the man and he felt foolish for falling into the man's trap. He would not control Albion but he would be controlled by its ways. The man's grip broke flesh and, in moments, the ghoulish form disappeared.

"Now," the man said, speaking from Kieran's mouth. "To find Jon and those who oppose me."

# CHAPTER 95

Lewiston stopped. Pain gripped him as he fell to the ground. Neither Sam nor Lucille knew what was happening. They rushed to his side, kneeling to the ground as their leader writhed in pain.

"Lewiston." Lucille gripped his arms. "What's going on?" She looked to Sam, hoping he might know. "What's happening to him?"

Sam thought for a moment. What he was seeing seemed familiar. As if this very same incident had taken place before. Shaking his head, he looked up to see if anyone was around. *No one,* he thought. This worried him even more. Only one great power could have brought Lewiston to his knees without being around.

"It's the city," Sam said. "My brother, to be exact."

"Your brother?" asked Lucille. "I didn't know you had a brother."

"I do but he's not the same," said Sam. "This was before I left the group. I only recently ran into him when I gunned it from the warehouse."

Sam thought back to when he had last seen him. His brother. A man who had managed to sneak up on him when Sam knew that no one was around. Something had seemed off about their meeting. Something had felt off about speaking to his brother again. He faced Lucille, telling her what had happened the night he first met Lewiston and Shelby.

"I was running. My brother and I were on Sentry Lane and were attacked. Not by any street thug or Albion assailant." He noticed Lewiston turning pale. "No, it was more than that. Pure evil. A ghoulish-looking group of guys who were out to get us."

Lucille couldn't believe what she was hearing. She knew the city gave off strange vibes but never did she believe it was more than violent deviants on the prowl for an innocent victim.

"He forced me to leave. Told me he'd be fine and that he'd hold them off," said Sam. "I knew better than to believe him but he's my big brother. He had protected me from worse."

"So you left him?" Lucille gathered. "You left your brother to a force you couldn't even explain?"

"No," Sam whispered. "I wish it were that simple. I stayed. Willing to hold my ground just like him. Willing to fight until the end, if that's what it came to. But when I looked to my right, he was gone. Vanished into thin air."

"Vanished?" asked Lucille. "Sam, what the hell is going on? What else is in this city?"

"There's more to it than what you see," said Sam. "That's why no one has been here. That's why the other cities have given up. Albion can't be saved because something bigger than Albion controls it."

He turned to face Lewiston. Their friend lay on the ground, barely breathing as he tried to speak.

"He's here," Lewiston whispered. "Kieran. He's coming."

# CHAPTER 96

Samson finally woke. A pool of sweat surrounded him. He was confused as to where he was until he looked down. The nightgown gave it away. And though he was alive, he was sad that the dream was over. He could no longer see his son. He looked over and saw Shirley asleep in the chair beside him. *She came,* he thought. *But why?* He knew she deserved better. He couldn't imagine forgiving himself, let alone her forgiving him. Still, he was happy to see her. So happy that he wept. Quietly at first. Uncontrollably moments later.

He couldn't stifle his feelings. He was overwhelmed with emotion at the loss of his son, yet he felt the love of his wife. *I don't deserve to be here,* he thought. *I don't deserve to be alive.* Yet he was. He wished Monty had taken his place. Giving his wife the person she deserved. Taking at least part of the pain away from her. It was then that Shirley woke up. She blinked, taking in the fact that her husband was alive.

"Sammy," she whispered. "You're okay."

Tears continued to stream down his face. He wasn't able to speak, yet he wanted to ask her why she had come. Why she hadn't ignored the call from the hospital. How she could forgive him for committing such an act of betrayal.

He watched as she rose and walked to him. Hugging him. Climbing into the hospital bed and weeping uncontrollably, just as he had. He hugged her. Never wanting to let go. Never wanting to hurt her again.

"I thought I lost you," she said. "I thought…"

"I know," he said. "I'm surprised myself."

He leaned in as they cried together. Weeping for each other. Finally understanding how much each other had suffered. Finally able to admit they were not okay. Minutes passed as the hurt flowed out. It wasn't until a half-hour later that Samson pulled back from his wife. He had something to tell her.

"I saw him," he said, tears still streaming. "I saw our son."

"Oh, Sammy." She lost her breath. "How? What did he say? How was he?"

Samson told her about his encounter with Monty. The mysterious man by his side. How Monty had continued telling him that they would see each other soon. How was Samson going to see his son soon?

"Are you dying, Sammy?" she asked cautiously. "Because he died, and he said he would see you soon. I can't lose both of you."

He kissed her forehead, pulling her in close. "No, I'm not dying. Or I don't believe I am. They probably pumped out enough alcohol to serve an entire bar, but I'll be fine."

She looked up at him. "Then what did he mean? How is he going to see you soon?"

"I don't know," he said. "But I have a feeling he wasn't lying. That somehow, I'll see our son again."

"He hasn't left us," she said, placing her hand on his heart. "He's in there. Still with us."

Samson nodded. Hoping she was right. Hoping he would see his son in every dream thereafter. If that was what it took to see his son, he would take it. He missed Monty, and that dream alone brought him hope.

"Or maybe it was God," his wife said. "Holding his hand. Protecting him."

Samson thought on this for a moment before speaking. "No," he said, "I don't think it was."

"Why not?" she asked. "Don't you think he went to heaven?"

Samson didn't know how to explain what he saw or what he felt. Yes, his son was dead. But the dream was real. More real than the hospital bed in which he lay. It didn't seem like a glimpse of his son in heaven because there was nothing else. No angels. No clouds. There was the possibility that everything he had been taught in church was false but he knew something was different.

"It didn't feel like the afterlife," he said, facing Shirley. "No angels were singing. There were no pearly gates. It was just the three of us. Talking."

He remembered his son's blank reaction when he first met them. The same went for the man. It was like they were waiting for him. As if speaking connected them. Yet, he still didn't understand what he had witnessed. He just knew there was more to it.

"Maybe it was God's way of telling you that Monty's all right," she said. "That when we do pass, we will see him. It says in Ecclesiastics that life is fleeting. Here one moment and gone the next. Time works differently for them."

Samson wasn't sold on this idea but he didn't want to argue. He didn't want to lose his wife again.

"Maybe," he said, holding her close. "Anything is possible at this point."

As they lay in bed, he thought about the past few days. His drinking. Her leaving. The affair. He was glad she had forgiven him. He was glad she was still by his side. But he couldn't ignore what he had done. He couldn't ignore the lie that stood between them.

"I'm sorry," he said, hoping she was still awake. He felt her stir as she looked into his eyes. "What I did…how I've hurt you. You deserve better and I messed up. You don't deserve any of this."

She looked into his eyes. Expressionless. He couldn't tell what she was thinking or sense what she might say. This was the part he feared. This was the part of telling the truth that scared him the most.

"You're right," she said. "I don't deserve this. Being lied to. Having another woman sleep with the man I love. But most importantly, I didn't deserve to have Monty taken from me."

Tears formed as Samson refused to look away. He could see the pain in her eyes. He could also sense her courage. Her perseverance through hard times. He wished he were as strong as she was. He wished he weren't so weak.

"But life," she said, "isn't about what we deserve. We make decisions and our actions have consequences. Doing the right thing doesn't guarantee a pain-free life. We suffer losses that no person should suffer. We are betrayed in unfathomable ways."

She sat up in the bed, facing him. Noticing, for the first time, her husband's true countenance. He wasn't going to shy away from the truth. He could have made some poor excuse but he didn't. He could have said it was an accident. Instead, he faced her, right there in the hospital bed, willing to suffer any consequence she dealt. And despite what he had done, she smiled.

"I'm choosing to forgive you, Samson," she said. "Not because you deserve it. Not even for Monty's sake. But because I refuse to let life dictate me or my happiness. I just hope you choose to do the same."

# CHAPTER 97

Elias made it back to the heart of the city. *What the hell am I doing,* he thought. *I won't survive one minute here.* Yet he knew he couldn't turn back. There was no *back* to return to. He continued forward until he witnessed his worst fear: a group of guys, each more menacing than the other, slowly approached. *A welcoming crew,* thought Elias. *Just what I wanted.* Regretting his decision to return, he continued forward. He knew he couldn't outrun them. And he knew there was no place to hide.

The man in the middle—the most menacing of the three—stepped forward.. His dirtied shirt was ripped at the shoulder. The man's appearance seemed to mirror his disgruntled manner. Elias would have to fight. If he didn't fight now, he would answer to another group just like them farther into the city.

"I don't have time for this," he said.

He swung at the man who had stepped forward and was thankful to have made contact. The other two men jumped at him, but Elias, as if by instinct, swung left and then right, managing to knock both men to the floor. Having never been the athletic type, Elias wasn't sure what was going on. It was like something greater was guiding his hands. His mind was sharper than it had been in years.

*Fight or flight,* he reasoned. *Or purely the desire to not die in this godforsaken place.* He watched as the first man charged at him. Elias felt fear yet he didn't run. He jumped to the side as the man charged by.

He noticed the two henchmen tried to surprise him. Thankfully, the men hadn't gathered weapons, which strangely made Elias feel better. As he turned to swing, he managed to make contact with both men.

The henchmen, having had enough sense knocked into them, ran away. The first man, apparently not getting the memo, stayed to fight. It was about pride at this point, and he wasn't going to let someone of a smaller stature scare him away.

"Okay," said Elias, sizing him up. "Would have rather fought them than you but I guess we don't always get what we want."

The man reached for Elias's throat. Elias, quickly nudging the bat, hit the man's wrist. The man pulled back his hand, yet surprised Elias by head-butting the judge so quickly that Elias could only fall back. The blow, harder than any hit he had ever taken, made him dizzy. He stumbled to the ground.

*That was less than ideal,* he thought. He looked up to see the man jump at him. Elias rolled to his side, barely missing the attack. Bat still in hand, he swung with all his might, which didn't amount to much, as he was still on the ground.

Yet he made contact, connecting with the man's throat. Elias could hear him gasping for air. Though he didn't condone violence, Elias knew this would be his last chance. He would have to finish off the man before the man could get to his feet. As he stood, wobbly at first, Elias raised the bat, then brought it down with all the force he could muster. He closed his eyes as he heard the crunch of the man's skull beneath the blow.

He turned. The man was no longer breathing. Stumbling away, Elias thought about what he had done. *I killed a man,* he thought. *I killed a man with a bat.* It wasn't something to be proud of, yet—strangely enough— he felt a certain confidence rise within.

Elias didn't believe in murder. As a judge, and simply as a person with a moral conscience, he knew that he should have been able to reason with the man. To talk things out in a manner that would enlighten both parties that violence was not the way to go. In a different situation, he wouldn't have brought a bat. Rather, logic would have been his weapon of choice.

But he was in Albion. Reasoning didn't take place here. Rationalizing and weighing the moral cost did not happen. That was his only excuse. And though he didn't feel great about it, he knew there was more to what had happened tonight than simply beating the supposed *better man.* A part of him he never knew existed had saved him. Protected him. Guided him so that he would survive. That was the instinct he never thought possible. The part of him he never thought he had.

He knew, when the mayor was still alive, he couldn't rely upon himself. Not being strong enough. Athletic enough. Smart enough. He thought himself prey in a city so taken by violence. Tonight proved otherwise. He could win. He was a man. Not because he could kill. Not because he could scare away two henchmen. But because he could fight. He could stand up for himself and win.

He made it a block away before he sat in the shelter of an alley. Elias didn't know if he could go another round with anyone else. As he gathered his breath, and as the adrenaline slowly faded, he thought about why he was still there. What he had come to do. *I'll tear this whole place apart,* he thought, *if that's what it's going to take to find Jon.*

There was no heading back. There was no friend to console him. It was just him, God, and the city of Albion. Night came fast but nothing would take him away. Nothing would stop him from doing what he had come to do.

As if on cue, he heard footsteps. Despite his strong belief and tenacious understanding of his newfound purpose, Elias cowered deeper into the alley. He was surprised to see that the footsteps revealed the boy he had witnessed earlier that week. He looked at the boy and the boy looked at him.

"Come on," said the boy. "I'll take you to him."

"To whom?" Elias asked.

The boy smiled. "To the man you're looking for."

# CHAPTER 98

Lewiston gradually got to his feet. Lucille kept guard, making sure they had not been followed. They were alone. Just the three of them in the heart of the city. Lewiston's warning had caught Lucille and Sam off guard. She turned to face him.

"I don't see anyone," she said. "And it doesn't sound like anyone is coming. So, what are you talking about?"

Lewiston winced in pain. Sam came to his aid, holding him up. Lewiston didn't know what had happened. He only knew that Kieran's presence could be felt. He could not see him, nor did he think Kieran was around the corner. But he was coming.

"He wanted to take over the city," he said, still in pain. "That's why he came."

"You're stating the obvious, Lewiston," Lucille said.

Lewiston looked up to face Lucille. "He failed."

"That's good then, right?" Sam asked. "He didn't get what he wanted. The city is still intact and Jon can still help."

Lewiston shook his head. "You don't get it. He didn't fail because he messed up. He failed because something happened. Something he didn't plan for."

"What happened?" demanded Lucille. "Lewiston, you're not making sense."

"What controls Albion is bigger than the people," Lewiston said, exasperated. "I can't explain it but the city has a mind of its own."

"A mind of its own?" Sam asked.

"Yes," said Lewiston. "But that's being threatened. First by Kieran and now by Jon. Kieran failed because he thought he could control it. He thought he was smart enough to take what he wanted." The pain diminished as Lewiston stood on his own. "Today changed all of that. Kieran remains but he's not in control. Something is controlling him."

"I feel like that might be a bad thing," said Sam. "But it could be worse, right?"

Lewiston looked at Sam as if he had missed the whole point. As if he didn't notice what made the people of Albion commit such heinous acts.

"You know there's more to this city," Lewiston said. "More to the violence. The murder. Everything here. I missed that in my calculations."

"What are you talking about?" Lucille asked. "We calculated for everything. Even to the aspect of leadership and stronger infrastructure."

"No," said Lewiston. "We didn't."

"What did we miss?" asked Sam. "What's so important that it threw off your plans?"

Lewiston didn't know how to explain because it was, in fact, unexplainable. The human psyche. The drive that made a person choose to do either good or bad. That piece of information no one knew. It could not be controlled or fixed by sheer willpower or by fear. He knew better than anyone that to change Albion would require changing the whole city. How many would be on board for a complete overhaul?

"This city and the people in it," he said. "Think about it. Don't you think that, after realizing they couldn't change the city, they would try to escape?" He turned to Sam. "You know better than all of us."

"I know what?" asked Sam. "That my city has problems?"

"That you don't care that your city has problems," Lewiston said. "What you care about is surviving. Making it to the next day and choosing what is best for you. No offense, Sam. You have that right. But the city wired you that way and now that's all you know."

Lucille, though she didn't completely grasp everything, was starting to understand Lewiston. She could grasp it because she felt the same way. Running to and fro. Looking for a person whom she didn't know in the hopes he might save them. But how close had they gotten to a solution? Were they any better today than they were when the group first started?

"This whole time," she said. "We've wasted so much of it. Distracted." She turned to face Lewiston. "We haven't gotten any closer to fixing the city because we are, ironically, now a part of it."

"Exactly!" Lewiston exclaimed. "Sam, this city is a complete mind scrambler. It doesn't want to be fixed. Nor anyone in it."

Sam refused to believe it. "No," he said. "You're wrong. You know why? Because I've wanted to get out of this city for years. Hoping it would change. Choosing to be a part of that change even it meant risking my life. And if I couldn't get my brother out, I'd escape to make sure his sacrifice wasn't in vain."

"Sam," Lucille said calmly, laying a hand on his shoulder. "Don't you hear yourself? You want to *escape*. To *get out* of the very city you hoped to save. But did you come close to leaving? Even as part of our group. Did we get any closer to rescuing you or the people of Albion?"

Sam wanted to deny it. To tell her she was wrong. To tell both of them that they were wrong about their time in Albion. But he didn't have a single memory pointing to a time when they had actually helped the city. They had built a warehouse to protect them from its corruption. They had accepted the help of a power-hungry Durrington citizen to speed up the process. But during their time together—as a group—they hadn't changed a single thing.

Lewiston could see it in Sam's eyes. The realization of it all. The understanding that shook even Lucille. They hadn't changed the city. Not even a small part of it. If anything, they had given into Albion. Its will. Its corruption.

"That power Kieran looked for. He found it." Lewiston thought about what they could do but he knew it was helpless now. "The city and Kieran are now one. And I don't know, guys. I'm thinking even Jon can't stop whatever they have planned."

"I'm thinking he can," said a voice.

It came from behind them. Not a familiar voice or one they hoped to hear. As they turned, they saw a balding man who seemed out of place. It was clear he was not from the city. His clothes were still tidy and his smile—well, they couldn't remember the last time they had witnessed someone smiling—made it seem as if he had just arrived.

"The person you're looking for is here," he said. He stepped closer to the group. The group, unsure of what he was talking about, became defensive. "You don't believe me," the man said. Still smiling. Still full of hope. "Come and see."

The man left. Surprisingly, the group followed.

# CHAPTER 99

As they were led by the bald man, Lewiston thought about Kieran. What he was up to. How he would try to overtake the city. Yet he continued to follow the bald man as he wound through alleys and streets, as if the city wasn't a threat. As if Albion had become his safe haven.

"I don't like this," said Sam. "Why's he so calm?"

Lucille agreed. The man seemed cheerful for reasons she couldn't understand. She poked Lewiston in the shoulder but her friend was anywhere but present.

"Lewiston," she whispered. "You with us?"

He didn't respond. She gave him a shove that almost knocked him over. He blinked a few times.

"What...what'd I miss?" he asked.

"This guy," she whispered. "Does something seem a little off to you?"

Lewiston shrugged. "I think this is a pretty nice change of pace considering all we've been through." He turned to Sam and could see his confused expression. "Look, he said he's going to lead us to the person we are seeking. Worst-case scenario, it ends up not being Jon and we run. Best case, it is Jon and we save ourselves the hassle searching for him ourselves."

"I think you're missing the middle-to-worst-case scenario," Lucille said. "The part where the violent citizen gets his vicious gang to attack us."

"Hey," Sam said, "they're not gangs. Just groups of bitter, violence-driven citizens who don't know better."

He could see the anger in her eyes and quickly stepped up to the bald man's side. "This might seem like a dumb question," Sam began, "but how can we trust you?"

The man smiled and walked ahead, yet turned to face Sam. "How can you not?"

Sam, creeped out by the response, fell back in line with the others.

"I'm with her on this," Sam said. "Something feels off."

"This city feels off," Lewiston said in a hushed tone. "Sam, we have no other options here. We're running out of time and Kieran is gaining power. If we don't find Jon, we are all dead. Or worse..."

"What could be worse than death?" Lucille asked.

"We could be stuck in this city," said Lewiston. "A city ruled by Kieran and his lunatic ideas."

"You're right," Sam agreed. "That is worse."

The bald man turned to his right. They faced a building that had once been an apartment complex. The man walked up the steps and opened the door for his three guests. His smile, though innocent, still creeped out Sam as they walked inside.

Once they had entered, the bald man took the lead, guiding them to the back of the room. The place reminded Lucille of a haunted house she had visited. The eerie fear of not knowing what came next. The panic of knowing there was no way out. If they were ambushed, they would have to race to the front of the building.

Lewiston wondered about the choice in décor. Not that he was much of a home decorator, but the place did give off weird vibes. He didn't like the fact that the hallways were so narrow, or that the light seemed to flicker as they made their way to the back.

"Only a few doors down and we'll be there," said the man. "He's waiting for you."

As they continued to follow, and as the man opened the door, Sam was the first to see him. At the side of the room sat a man with a dark complexion, leaning forward, awaiting their arrival. Sam was thankful that the man didn't show the same smile. Instead, the man actually frowned, as if his guests were late and they were the ones to blame.

"I still don't get why you do that," said Jon. "Probably scared these people half to death with that weird look on your face."

Elias laughed. "Couldn't help it," he said. "And look at this place. I'm sure they already thought they were being led to their deaths. It's like a haunted house here."

Lucille let out a sigh of relief. "Thank God," she said.

"I thought the same when you guys captured me," said Jon. "Funny how things work out."

"How'd you know to get us?" asked Sam. "I thought we'd be the last people you'd want to run into again."

"I thought the same," said Jon. "Until the spirit said otherwise."

The group stared at Jon for a second, then looked around to make sure there wasn't some ghost they were supposed to see. When they realized there wasn't, and that Jon was, in fact, talking about a spirit, they remained quiet. All except for Lewiston.

"When you escaped, you said a few phrases that froze us in our place." He took a step forward. "What were they?"

"The phrases?" asked Jon. "They're scriptures."

"Scriptures?" asked Lewiston.

"Yes," said Jon. "You know? Bible verses? From the bible?"

"Of all my reading, I suppose that book must've gotten past me," said Lewiston. "But that doesn't make sense. How could a few phrases stop us from going after you?"

"Seeing that you are here now makes me think they haven't," said Jon, rising from the chair. "But to tell you the truth, they shouldn't have. They usually don't if a person just says them aloud. But if they're impacted by the spirit, and if it carries out His will, they will do what they are meant to do."

Lewiston understood. "That must be what Kieran is afraid of. He knows you know those...what are they again?"

"Scriptures," said Jon, agitated that he had to repeat himself. "Just call it the Word."

"Right," said Lewiston. "He's afraid because you know the Word and he doesn't. That's why he wanted to capture you. To get you to use the Word for his benefit."

"And I'm guessing his benefit doesn't serve us well," said Jon.

Sam shook his head. "But I don't get it. You didn't come all this way to use the Word, or to save Albion."

Jon turned to face him. He stood a foot taller than Sam. The Albion citizen, feeling a bit intimidated, took a step back.

"What I'm trying to ask is...why are you here?"

Jon sighed and turned around. As he did, a boy entered from another room. The boy waved. The group, now understanding, waved back.

"We have to get him home," said Jon. "We also have to save this city."

# CHAPTER 100

Kieran couldn't move. He tried to turn left or right, but nothing happened. He also could no longer see the ghoulish man who had stood before him. All he could see were those surrounding him. The thugs. The misfits. And yet, they stood still. No longer taunting, but holding solemn expressions. Kieran didn't know why.

He tried to run. To flee. But he couldn't. He felt paralyzed but he wasn't. He then heard a familiar voice but it came from within. Worse yet, it came from his mind.

"Keep struggling," said the voice. "It will do you no good. Funny, isn't it? The thirst for power. The desire to have more than you can handle. And where has that led you?"

Kieran couldn't understand why he couldn't move. Why he was hearing the voice so clearly whereas moments before it had seemed muffled.

"It's no use, Kieran," said the voice. "You can't move because you no longer have control of this vessel."

"If I don't have control, then how am I here?" he asked. "And why is it that I hear you clearer than I did moments before?"

"Because I'm here, Kieran. With you. In this mortal body of yours," said the voice. "You wanted power, didn't you? Well, I am that which you seek."

"No," said Kieran, unable to understand why this was happening. "I wanted to help you. To help the city. To help—"

"Yourself?" interrupted the voice. "Yes, Kieran. I know your schemes. Your plan and your group who abandoned you. Did you believe I was fooled? That I couldn't figure out what you were up to?"

"You're mistaken," said Kieran.

"Am I a liar?" asked the voice. "Search your words. Remember your actions. Who has lied to whom? If you search deep enough, long enough, hard enough, you'll realize the only person telling the truth is me."

It was then that Kieran felt his body shift. He was walking but not on his own. He still wasn't able to control his movements. No, it was the voice. The man who had once stood before him and who was now in control of his body.

"It appears your body agrees with me," said the voice. "And now I will rule the city as a man. Though, I think we both know I am more than that."

"You can't," demanded Kieran. "This is still my body. My mind. I control what it does. I have a say over where I go and what I do."

He could hear the voice laughing. It echoed in his mind. For the first time in a long while, Kieran was afraid. The man and his ghouls had intimidated him but now, at the moment when he should have left, he couldn't. He was helpless. He was no longer in control of anything.

"You should have left, Kieran," said the voice. "You couldn't possibly understand the power you seek. But I do. I can, because I am power. And though your pompous plan to take over the city has failed, you aren't without a good idea."

Kieran didn't speak. Couldn't speak. Fear gripped him. He was helpless. All he could do was listen.

"Oh, Kieran, this is no fun," said the voice. "Where is that witty banter? That suave genius of yours that has rescued you so many times in the past?"

Kieran would have cried if he were still in control. He felt like a kid who had lost his parents. Unable to fend for himself. Unable to control what was.

"So be it," said the voice, disappointed in his host's hospitality. "I suppose I should at least let you know what idea of yours I found best. It would be rude to take credit where credit is due."

Kieran could feel the voice now. Moving around in his mind. Roaming the very cortex of his brain as if pacing around. He became worried, unknowing what would come next.

"The four cities surrounding Albion. I have no use for them," said the voice. "And they do not know this city's power. If they did, they would have wiped us off the map. Instead, they retreat to their cozy homes. Hidden away from the truth. Knowing that if they came to my city, I would eat them whole and leave nothing behind."

The very tone made Kieran cower. If he could cower in his own mind. Yet the voice continued.

"But today is a new day. A promising day. A day in which fear, chaos, and violence may rule. A day in which the mighty Kieran," the voice broke into laughter, "may show the world a newfound Albion. A city without limits and boundless potential."

"You wo-won't win," Kieran sputtered. "You c-can't."

He couldn't see the voice but felt something come close. An eerie sensation came within inches of his soul.

"You threaten me?" asked the voice. "You think you can take back what's no longer yours?"

"Not me," Kieran whispered. "But Jon? He can stop you."

A booming laugh echoed again in Kieran's mind, this time causing pain. This time causing Kieran's mind to ache as if it had been hit by a bat.

"You really are entertaining, Kieran, that much I must admit." The voice was quiet for a moment before it spoke again. "I don't know Jon, and I don't know whom he brought along. So you are right in that I am at a disadvantage. But you forget that he is in my city. Under my rule. No one escapes Albion. I have ruled this city for centuries. Any person that manages to escape my grip loses his soul."

"He won't let you," croaked Kieran. "He will beat you."

"Oh, he will try," said the voice. "But remember, Kieran. You once thought so little of me. Believed that you, in your infinite wisdom, might best the city. Look where that has landed you. Now you have a front-row seat to destruction. And who knows? You may witness, from my eyes, the very evil you overlooked. The very chaos you still fear and know."

Kieran shuddered at the thought as the voice continued laughing. The sound grew louder. Kieran hoped to God that Jon would win. He hoped, for his own sake, that Jon wouldn't let the voice take over any of the four cities.

# CHAPTER 101

They crossed the road. No citizens were in sight. There was no Kieran to be found. It wasn't that they were looking for a fight but they knew it was now or never. Each of them knew that the fight for Albion was now. They didn't know what Kieran was up to but they knew they couldn't hide in a building. That wasn't how this city worked. That wasn't how evil worked.

"What exactly are we up against?" asked Sam. "Kieran is bad news but he's siphoned power from this city. I can only imagine how he plans to use it."

"No one has answers, Sam," said Jon. Sam still wondered how Jon knew his name. "We confront him and let the spirit take over from there, right?" Jon asked, looking at the boy.

The boy, who had remained silent, nodded.

"It's not magic and it's not luck," said Jon, leading the group to the next street. "What brought us here can't be explained but it is on our side."

"Can it be exploited?" asked Lewiston.

"No," Jon said sternly. "Though I wish it could."

"What is it?" asked Lucille.

The rest of the group remained silent. It was the question on everyone's mind. Jon didn't appear any different from them, and they didn't know how he could defeat a person who was backed by the city's power. They wanted answers.

"You can't tell me a judge, a kid, and our group were all lured here for some destined plan," Lucille continued.

Jon smiled. "You'd be surprised what the spirit can do."

"So it's this *spirit,*" said Lucille. "Figures. The world's going to hell and this *spirit* will save us."

"Not this spirit," Jon corrected. "The spirit. As in, nothing else like it."

"As in, we better hope to God that it doesn't get us killed," Lucille retorted.

"The spirit and God go hand-in-hand," Jon said with a smile. "So you're not wrong."

He looked both ways before crossing, as if a car might come. But he wasn't on the lookout for a car. He felt Kieran's presence. He just didn't know where the man was. The air held a heaviness that let him know they were close.

"But you'll make sure we'll win?" asked Elias, doubting Jon's plan. "Because all I have is a bat."

"You're wrong," said Jon. "You have more to offer than you know. All of you. This wasn't placed on me, or you, or the boy. It was put on all of us. Remember that."

Jon had been facing the group while Sam made out the street sign behind him: Sentry Lane. Jon could sense his fear. He knew, as well as Sam did, that the very fabric of evil sat on this street.

"Sam," Jon said calmly. "You know this street better than any of us do. The spirit led me here. You'll have to lead us the rest of the way."

Sam felt himself turn pale. He did not want to be back here. Yet, a part of him knew he would. His brother. This was the last place Sam had seen him. This was the last confirmation he had received. His brother was alive but no longer the brother he knew. Sam couldn't rescue him. He could only hope that saving Albion would bring back his brother.

"Okay," he said, taking a deep breath. "Though I'm not sure what you're expecting.

"I suppose we'll just have to look and see," said Jon.

He held out his hand toward the boy. Though Monty was nine, his maturity made him seem older. Wiser. Calmer in the face of danger. Yet at this moment, faced with the reality of evil and chaos, Jon was reminded of how young Monty really was. The very fears that played on every boy's mind. This was no different.

Bedtime stories were fictitious. There were no monsters under your bed—only dirty clothes and worn socks. Your closet didn't contain monsters—just school clothes and scuffed-up shoes. The monsters in Albion, however, were real. Crazed thugs and chaotic acts of violence took place daily. In Albion, the monsters were up close and personal.

Monty held on tight as they followed Sam. Lewiston looked around, observing what made this street so prevalent. There were no lights yet plenty of life. Citizens he hadn't seen before cowered behind dumpsters, hissing and throwing trash. A man to his right banged away on a trash can. A woman crossed the group's path, giggling to herself. Creeping him out and causing him to wonder if this was such a good idea.

Sam continued, glad he was not alone. Glad that Jon was by his side. He didn't know much about the man but he could sense his presence. Jon remained calm and at peace despite the very real situation they were in. Sam wanted to believe that Jon knew what was he was doing. He hoped Jon was all they had made him out to be.

Lucille remained quiet. Wishing Kieran wasn't such a coward. Hoping she would be able to take him down. She wanted to make him pay for leaving her to die. The group had been created to have each other's back. She had made peace with Kieran joining the group for that simple principle.

No one would get left behind.

Clearly, he had other ideas and more important lives to save. She wanted revenge. And though fear should have been pumping through her veins, she felt only rage. Lucille knew she would need it for what came next.

When Sam stopped, the group looked ahead. No one could see anything, yet silence had replaced the scurrying around Sentry Lane. Something was wrong. Both Sam and Jon could feel it.

"Why'd we stop?" asked Lewiston.

A strange laugh came from behind them. It echoed off the buildings and grew louder as the group wheeled around. They noticed a man standing by himself.

"It looks like you've found me," said the man. "And you've brought the boy."

"Kieran," said Jon. "You seem…out of sorts."

No one knew what Jon meant until the man stepped forward. Kieran now seemed a bit crazed, with eyes that had sunken to the back of his skull and a smile that revealed teeth more yellow than white. No longer was he the neat, tidy man from Durrington. He was a true citizen of Albion. A true citizen of complete and utter chaos.

# CHAPTER 102

Sosa returned home. The media speculated as best it could about the overnight hospitalization of Durrington's favorite athlete. Some speculated the loss of his son had taken its toll, driving the star to try taking his own life. Yet no one knew what had taken place. No interviews were given. And though no answers were provided, Sosa was happy his wife stuck by his side. Shielding him from the reporters. Keeping the doors locked to everyone, even family. The General Manager of Sosa's team reached out but Shirley had already disconnected the phone.

"Do you think this is too much?" Sosa asked his wife. "Not for them, of course, but for you. Isn't this becoming too big a burden?"

Shirley smiled. Knowing her husband cared. Also knowing how the media fed on this. And though she knew the truth, she knew better than to feed the frenzy. They would know the truth soon enough.

"They'll find out either way," said Shirley. "And when they do, all hell will break loose. I'm not ready for that kind of attention just yet."

"I know," Sosa said, his head bowed in shame. "It won't be easy, and it's my fault. I just know we can't live in the shadows forever. Not like I have." He held her hand. "And I've kept you in the shadows far too long."

She smiled yet pulled back. The sting of betrayal was fresh on her mind and the loss of her son was still taking its toll. She forgave Sosa but she couldn't shake the hurt. It was deep, like a thorn that only sank deeper as the truth came to mind.

"You're right," she said, getting up to retrieve something from the kitchen. "But that's what makes us better, right? We learn from our mistakes.

We make better choices. That's what we're meant to do. That's what Monty would have wanted."

At hearing his dead son's name, Sosa did his best to hold it together. To not shed any more tears. But that wasn't him. He was no longer the stone that nothing could penetrate. He was in pain, unable to get over the loss. Shirley, seeing his hurt expression, brought some popcorn back with her.

"You're hurt," she said, "and so am I. That's nothing to be ashamed of."

Sosa wanted to reach out for his wife. To hold her. To let her touch become his comfort. But he couldn't. Something was still there. A defense mechanism that wouldn't let him show who he really was. How much his heart had suffered.

He smiled. This time was the one who got up and went to the kitchen. As he looked around, he feared what was not there. Ashamed, he returned to the sofa with his wife. His head was still bowed. He had no words left to say.

"I had them take it away," said Shirley. She hadn't known how her husband would react. "I thought it best to start fresh. To come clean with what's really going on."

"You're right," Sosa said, to Shirley's surprise. "It didn't help. It never helped." He turned to face his wife. "I don't know when this happened or how. Maybe since we lost Monty. Maybe even before that."

"The drinking?" asked Shirley. "I don't recall you ever drinking this much."

Sosa, feeling more shame, faced the other way. Looking at the pictures of their family. Noticing his son's bright smile and innocent eyes. He knew that if he was going to get over this, he would have to tell the truth. He would have to tell his wife why Monty's loss meant so much to him.

"When he was born and I couldn't be there for you, I knew I'd let you down," said Sosa. "And every night when I was on the road, and not with you, I kept feeling as if I was failing. As if I wasn't the father I was supposed to be. And when the…"

He didn't want to admit it. He wanted to make the affair an accident. But they knew better. He knew better. "When I came to Emilia, there was no longer an opinion on the matter. I knew I failed. I knew I wasn't the father I was meant to be."

Shirley didn't turn away. She knew how hard it was for him to admit it and how much harder it would be if she didn't let him explain. She knew healing didn't come from avoiding pain. She also knew this would cause her a great deal more pain. Yet, she listened patiently, waiting for Samson to finish.

"So," he said, rubbing his chin nervously, "I turned to him. I made Monty my only focus. And if that meant facing you—lying to you—I was going to do it. For his sake. Because I knew that if he didn't have a father, I wouldn't have a reason to live. I knew once you found out about the affair, you would leave me. I was afraid you'd find out, Shirley. I just...I couldn't let that happen."

It took everything for Shirley to not leave. To stay. To hear the admittance of a man she once thought the world of. A man she was proud to call her husband. It was like her world was crashing around her. And at the center, its cause was Samson. Yet an eerie strength kept her still. Allowing her to endure. Allowing her to think and hear him clearly without letting her feelings of betrayal get the best of her.

Samson felt ashamed but also more than that. He was embarrassed. As a man. As a husband. As a father. He had failed on all fronts. Even as a role model to those who looked up to him. He wasn't the man he thought he was. Time and truth revealed his deepest hurts and his foolish mistakes. Yet, he noticed she was still there. By his side. Sitting on the sofa, listening patiently as he told all.

"When he passed, nothing else seemed to matter," he said. "You left to see your sister—which I had no problem with. I wanted to be alone. Needed to be alone, to gather my thoughts and figure out what I'd do next. That's when I started." He looked up, feeling as if a weight had lifted. Feeling as if he had just enough courage to face his wife. "That's when I decided none of this was worth living for."

Tears streamed down Shirley's face, yet she held her solemn expression. She felt everything. His words. His hurt. Her betrayal. Her loss. Everything. Yet she knew there was more. She knew Samson wasn't finished.

"I don't know what I have left, Shirley," he said. "But I know the dream I had last night was enough. Real enough for me to want more. Real enough for me to realize it's not about what I've lost but about what I have left to give and who I have something to give to."

He wanted to reach for her hand but thought better. This wasn't the time and he knew it. Now was the time to talk. Now was the time to tell the truth.

"I don't know if I'll ever be okay with what happened," he said. "I know that now. Before, I thought I'd shrug it off. As if losing Monty could be a motivator or career-changer. But I was wrong. I'm going to feel this loss for as long as I live. So if this is too much—if I am too much for what you had planned—I will understand. You deserve better than me."

Shirley wiped the tears from her eyes. Still feeling pain. Anger. The desire to mourn her loss. Yet she faced her husband. Thankful to finally hear the truth. Hopeful that something good could still come from this.

"I'll be called a fool, you know. For sticking with you." Sosa felt the sting of her words, yet when he looked up, he noticed her smile. It was a faint smile but one he recognized. "It will be okay, Sammy. Not because nothing bad will ever happen to us. Not because we are who we are. But because I care. You care. And more importantly, God cares. I'm not going to say everything happens for a reason. That's too simple. But we can still make the best of this." She held out her hand. Sosa took it.

As she straightened up, Shirley looked her husband in the eyes. "We can still make Monty proud."

# CHAPTER 103

The group looked at Jon. No one knew what to do. None of them wanted to step forward except Lucille, but Lewiston held her back. Reassuring her that this wasn't the time. They could tell this wasn't the same Kieran they knew.

Jon let go of the boy's hand and stepped forward, facing Kieran with a blank expression. He had changed, and though Jon couldn't explain the change in his former kidnapper, the spirit revealed who was there. Kieran was only the mask hiding the true evil within.

"You call this your city but all I see is blood and violence," said Jon. "Maybe you missed your calling."

Kieran smiled. "Your opinion matters little, Jonathan."

"I think it best to listen," said Jon. "Because as you parade around this city—inciting chaos and bringing death—the citizens of Albion continue to suffer. There are those who wish to escape. Those whom you refuse to let go. And all of this for what? Power? Inequality? What's the purpose behind this?"

Jon spoke to the man as if evil didn't exist. As if the man couldn't call one of his henchmen to take him out. The very presence residing in Kieran wasn't a mere ghost. He was more than that. He was evil incarnate. The very representation of everything that was wrong with Albion. Jon knew that if he didn't take a stand now, the city would be lost. And though he didn't feel qualified to call out such evil, he didn't have much of a choice. The spirit had led him this far. The spirit would have to lead him back.

"You think little of this city, Jon," said the man in Kieran's body. "We both know it. And here you come. Rescuing a lost child and rebellious adults. For what, Mr. Buckley? What is your cause?"

"I have none," answered Jon. "In fact, if it were up to me, I'd still be sitting on my couch, drinking and watching the day pass by. Waving to neighbors I dislike and staying away from the people of Brevington as a whole." Jon spread his arms wide. "I didn't want any of this."

He looked around, noticing the lost souls of Sentry Lane. They no longer seemed menacing. In this light—under the rule of the person controlling Kieran—Jon could see they were victims, not the problem. They didn't want to be there. But what choice did they have? They were citizens of Albion. They weren't allowed to escape.

"Awful long way to travel for a man who wanted nothing more than a drink," said the man. "Yet you still cause a fuss in my city. For that, I should have—"

"Hold on now," Jon interrupted. "As I said, this wasn't my choice. This wasn't my idea. But you know whose idea it was?" He held up a picture of his friend, Mr. Barrister. No one in the group knew the man. Neither did the man before them.

"It's because of him," said Jon. "A man who could have lived. A man who chose another instead of himself. His name was Charles Barrister and he was my friend."

The man laughed so loud that the citizens laughed along with him. Not knowing what was so funny, yet not risking disobedience of the man's power. The rest of the group watched as Jon remained still. There was a calmness to him. He wasn't afraid and the group could sense that. The group was grateful they had found the right man.

"Your friend was a good person, I am sure," said the voice. "But how did his death bring you here?"

"It didn't," said Jon, puzzling the man before him. "His death left me with a promise. A promise I'm now glad I agreed to keep. A promise Mr. Barrister knew I could fulfill. And though it meant saving a life, I knew it would get me off the couch and out of my city."

"And my city?" questioned the man. "You sought a life to save from Albion? Quite foolish, Jon. Seeing that they belong to me."

Jon took another step forward. "They belong to you?" Jon pointed at the man. "As what? Your slaves? Your minions? Your souls to control?"

The man smiled but didn't speak. Instead, he looked Jon in the eyes, as if searching for something. Something missing. Something he could recognize in any other man. Yet it wasn't there.

"You don't fear my city, do you?" asked the man. "Yet I can see much has happened to you since your arrival."

"I wouldn't say Albion is known for its hospitality," said Jon. "But yes, a few hiccups occurred here and there."

"And the people of Albion?" questioned the man. "Have none suffered death at your hand?"

"They have," said Jon. His tone held no apology. He stared the man down until they locked eyes. "There are a few in this city still under your influence. I think it's safe to say they didn't choose wisely."

"And yet you are here to save them?" The man laughed. "Jon, you are a complicated soul. You vow to save what you destroy, and take penance as if you are controlled by the worst kind of evil. Tell me, because I am curious, what makes you so sure you'll make it out alive?"

At this, Jon smiled. "I have no plans later," he said. "Nothing is guaranteed. Everyone dies eventually. But here is one thing I can promise. By the end of tonight, you will relinquish your hold on these people. So maybe I should give you some time to settle your arrangements."

The man, no longer amused, clenched his fists. "You threaten me, Jon Buckley?"

"No," said Jon. "I just speak for someone greater. Someone who's grown tired of your charades and your hurt. The violence you've inspired and the destruction you've caused. I think you know who that someone is. And more importantly, I think you know as well as I that once the spirit gets going, nothing can stop its will."

# CHAPTER 104

The man rushed Jon, anger fueling his rage, violence filling his mind. Kieran watched as everything took place. Unable to control his movements. A prisoner in his own mind. But he was surprised that Jon didn't seem the least bit worried. He watched his body grab for the Brevington savior. Jon stepped aside.

Kieran didn't know how, but as quickly as his body lunged for him, Mr. Buckley shifted to the side, stuck out his foot, and tripped him. Kieran felt his body collide with the ground and pain shot up his shoulder. He winced as only one trapped inside his own mind could, then watched as the corrupted spirit brought him back to his feet.

Kieran wanted to interfere. To stop what was taking place. Partially because he wanted free of this spirit but mostly because that fall had really hurt. And if Jon was as formidable as he appeared to be, Kieran was in for a world of pain.

Jon watched the man get up. Sensing Kieran was still inside. Knowing the evil controlling his movements was willing to take a beating. It wasn't his body, after all. He also noticed the smile creeping upon the man's face.

"You really do think I'm a fool," said Jon. "Kieran, I know you're in there. Would be nice to get some help, though I'm sure you're a bit occupied at the moment."

The man's smile widened. "He can't help you." The man stepped toward Jon. "You'll receive no aid in this fight."

"That's where you're wrong," said Jon. "Greater is he that is in you than he that is in the world."

The man, though attempting to attack again, remained still. He was unable to move. Kieran, watching this take place, took this opportunity to gain back control. He tried to move his leg. To his surprise, it did move. He took a few steps back, then lifted his hands to see how much control he had regained.

"I'm back!" Kieran said. "Thank you, Jon. You have no idea how..."

Jon watched patiently as Kieran collapsed to the ground. "You fool!" the man cried. "You thought a few words could free him? I'll own this vessel if it's the last thing I do!"

"I knew that seemed too easy," Sam whispered to Lucille.

Lucille, though still wanting to pound Kieran's face into the ground, knew this was a far worse punishment. She wouldn't wish this on her worst enemy. But she didn't know what to do. She felt they were there for a reason. To aid in this fight instead of being spectators.

"What do we do?" she asked, facing Lewiston. "There has to be something."

Lewiston, as if waking from a daze, blinked quickly. He thought but came up with no solution. He wanted to give an answer but didn't know what to say. He looked around as if hoping some clue would spark his genius mind. But it was to no avail. Lewiston closed his eyes for a moment, hoping the same spirit that had led them to Jon would lead him to an answer.

"Lucille," he said, his eyes now open. "Have you heard of the big three?"

"The big what?" asked Lucille.

"The big three," said Lewiston. "I'm not sure that's the technical term for them but they were the greatest warriors in King David's army: Josheb, Eleazar, and Shammah."

Sam, hoping once again that his friend hadn't lost his mind, came to Lewiston's side. He rested his hand lightly on Lewiston's shoulder.

"You okay, buddy?" Sam asked. "Cause you're not making a lot of sense."

"For Christ's sake, it's in the bible," said Lewiston.

"You mean the book you've never read?" remarked Lucille. "At least that's what you said only moments ago."

"I know, I know," said Lewiston. "It's this spirit thing."

"*The* spirit," corrected Sam.

"Whatever. You had a question and I think that's our answer," said Lewiston. "We are the big three. Fighting for a king greater than this earth. I know it sounds odd. But we're supposed to help. It's not just Jon fighting for this city. We're in this, too."

"So," said Lucille, "what do we do?"

"Hard to say," said Lewiston. "Kieran is trapped in his own body and the evil that corrupts him can jump from one host to the other."

"Except for us," said Sam, "because of the spirit."

"Exactly," Lewiston said, "so we have to pin him down."

"Easier said than done," said Lucille. "He'll see us coming a mile away."

"Unless we distract him."

The words came from the boy. He had been listening the whole time. Hoping they would come up with a plan, yet realizing it wasn't just them who were there for a reason. Though he was afraid, he wanted to help. Jon had risked his life to rescue him. He wanted to return the favor.

"What are you proposing?" asked Lewiston.

"Well," said the boy, "that man knows I'm the reason why Jon is here. If I go out there and give myself up, he'll go straight for me."

"Because if he gets you, then Jon fails," Sam said. "But wait. Isn't that a little risky?"

"Only if we don't work together."

This time, it was Elias who spoke up.

"This isn't going to be easy," said the judge, "but we have to believe."

"Believe in what?" asked the boy.

Elias smiled. "In the spirit. Look, I've already lost a friend to this city. I'm not losing anyone else. If we do this, we have to believe it will work. No doubting yourself. No fearing the worst. We have to be all in. Do you guys agree?"

Everyone nodded. They were going to help Jon, whether he wanted their help or not. All of them, reinvigorated by the spirit, waited for the opportune moment. Monty, as if on cue, stepped up to Jon's side.

The man noticed him and lunged forward. As the Brevington savior dodged out of the way, he realized he wasn't the target. The man took the boy, holding him hostage. Jon felt a wave of panic take over.

# CHAPTER 105

Emilia sat in her hotel room. No family to see. No friends to comfort her. Thankfully, she still had access to her and Elias's shared debit account. She found no reason to stay in Durrington now that Shirley wanted nothing to do with her. She also knew she couldn't show her face back in Brevington.

She now stayed in Jameson. Though not a citizen or accustomed to the city's peculiar ways, she took it upon herself to get a drink. The bar, located on the first floor of the Franklin Jameson Hotel, would be her first stop. While there, she purchased one glass of expensive wine after another until the bill resembled the year she graduated from high school. From there, at the suggestion of the bartender, she headed back to her room.

The hotel was friendly but any woman under duress, especially at the bar, could be seen as a target. And though the bartender was not at hand to speak on her situation, he knew a sad soul when he saw one. Plus, he didn't want to fend off predators who were more drunk than she was. That would cause a situation he simply wasn't willing to handle.

Emilia, stumbling and watching her fingers slide off the elevator button, thought about her honeymoon, when Elias had taken her to a hotel in Durrington. The hotel, in all of its architectural feats, resembled a swan quietly landing on a pond. She didn't know why the thought arose, yet she recalled the gallant spectacle.

*"Who mathes bildngs ly tha?"* she asked, as another hotel guest waited alongside her.

The man, knowing better than to speak, coughed. They waited in silence, though the man could see her waiting impatiently for his answer. Sensing that an answer would not be given, Emilia stuck out her tongue and turned, entering the elevator as the gentleman beside her decided to wait for the next one.

*"Suh yorselth,"* she said, pressing the button to the floor on which she thought she was staying. A moment later, she realized she had hit the wrong button. She tried to press another only to realize she had pressed the button for the floor that was her favorite number and not the floor where she was residing.

An elevator ride that should have taken less than a minute turned into half an hour as the befuddled Emilia sat in the corner. When it next opened, she dashed out, heels in hand. Surprisingly, the floor seemed familiar. As she ran down the hallway with worried guests walking around her, she came to a door that seemed familiar.

Using her card to get in, she realized that the door was already unlocked, though the couple inside, who were watching a pleasant movie, seemed less familiar as she was shooed back into the hall.

Another five minutes later, she had made it to her room. The adventure, as treacherous and enduring as it was, had caused her to sober up. She remembered Elias divorcing her and Shirley kicking her to the curb. It was enough to cause Emilia to drink further. She raided the mini-bar, which contained a few cartons of wine.

She wasn't much of a fan, seeing that a carton would not have the same potency as a more fervent, bottled wine. However, she hoped two or three would be as effective. Emilia poured carton after carton, watching some of it land in her mouth while some splashed on the floor.

*"Oh fell,"* she slurred, knowing there was enough in the shared account to cover the damages.

Strangely enough, the more she drank, the more she thought about how much was in the debit account. It wasn't until she threw the glass across the room that she realized there was probably, at most, fifty dollars' worth of damage.

Believing she could do better, she stood, grabbed the hotel chair beside her, and picked it up. Quickly realizing how heavy it was, Emilia chucked it with all of her might. She watched it soar across the room. To her surprise, it hit the window to her sixth-floor hotel suite, causing a crack down the middle.

Bringing her hand to her face, forgetting she had broken the glass that contained her drink, Emilia headed back to the mini-bar. This next feat would take more liquid courage and she wasn't quite in the mood to give up just yet.

It didn't take long for her to find four more mini-bottles: two whiskeys and two bourbons. Each cost twenty dollars. This brought her damage to the apartment to around three hundred and eighty dollars—the cracked glass totaling two hundred and fifty or so, because she knew a guy.

As she downed the mini-bottles, she remained sitting on the floor, thinking of something more daring. Hoping this next feat would drain the account. She wanted this to cause Elias more pain than he'd caused her, as she knew she wasn't going to foot the bill.

She got to her feet and climbed on top of the bed. She jumped for a while, knowing that the key to this would be momentum. She thought of Shirley and Sosa. Of Elias and her home. Of the boy the Barnetts had lost and the daughter she could never have. The sobering effect was coming back to her. It was then that she lost interest and stopped jumping. Now she sat at the edge of her bed.

It was three in the morning. No other guests were up, as far as she could tell. But her mind raced, going to and fro from one loss to another. It was then that she noticed, out of the corner of her eye, a bottle of whiskey right next to the mini-bar. She had missed it while searching for more to drink. Not long after this discovery, she made a decision. Emilia popped the cork, took a long drink, jumped back on the bed, and jumped full force through the hotel window.

# CHAPTER 106

Shirley's sister came over. She was worried about Shirley's choice to stay with Sosa and she stared holes through the man whenever they crossed paths. He thought better of it. Knowing that if he uttered even a word, she would give him a piece of her mind and more. He knew how close Shirley and her sister were, and he knew what he had done. He knew that she, like Shirley, had every right to be mad at him. He decided to stay upstairs, giving Shirley's sister a chance to talk some sense into her younger sister.

"You need help getting him out?" she stated more than asked. "I know people who can help."

Shirley laughed. "No, sis, I don't think that'll be necessary." She was folding clothes on the living room couch. Her sister, refusing to help, fumed. Watching her sister pretend that everything was okay. Shirley could tell her sister was upset. She also knew that if she didn't say something, her sister would do something dumb.

"Look," Shirley said, "we've been through a lot this year. We both know that."

"You're right, *I* do," said her sister. "But it doesn't seem like you do. You going through a lot doesn't excuse his actions. If Dad were still here, he would have skinned that boy alive!"

"God rest his soul," Shirley said, continuing to fold clothes. "I'm not saying I excuse his behavior. Sis, I'm not even saying I'm okay with everything or even how it went down. My mind still wonders why."

"You know why," her sister said. "Because you deserve better. And men never appreciate a good woman. They never know what they have until it's gone."

Shirley smiled. "Says the woman who abhors the idea of marriage."

Her sister snorted. "Men are pigs." She kicked over a stack of Sosa's shirts. "Why would I subject myself to being underappreciated?"

Shirley took notice of the knocked-over stack of shirts and smacked her sister's leg. Her sister winced in pain and took her leg out of Shirley's reach so it wouldn't happen again.

"Some men don't," Shirley said, "but others do. Just because you've run into your string of bad luck doesn't make all men pigs."

Her sister rubbed her bruising leg. "Tell me, sis, what makes what he did different from any other man caught in the same situation?"

"He learned from his mistake," answered Shirley, quicker than her sister would have liked. "It was wrong but who can say they're perfect?"

"Sis, you're missing the point." Her sister walked over to counter. "Men are like fruit," she said, holding up an apple. "They look great, and God, they're good for you, but if you keep them too long, they get ripe. You get to see what's really inside."

Shirley wondered where her sister came up with such examples. She wanted to tell her sister what love was like. How it changed a person, and how much different it was from lust. Shirley knew love was a choice. That it required forgiveness even in the face of hurt. She knew its power to heal a person despite the pain and heartache it might cause. Love was always one in her book.

But she knew her sister wouldn't understand. She had never been in love. Had never appreciated a person, other than herself, past the flaws and mistakes that person made. Shirley was the closest thing her sister had come to loving, but only as much as an older sister could. Had they not been related, Shirley wondered if they would even be friends.

"You wouldn't understand," Shirley said. "It's not that I forgive him. But the reason *why* I forgive him is what matters most."

"Then explain it," her sister demanded. "Explain why you would choose to forgive someone who purposely stabbed you in the back. Who betrayed you. Who did something he knew would hurt you."

"Simple," said Shirley, putting one of her favorite blouses on a hanger. "He was weak."

Her sister stood, eyes wide open, wondering what was going through Shirley's mind. Weak was something she associated with wimpiness. Being feeble-minded. Something only a child would admit to in times of being bullied or getting punished.

"Weak?" she said incredulously. "How can a man, who claims to be the head of the household, be weak? Did he even know what he was getting into when he proposed to you?"

"Of course he did," Shirley said defensively. "But that doesn't mean we don't have our moments of weakness."

"In that case, we all should have moments of weakness," her sister said. "But we don't. You know why? Because we have morals!"

"You're right," said Shirley. "But think about what you would do if every man hung on your every word. Desiring you day in and day out. Approaching you in complete adoration of you, simply because of who you are."

"You think that's what his life is like," her sister scoffed. "He's an athlete, sis. He might get attention but—"

"But what?" Shirley gently interrupted. "Don't they have fans? Don't they get endorsements just for shooting a ball into a hoop?"

"Well, yeah, but that's not an excuse for lost self-control," her sister said. "They are not above the law of morality."

"You're right. They aren't," Shirley said. "But it would be tempting. Just think about it. Having the man of your dreams approach you, just because you're you. But on a nightly basis. Yes, you might fight off your pursuers at first but do you really think you could fight them off the rest of your life?"

"Of course I could," her sister said quietly. Her confidence was gone. "It would be hard but I'd find a way."

"And he did," Shirley said. "Until he didn't. Until he had a moment of weakness. Forget about who it was with. Forget that he's married to me. If this happened to any of your friends, do you really think you'd be that surprised?"

"No, but that's them," her sister said. "And you're his wife."

"Sis, I've seen men and women do worse for less," Shirley said. "But this isn't about him. Nor is it about what he did. I'm being selfish on this one."

"How so?" her sister asked.

"Because I choose who I forgive and who I don't," Shirley said. "And I'm not going to let my heart be wrecked because of him. I choose to remain in control of my actions no matter how life tries to bring me down."

# CHAPTER 107

Jon looked back to see that the rest of his group had left. He was alone. He knew he had failed. That was when he realized the citizens surrounding them had closed in. Jon, Monty, and the man were the only ones left. There was no backup.

More importantly, there was nothing left for Jon to do. The man had the kid. Kieran couldn't regain control of his body. And Jon knew any sudden movements could result in Monty's death. He wouldn't let that happen. He wouldn't be the reason for the boy's death.

"Okay," Jon said. "You have the boy."

"Very observant, Mr. Buckley," said the man. "And the boy? How could someone so insignificant mean so..."

The man's words trailed off. As if he understood. The man no longer recognized his captive as a boy but as *the* boy. The one who was supposed to be dead. The one who had been kidnapped and brought to his city.

"Oh, Jon," the man said. "You came all this way for this?" He held out Monty by his collar. "The Durrington boy of some famed basketball player?"

The man laughed wildly. Jon could only watch. Wishing he had made this trip alone. Realizing that no one would be in danger if he had. But then again, he never would have found Kieran. He recalled the spirit guiding Sam, not him. The spirit brought Monty, Elias, Lucille, Sam, and Lewiston to his aid. He hadn't recruited them. He hadn't cried out for any help in this venture.

He couldn't have prevented this from happening because it was what the spirit willed. The spirit called for his capture, and it happened. The spirit called these lost souls to his aid, and no argument could have convinced them otherwise.

After doing some thinking, Jon began to smile. He didn't know what would come next. But that was the best part. It wasn't on him to get the boy back, just like it wasn't on him to provide a proper escape when Kieran had first captured him. It was up to the spirit.

The man, seeing Jon's amusement, frowned. He snatched the boy back, pulling him in close so that Jon wouldn't try anything funny.

"I don't see what has you so happy," the man said. "You've lost, Jonathan C. Buckley. There's no way out this time."

The man reached into his pocket and pulled out a knife, which he held to Monty's neck. Jon, though a bit worried, didn't change his expression. A smile remained. The man's temper began to rise.

"You don't think I'll do it, do you?" the man asked. "Oh, Jon. This is Albion. My home. My city. What I say goes. You know this."

"You're right," Jon said. "I do know this. I also know you're a murderer, and the very violence you cause has disastrous effects."

"It does." The man smiled. "And nothing within these walls can prevent such acts from taking place."

Jon rubbed his chin. "I don't think you see the flaw in your plan."

"Oh?" asked the man. "And what might that be?"

"Well, we are in Albion but those from other cities are here, too," said Jon. "Which means we do not succumb to the same rules. Your laws are lawful only to your citizens."

The man, puzzled by Jon's remarks, refused to waver. He pressed the knife to the boy's neck. Jon held up a hand.

"Now hold on," he said, "I mean no offense by this. We are in your home, after all. Albion is yours along with those who live in it. All I am saying is that the same rules that govern your city do not govern us."

"If you are in my city, then you will obey my rules!" the man spat. "Those who refuse will lose that which they value most!"

"But that's the thing," said Jon. "You believe we value one thing above another. That life is the end-all-be-all for each of us. Yet how often do you see outsiders walk into your town? How often do you run into citizens of Jameson, or Germantown, or Brevington, who came here willingly? With a larger purpose in mind?"

"You're a fool," the man said. He didn't know what else to do. He followed Buckley's logic, yet he didn't like where it was going. "If I say you die, and you are in my city, that is what will be done."

"You're right," Jon said, his hands raised. He didn't want the man to think he had bested him. Not just yet. "We die if you say die. This is, after all, your city. But you forget one thing about me. About all of us. It's the one thing that makes us more dangerous than you."

The man hesitated. "What might that be?"

Jon smiled. "We're not afraid to give up what we value most. Nor are we afraid to try something stupid."

"Something like—"

Before the man could finish the thought, Monty ducked to the ground. As the man began to pull him up, Lucille kicked the knife from his hand. What the man hadn't noticed, in his attempt to retain the boy, was that the group had returned. In sync with their attacks. Led by the very spirit that had brought them there.

"NO!" the man yelled.

As he wheeled around, he noticed a balding man running toward him. Before the man could move, he had been speared to the ground. As the balding man rolled off of him, the man tried to scramble to his feet. That was when Lewiston, with all of his might, punched the man back to the ground.

"Hey," Lucille said. "I called first dibs."

Lewiston clutched his hand, wishing she—and not him—had punched the man. The group then huddled behind Jon. The boy was now by his side. Jon smiled as the man finally rose to his feet but the smile slowly faded when he realized someone was missing. Sam was no longer with the group.

# CHAPTER 108

He ran. Unsure of where to go. Not really understanding why he had left. Yet something pulled him. When the group attacked, he left. Thinking that fear, once again, had a hold on him. He felt like a coward. He felt unworthy of the group.

Yet, he was wrong. He wasn't afraid. He knew the man controlling Kieran would lose. He knew that with Jon, and the spirit, they would win. But they were missing one thing.

He ran down Sentry Lane. Searching left and right. *Where is it,* he thought. He didn't know what he was looking for, yet he felt something. Something other than the pulling motion. The spirit may have led him here but he would have to find the item.

He stopped at a dumpster. Climbing in. Disregarding the trash. Disregarding the fact that he, Sam Cowell, had climbed into a dumpster based on a hunch. He hoped the item he needed was there.

As he continued digging through the trash, throwing out items left and right, he heard footsteps. He stopped digging. He didn't need to know who it was. He was sure it was no one from his group. And as he awaited his certain fate, he noticed a woman peeking in.

A smile of recognition was on her face. Sam blinked. It was the woman who had helped nurse Lucille back to health. She held out a hand, which was clutching an item. Sam moved to exit the dumpster. When he climbed out, the woman gave him the item. He examined it for a moment before realizing what it was.

He looked up. The woman was still smiling. The boy who had been with her in the grocery store was still by her side. It was then that the boy let go of her hand and walked over to Sam. Without warning, the boy hugged Sam's leg. The mother, now tearing up, watched as her son, the one who trusted no one in Albion, had finally left her side. Sam patted the boy on the head.

"Thank you," Sam said, looking at the woman. "For everything."

The boy, now having let go of Sam's leg, returned to his mother and smiled. It was the first time Sam had seen anything but fear on the boy's face. The boy reminded Sam of himself at a younger age. Following his older brother around the city. Fearing for his life when he lost track of his brother.

Yet his brother always came back. By his side. Assuring him that everything would be okay. And Sam, with happiness in his eyes, would act as if there had never been a threat. As if his life was protected by his brother's hands. Hands big enough to make sure nothing else would get through.

He realized that was what the spirit was doing. Protecting him. Leading him to where he needed to be instead of where he wanted to go. And though he thought himself a coward, the spirit made him into the hero. The necessary key to defeating Kieran. Only then did he remember why he was there.

He quickly turned and headed back the way he had come. The woman and boy waved, though Sam didn't look back. Yet they weren't waving at the man. They were waving at the presence that surrounded him.

Hope filled the woman's eyes. Finally, they would be saved from the city that had brought so much chaos and violence into their lives.

# CHAPTER 109

Shirley's sister left. The house seemed back to normal. Yet there was anger and there was also doubt. Shirley knew she had the right to be mad at Sosa but she wouldn't give into it. She would fight her anger and frustration until she couldn't any longer.

Sosa felt everything but peace. He worried frequently that his wife would leave him. That he didn't deserve her. That she would realize she could do better. It didn't help that Monty was no longer in the picture. It was their son who had brought them together. In his mind, nothing kept them together except the hurt they shared.

They made pleasant conversation, yet they were afraid. Afraid words would break them apart. Afraid their feelings would overwhelm them. And though they feared hurting one another, neither realized what they had bottled up. They didn't realize what they kept in the dark would eventually come to light.

It took a few weeks until that exact thing happened. Shirley was washing dishes as Sosa shot around in the driveway. As she looked out the window, Shirley could see a neighbor staring. The man was looking at Sosa. For whatever reason, she believed he had bad intentions. It wasn't until the neighbor pulled out a phone and aimed it at her husband that she knew: The man was trying to exploit their circumstance.

She slammed down the plate and headed toward the driveway. As she approached the man who was snapping photos of her husband, she let everything out.

"Don't you think we've been through enough?" she questioned. "And yet here you are, our neighbors, snapping photos of a man who is trying to grieve in peace."

Sosa looked back to see what was happening. Dropping the basketball, he rushed over. He could tell from the shocked expression on the man's face that Shirley had scared him. What she said, Sosa didn't know. The man took a few steps back.

"I'm sorry," Sosa said. "It has been a rough time. Please excuse us."

Knowing better than to force his wife away from the situation, Sosa waited, hoping she would walk back with him. Hoping she would understand what he was saying and make the right choice. He knew this was what the media wanted. He also knew the man in their driveway hadn't been taking pictures.

As the man spoke directions into his phone, having dark shades on, Sosa heard the phone talk back, telling the lost man how to get back home.

"Shirley," Sosa said, worried about what had taken place. "We need to talk."

# CHAPTER 110

Jon waited. The next move was on the man. Kieran, still controlled by the spirit, was snarling and foaming from the mouth. Jon wasn't sure what to make of this. He knew Kieran was no longer in control. He knew the spirit controlling him was evil. Yet, Jon hadn't expected the spirit to be so animalistic.

Yet, it made sense. If it were human, it wouldn't have slaughtered so many citizens. If it were human, it would have seen the fault in its way, releasing the citizens to do as they pleased. But no, the spirit was animalistic. A beast that couldn't be controlled.

"You think you've got me?" asked the man through gritted teeth. "You forget that this is my city!"

Jon, along with the group, noticed the citizens who surrounded them. They were creeping in. Closing the circle. There was nowhere left for them to go. No place to escape. No point in surrendering. Tonight was out of Jon's control. He knew it was up to the spirit. He knew it was up to the big man himself.

As the citizens closed in, the man began to laugh. Calmly at first. Hysterically only moments later. Jon studied the man. Ignoring the citizens. Ignoring their impending doom. He wondered what had caused such evil to exist. And, worse yet, what had caused Kieran to seek such evil. Was this all for power? He couldn't understand it.

He could see the man's eyes. He could sense Kieran inside. Cowering. Fearing the worst. To Kieran, all hope seemed lost. Jon could empathize with Kieran. *A repentant soul,* he thought. *It's still not too late.*

# CHAPTER 111

Lucille nudged Lewiston. Hoping he had a plan. Hoping, if all else failed, that this spirit would guide them. Part of her wanted to fight her wait. To leave the city a bloody mess in her wake. Yet, it was the citizens surrounding them. They weren't bloodthirsty criminals. They were victims.

Mothers and fathers. Sons. Friends. Daughters. They were controlled by evil. By the man who now controlled their fate. This corrupt soul seemed to have them wrapped around his finger. That was when Lucille thought it best to run. That was the most reasonable option. To not hurt the people. To go and not look back.

She knew the city could not be saved. They had failed. *I have failed,* she thought. And yet she didn't run. She didn't leave like Sam had done. *Where is he, anyway?* She couldn't believe he had done this again.

Not after saving her. Not after restoring her to health after a group of thugs had bludgeoned her to a pulp. She knew he cared. Not only for her but for the group. For those who meant to save the city. *That must be it,* she thought. *We failed and he bailed.* It made sense.

They couldn't do it. They couldn't save his city. Lucille remembered when he had first bailed after seeing Kieran for who he was. He wasn't abandoning them but choosing the only reasonable option.

He knew Kieran's intentions. And though the group knew Kieran was out of control, no one had tried to stop him. *Sam knew,* she thought. *He knew we couldn't stop Kieran.* And just as they hadn't then, they couldn't now.

The man controlling Kieran was too powerful. Common sense dictated that if one spirit could control a whole city, he could also summon the citizens to come to his aid. The group was outmatched. Outwitted. All by a corrupt spirit. All by something they couldn't fight. She let her hands fall to her side. This was no longer up to her. It wasn't up to the group. They would need more than logic and force to get out of this.

# CHAPTER 112

Lewiston froze. Unable to move. Overwhelmed with fear. He knew this was inevitable. *We're going to die,* he thought. *We never had a chance.* His belief in Jon, in the spirit, in his group. All of it dissipated. Now understanding they could do only so much. Understanding that the evil they faced was more than man. More than logic.

It was power. Raw power. Power that was able to corrupt an entire city. *What chance did we have?* he thought. *I should have seen this coming.* But he hadn't. And each similar thought laid the groundwork for blame. Blame that he upheld. Blame for which he took responsibility.

Had he not recruited each person in the group, they wouldn't have been put in this situation. Had he not recruited each person in the group, Sam wouldn't have run for his life. It was his fault. Yet, a new question came to mind. *Where are you?* he thought. Lewiston had believed that he understood Sam. His intentions. His desire to save Albion.

Yet Lewiston also understood why he had left. It was the same situation as before. *But weren't we on the same page?* he thought. *Weren't we here to fight for the same cause?* The question drifted from his mind. It didn't matter. Lewiston knew they were going to die. After having followed the spirit. After having found Jon.

He knew this would be it. Here on Sentry Lane. In a city he thought he could save. He had overpromised and, in the process, lost a friend. Shelby was nowhere to be found, and at this point, Lewiston didn't want to find him. If he were alive, the city would have already corrupted him. And if he had found a way to fight the city's corruption, then he was surely dead. That was the only way out. That was the reason why no one could escape Albion.

Death tracked each victim. Any person daring enough to try to leave. And those who remained in the city, who were not corrupted by it, stayed hidden. Hidden in the shadows. Hidden in the shelter of the abandoned buildings. Lewiston knew they were there, though he had no proof.

He could sense it, just like when the spirit had guided him to Jon. *Jon,* Lewiston finally thought. *Please, Jon, save us one last time.*

# CHAPTER 113

Elias watched. Unable to understand. Unable to figure out where they'd gone wrong. How was one spirit more powerful than the other? Why had they been led into a trap? They were powerless. Defeated. But Elias didn't want to give up. He wanted to take a chance. To go after the man. To take the man's life even if it meant losing his. He didn't want to admit it but Albion had changed his perspective.

There was always one fight after another where he hoped to escape. Hoped to outlast the latest assailant only to come up short. *I won't waste this life,* he thought. *I didn't lose a friend only to die now.*

He thought about what the mayor would have done. How his friend would have approached this situation. Would he have hesitated? *Maybe,* Elias thought. *Maybe not.* He knew Wade cared about others more than himself. Yes, Wade's ego had gotten his name on the door to the mayor's office, but his caring belief and attitude toward the people of Brevington had made him the leader they needed. He committed to action even if it meant making a mistake.

He delegated what wasn't important and sought to do what was necessary. Even when people disagreed. Even when people, like Jon, became the beacon of hope in a city that didn't have worth. That was also what had landed them here: pushing Jon away.

Elias loved his friend and missed him dearly, but he knew he would take a different approach. He wasn't Wade. He wasn't a mayor. And he wasn't Jon or anyone else in the group. He was Elias Andreas. Judge Andreas to the people of Brevington. And he ruled with moral conviction, no matter the cost.

Whatever sentence he gave, whatever punishment he assigned, he did so out of integrity. Most of all, he did it to protect the people. Not just the citizens of Brevington, but those who were behind bars.

He wouldn't let them rot in a jail cell. The times he had sentenced Jon to a day, or even a week, in jail were times when he intended to show that he cared. He knew that Jon, unlike the other criminals, didn't need months or years at their correctional facility. He knew that all Jon needed was time.

Time to sober up. Time to think about what came next. And though Elias hated seeing Jon there, he would always visit. Elias visited all of the criminals who were behind bars. That was what made him different. That was what most criminals remembered and what most families of the incriminated never witnessed.

He was a good guy, despite what they said. Despite what his wife thought. *Emilia.* How long it had been since he had thought of her. How long it had been since he had remembered his initial reasoning for coming here. The city needed Jon. Elias needed hope.

Hope that he wasn't worthless. Hope that his wife had made a mistake and that he wasn't the one coming up short. Hope that he was as good as his friend believed. Hope that he could find Jon, and now, that he could help save Albion. There was a cost that came with doing the right thing, and Elias had paid the toll.

He had left his wife who had cheated on him. He had lost his friend who, although unwillingly at first, had decided to come with Elias to Albion. And now he would lose his life. He looked around, noticing the people he was with. A boy who had been presumed dead. A genius who was led by the spirit. A man whom many considered Brevington's savior. And a self-sufficient woman choosing to stand by their ragtag group instead of booking it to the next city.

He knew they weren't going to make it. That he would lose his life fighting for a city he didn't even belong to. And that was okay. He was okay with this. What he couldn't do was live a lie. To fight for nothing more than pride or power. And though he didn't know this Kieran fellow, Elias could see how going after such things caused damage. Irreparable damage. Damage bad enough that a man could lose his soul.

He didn't want that. Elias knew there was nothing left to prove. He would die with his integrity, alongside a group of men and women who believed saving lives was more important than greed.

*Not the worst way to go out,* he thought. *Not ideal, but definitely not the worst.*

# CHAPTER 114

Sam ran as fast as he could. Tightly, he gripped the item. His hope was restored as he made his way back. He now realized how far away the spirit had led him. How far away he was from the fight. How far away he was from Kieran.

A part of him felt bad. He wanted to help the man imprisoned by an evil spirit. Yet there was another part to Sam. A part that said Kieran had gotten what he deserved in merging with evil. It was the evil that had caused him hell growing up. Sam knew he didn't deserve that kind of childhood, and he knew he didn't deserve to lose his brother.

Thankfully, he had managed to see his brother alive, though his brother hadn't been the same. The evil had corrupted him, too. Sam knew that this was his chance to bring his brother back. The brother he remembered. Even if it meant risking his life. Even if it meant saving the city and not himself.

*That must be the lesson,* he thought while running down Sentry Lane. *To lose my life in order to gain a new one.* He wasn't sure if this made sense, but he wanted to believe it did. He wanted to believe making the ultimate sacrifice deserved some kind of reward. Regardless, he would have no regrets.

He would get the item to Jon just as the spirit planned. Even if he didn't understand how this was supposed to help. Sam eyed the item as he neared the crowd. Looking over the crowd, he could see his friends in the middle. The crowd was closing in.

He looked back at the item. "Not sure how a book is going to get us out of this," he said, "but it's worth a try."

# CHAPTER 115

Shirley went into the house with Sosa at her side. Once inside, they sat on the couch. Lately, this had been their place to discuss what bothered them. Since their last talk, spilling what was on their minds and hoping to somehow make their late son proud, they hadn't had any further discussions.

Both had bottled-up feelings. An inner battle was taking place. It seemed too much to bear. And though it hadn't been Sosa who had confronted the man, his thoughts were not far from Shirley's. It took a while for him to realize the man wasn't paparazzi, but the first few moments he believed otherwise.

Sosa had chosen to keep shooting instead of confronting the man. It would be a show of false strength. To keep doing what he knew how to do. Unafraid of the media. Unafraid of life finding ways to get worse. He was sick of being caged in, restricted from the world going on outside. At the same time, he knew there would be stories about him.

Lies and deceit. Some of which would probably be about his affair. He knew he would have to face it sooner or later. That was how the media worked. He knew that hiding from it didn't make it any better.

Yet here they were, sitting together. Shirley, still ashamed of the incident, held a pillow to her chest. Sosa, wondering what he could possibly say, sat idly, hoping she would speak first. He knew it would be hard. She was never afraid of admitting when she was wrong but today was different.

Today she showed a side of herself Sosa thought had been resolved. He thought his wife would understand that no matter how long they stayed in hiding, the media would find them, whether they made the occasional trip to the grocery store or went to a counseling session.

Eventually, the media would find them. Yet because he was the one who had caused this mess, he knew he couldn't fix it. Not on his own. Not without his wife trusting him. Trusting that things would be okay.

Her voice surprised him as she began to talk. "I know what you're going to say," said Shirley. "You're wondering why I snapped on that guy and—if I was really okay with continuing our marriage—why it was so troublesome to me."

She looked ahead. Too ashamed to face Sammy. Too afraid that she, the innocent one, was losing confidence. Both in her husband and in herself. She wanted to say that she was defending him. That she was making sure no one took advantage of his life or his fame.

But that wasn't true. She finally turned to face her husband.

"I was ashamed, Sammy," Shirley said. "I was afraid he would take pictures and see you, playing basketball as usual, and me, the housewife, inside. Doing what all housewives do when something out of their control takes place."

Sosa nodded. He knew it wasn't his time to talk just yet. He knew Shirley had more to say.

"And it just bugs me, you know?" Shirley squirmed in her seat. "I never saw myself as this person. The victim. The one remaining in a mess. It's just never been me."

She threw the pillow down in both anger and shame. Knowing she had lost control when she had spent the previous afternoon preaching to her sister about why she had stayed. That she had made the choice. That she was the one deciding to take the moral route instead of giving up. She wanted to believe that was still true. That she was in charge of her actions. That she would make it past this.

As she turned from Sosa, she realized that life would be hard, at least for a while. Accepting him back wasn't easy. She'd never had to forgive someone who lived with her. Who shared her bed. Who shared her heart. And she had never gone to such lengths to make sure that person, the only person in the world capable of hurting her so deeply, would be okay after trying to kill himself.

"I'm trying," she said between tears. "I really am. But this is so hard, Sammy! With Monty, and now this? I just feel like I don't know who I am."

Sosa decided to speak his mind. His whole mind, without leaving anything to be interpreted.

"Shirley, I've known you for so long, and I've seen what you've become." He moved slowly to her side though she still looked away. "Trust me when I say you haven't changed. You're still the strong woman I know. The strong woman I married."

She plucked a tissue from the coffee table and blew into it. Her makeup ran down her face. The strength she once felt now melted away.

"I put us here," said Sosa. "I've caused you to question yourself and what we are doing. I've also been hospitalized because of my mistakes. My drinking. Trust me, I know what it's like to view yourself one way and realize something else."

He didn't know if it was a good idea, but realizing that she was his wife and that she had stuck by his side despite the mess he had caused, he held her hand. Slowly, Shirley turned, yet still she didn't face him.

"You are strong, Shirley," Sosa said. "But now, after life has dealt its beating, and after the person you trusted most betrayed you, you have to show a different strength. A strength that doesn't seem to make sense to the world. A strength that shows you still have control over yourself. Isn't that strength worth showing?"

Shirley leaned over. Understanding her husband's words. Understanding this strength would be different. That she would have to face the world, her son's death, and her husband's betrayal, all at once. And as she did, she sobbed into Sosa's shoulder. She wasn't sure she could do it. More than anything, she wished Monty was still there.

# CHAPTER 116

Sam drew closer. The crowd didn't notice. A sudden truth came to mind: If he left, no one would know. No one would care. He didn't have to join the fight. He could return to the life he had once lived. Living more aware. More understanding of how the city worked and who was in charge. He could simply disappear and nothing would change.

He thought this over. The idea seemed appealing. But when the crowd didn't notice him, he noticed his friends. He wondered if he could walk away from this. If he could simply forget about the people he had met and the reason they had come together.

There was more to this. More of an investment. More tying him to the cause than a mere fantasy or wish. These were people who had given up everything to save his city. People who, upon first meeting him, should have punished him for trespassing. People like Shelby, who didn't know the city's power. Or Lewiston, who gave up all other pursuits of a genius's life to change what seemed impossible.

And Lucille. What couldn't he say about her? She was the sister he had always wanted. A fearless fighter who never took "no" for an answer. She remained by his side even when he left hers. Even after he abandoned her and the group, only to carry her on his back when she needed him most.

He didn't know Jon or the boy or the bald man. But he knew the others. He knew enough of them to not turn away. No matter how things ended. No matter whether they succeeded or failed.

He took a few steps forward. Those few turned to more. And to more until, after a moment, he was close enough to be heard.

"Jon!" he yelled. "Heads up!"

Sam noticed Jon. He was the only one from the group who seemed to hear, and yet the crowd turned as if Sam had spoken directly to them. As Sam tossed the book, Jon eyed the item. It glowed in the darkness and caught everyone's attention. No one other than Jon and Sam knew what it was. Only Jon knew of its power.

He reached out to catch it. As it landed in his hands, the man controlling Kieran turned. Not seeing how this could change their outcome. Not realizing that Jon had been handed the only thing that could stop the man from keeping Albion under his control.

Jon held the item as if it were an old friend. He didn't much care for reading it, but he knew that this was the time. This was the only way he would reach the citizens amidst the evil that surrounded him. This was the only thing, aside from the spirit, that could help him protect the boy. As he skimmed a few pages, parts of the crowd broke off, deciding it best to chase Sam.

Sam, already knowing the lay of the land, dodged them. He ran from one side to the other, doing what he did best, making sure they were not able to catch him. And while he was running, he realized the citizens were still under the man's influence. This made them sluggish and helped Sam avoid being captured.

Sam relished this and hoped it would give Jon enough time to find what he needed. The rest of the group watched as the crowd, no longer feeling the need to wait, collapsed in on them. Elias swung his bat with precision to make sure no one came close to the boy.

Lucille fought off the citizens, forbidding anyone from getting too close. Lewiston, though still in pain from having punched Kieran, grabbed hold of the collar of an oncoming citizen and, using the assailant's momentum, guided them away from the group.

Monty watched everything take place. He didn't want to fight. He didn't want to risk getting lost in the mayhem taking place. Instead, he remained by Jon's side, hoping Jon would keep his word and not let anything happen to him.

Kieran watched from within his body. Unsure of what was happening. Unable to comprehend how a book was going to help them. It never registered to him that the words Jon spoke to his guards—the group—were the same words that lay between Jon's hands. Yet as he watched the rest of the group fight off the crowd, Kieran noticed Jon and the boy.

Though they were in the middle of the fray, they remained untouched. The crowd didn't simply go around them but, in fact, found it impossible to reach them. Something protected them. Something not seen but clearly felt, as the many from the crowd bounced off it. Yet it wasn't just Kieran who noticed this. The evil that controlled him noticed, too.

Instead of waiting to see what would happen, he charged forward, throwing citizens aside, creating a path to Jon. Still, he found it hard to get through. There were too many in the crowd. When he threw one to the side, there was another to replace him. The man found this cumbersome, yet he knew that if he were to kill too many, he would have few in the city to rule.

Jon searched, flipping through pages, hoping to stumble upon something, anything, that might help them. Time was running out. His new friends could hold off the citizens for only so long. And though he yearned to find the right words, nothing seemed to come. Nothing jumped off the pages.

"Come on," he said to himself. "Show me something. Anything!"

It was then that he noticed a phrase. Something simple yet powerful. It didn't seem to help their situation but it brought him a certain peace. He looked up in time to see the man quickly approaching. The sea of people kept him from the group. Jon watched the desperation on the man's face, the fear that gripped him. The man realized this was no ordinary book. If it kept his people from getting to them, then something more was taking place. Another spirit opposing him. He might not have known its power, but he, and Kieran, now knew what gave Jon his power.

# CHAPTER 117

The ambulance arrived late. Few people noticed the woman sprawled on the sidewalk. Those who did, like many others in Jameson, believed the woman couldn't handle her liquor and wrote it off as her sleeping off the rest of the alcohol. They noticed the woman's condition. No one understood her plight.

Luckily for Emilia, the front desk worker had called an ambulance upon finishing his shift. He noticed the pool of blood beside the woman's body and decided, before making the call, to finish his smoke.

The ambulance completed the necessary protocol. A body bag. A detailed call to the local law enforcement. The department identified the woman, pulling her information from its database to find an emergency contact. When they called the number of one Elias Andreas, it ringed to voicemail. The voicemail was full. Upon hearing the judge's declarative message, the officers put two and two together: This was Judge Andreas's wife.

Her death made the news. Members of the Andreas family—Uncle Dario and Aunt Celia—were in awe. Many wondered why such a beautiful woman, the wife of Brevington's judge, was staying at a hotel in Jameson.

When questions were left unanswered, and Elias himself could not be found, the media began to speculate. Some said her death was due to another affair. Some believed the judge had ordered his wife to jump because of the humiliation he had endured. But in the end, most claimed alcoholism. It was cleaner that way. Especially when a woman leaped to her death in the city of Jameson.

A memorial was held, though the only ones in attendance were the funeral director and the janitor. Both found this to be very awkward. Both believed that at least one relative should have shown.

Because no one spoke on the woman's behalf, and no pre-paid plot had been purchased, the funeral director thought it best to have her cremated. As the cremation began, he brought over an urn. It wasn't much more than a plain vase with a lid concealing the ashes. Yet the only thing more difficult than setting up a funeral for a woman who had no next of kin or nearby family was figuring out who would keep her ashes.

"My God!" the director exclaimed after his twentieth attempt to contact a relative. "Did no one care for this woman?"

He decided to return the ashes to her home in Brevington. Upon delivery, the packaged vase was concealed enough to not tip over, yet not sturdy enough to avoid the collapsing weight of the other packages. The funeral director forgot to mark the package "fragile."

As the delivery man made his rounds, it slipped his mind that one more item remained. Two days later, he realized the delivery had not been made, as the package was brought back to shipping. Being the good Samaritan that he was, he took it upon himself to make the delivery.

After he found the address, he rang the front doorbell. No answer. He knocked a few times. Still, no answer. Believing the person receiving the package was not home, and not wanting to take the urn back to his home, he tried the front door.

To his surprise, it was unlocked. As he walked through the house, he noticed everything was out of sorts. Tissues lay all over the floor. Old food, which he believed needed to be thrown out, made the living room smell as if someone had died. He found this ironic, seeing that he was holding the remains of one of the owners of this house.

Finally, after moments of thought, he decided it would be best for the remaining owner to choose where the woman's remains should be. He set the urn on the counter. Happy that the job was done, he clasped his hands. It was, however, inconvenient that at the same time, he noticed something moving out of the corner of his eye. Fear jolted him as the creature moved closer, causing him to knock over the vase.

The ashes landed on the carpet—a cleaning task the good Samaritan didn't find it possible to undertake at the time. He soon realized the creature moving was the owner's cat, which appeared to not have been fed before the resident's departure. This sent a tingle down his spine.

"Okay," he said, looking down at the spilled ashes, then at the cat from hell. "Time to go."

And he did just that, leaving the house the way he had found it—besides the woman's remains spread over the floor. He locked the door on his way out, hopped into his car, and drove away, vowing to never make a personal delivery again. That was how Emilia would be remembered. That was how she would remain.

# CHAPTER 118

When the news spread of her friend's death, Shirley thought little of it. A part of her, the shameful part she would never admit to, thought that was what Emilia deserved. Another part of her was saddened that it had come to this. *That is rock bottom,* she thought. *Literally.*

Sosa, like his wife, didn't think much of it. Part of him—a part that he was less ashamed to admit—was happy Emilia wouldn't be able to benefit from their affair. He didn't know why she had told Shirley in the first place, but he guessed revenge might have been on her mind. He knew plenty of professional athletes endured lawsuits and blackmail so their secrets never came out.

Some went even further, as publishers and magazine writers offered large sums for such spilled tea. Sosa felt this was to her advantage. And yet another part, one saddened by her death, believed this was it. This was what it looked like to have no friends, no family, and no one to support you during difficult times.

In Emilia, he saw a glimpse of what his life could have been. Alone in a hotel. Drinking himself to death. Making the leap that would end it all. He realized he had practically completed two of those three things. Thankfully, he had survived. Thankfully, his wife hadn't left him. Long live Sosa.

# CHAPTER 119

Lucille continued fighting. Protecting the rest of the group. Holding her ground as the citizens tried their best to take her down. Lewiston did his best to make it to the other side of the street. Dodging the citizens. Doing his best Cowell impression, yet having no such luck. A person from the crowd snatched his leg, causing him to fall forward. He kicked off the man and rose to his feet.

Sam continued to round each corner, avoiding the citizens. Moving with ease as each citizen failed to catch him. He managed to see Jon reading. Sam hoped Jon would do something soon, that he would cause this to stop. Sam was getting tired. And though he was happy to be back with the group, Sam still wondered how this would turn out.

Elias swung his bat, hoping to only knock out the citizens. He didn't want to kill anyone. He didn't want to punish the citizens for the evil spirit's doing. He knew they were innocent. He knew they were under some type of spell. He also knew that, if given a choice, they would run away from all of this. From the violence. From the corruption. From the city.

Yet he couldn't help looking over his shoulder. Sneaking a peek. Wondering what Jon was up to. He wanted to help. To decipher the words. To give advice as only a moral judge could. But he didn't. This was Jon's arena. His area of expertise would have to suffice if they were going to make it out alive.

Monty waited by Jon's side, watching each citizen, noticing they couldn't get too close. Something stopped them. He didn't understand what, but he was glad for it. He tried to understand what Jon was doing. Monty recognized the Bible in Jon's hands but couldn't comprehend how a book was supposed to save them. He knew about God. His mom always brought him to church, even if dad had a home game. He understood certain aspects of Christianity. What it meant to be kind. Helping others even when it was inconvenient.

But this seemed different. They didn't teach this in kid's ministry, and it made Jon appear to be more than a hero. Not a savior, yet somewhere in between. Jon didn't lead them back to the city. He didn't even know how to avoid the many traps that the merciless killers set throughout the city. Monty had shown him the way. He had also shown Jon what alleys to not go down. How to avoid the chaos of the city.

In many ways, he thought he was more of a savior. This wasn't his home, but Albion wasn't hard to figure out: Everyone would hurt, betray, or steal from you. And even though he noticed Jon's struggle to get around the city, here—in the face of evil—Monty witnessed a man at peace. A man who was either foolish enough to believe this could work or smart enough to know they were going to die.

Jon held confidence in a way Monty had never seen. He didn't quickly flip through pages. No, Monty noticed the man slowly read the words. Jumping to chapters only after the last line had been read. He wanted to tell Jon to hurry up. That their lives were in danger.

But he couldn't. The very protection they held was because of him. Or the spirit. Monty didn't know. He couldn't tell who was in control because, of all the people there, the spirit had never personally led him. Not that he could feel. Not that he could tell. The closest he had come to the spirit was when he had found Jon.

Still, the only reason he had taken Jon up on his offer was that he was tired of being alone. Tired of rummaging through the trash by himself while other scroungers and thieves stole what he found. Going from a life of luxury to this made Monty think, *How did I get here? Am I really going home? Will they even remember me?*

There was no concept of time in Albion, so he didn't know whether days, weeks, or months had passed. All he knew was that he wanted to leave. To go home. To run into his dad's arms. Protected by his love and strength. It was only at that moment that Monty knew how to describe Jon: a father.

Like his father, Jon wouldn't let harm come to Monty. Like his father, Jon never abandoned him nor gave up on him when he was being stubborn.

Monty could see that there were more similarities than differences. The only conclusion he could reach was this: The spirit had led Jon here and God answered his prayers. He appreciated the spirit because of who he sent. He appreciated God because he was no longer alone.

# CHAPTER 120

Jon read the scripture twice. Peace washed over him. The Holy Spirit guided his thoughts. He knew this was the word he needed. He knew it had to be said. As he noticed Kieran about five feet away, Jon turned, choosing instead to look at the boy. The boy, already looking up, met his gaze. Jon could tell he was afraid. Unsure of how this would turn out. Unsure of the person who was supposed to save him.

"Do not fear, for he is with you." Jon knelt to the boy's height. "Do not be dismayed, for he is our God. He will strengthen you and help you."

He turned to see Kieran a foot away. He didn't bother moving. He just continued to speak as the man dove toward him.

"He will uphold us with his righteous hand."

Jon watched the man, inches away, fall to the ground. The man tried to get to his feet, yet he couldn't move. He was stuck.

Jon waited, crouching on bended knees.

"This was never up to me," he reminded the man. "To meet you here. To rescue this city. It was never my plan. I came only as a favor to a friend."

He turned to face the boy. Monty, relieved they weren't dead, let a tear fall down his cheek. It was the first time he had cried since being in Albion.

"You've done enough," Jon said to the evil spirit. "This city is no longer yours."

His last words proved fatal. The spirit controlling Kieran howled loudly. It was an ungodly sound that echoed off the buildings. Lewiston and Lucille clutched their ears and Elias collapsed to his knees. The power from the evil spirit blew by like a gust of wind.

Jon simply remained. Watching Kieran pass out. Knowing the spirit that once controlled him had relinquished its hold. Kieran was saved. Albion was finally saved.

# CHAPTER 121

Their feat produced little fanfare. Though they were timid at first, the citizens slowly made their way out of hiding. Sensing something had changed. Believing it was safe to finally show their faces. Jon greeted those who came out, assuring them the city was safe and no harm would be done. The citizens, not knowing Jon but sensing a different presence, took the man at his word. Families took to the street, happy to finally go outside. To finally see the city without fear. No one remembered the last time they had been able to simply live. To roam the city and see it for what it was. A peaceful place. A beautiful home.

Lewiston, after finding the corpse of his friend, held a burial for Shelby. The city, quickly coming to know those who had come to its rescue, attended. It was the largest turnout Jon had ever seen. And though he didn't know the man, Jon could piece together what had happened. *Another soul lost to the past,* he thought.

He was glad those days were over. He was glad the Holy Spirit, after all his bemoaning and doubts, had kept him alive. He had been sure he wouldn't make it through this. He had been sure this would be the last deed he'd be afforded before his death.

Now that he hadn't died and would be sticking around for quite some time, he decided to stay in Albion.

"I think you can understand my decision," he said to the judge. "I've done all I can for Brevington."

Elias nodded. "That you have, and we're proud to have had you." The judge looked around. Taking in the city. Seeing Albion for the first time without fear. Seeing the city, which had been lost to chaos and violence, finally at peace.

"I take it you'll lead them?" he asked.

Jon shrugged. "I don't know anything about leading people, judge. All I know is the spirit."

He held out his hand as a gentle breeze spread throughout the city. Elias, still in awe of their feat, simply nodded. He didn't know what would come next for his friend. He was just glad Jon had found his home. He had never liked seeing him in jail or drunk, which happened more frequently after the city hall incident, believing he was the cause for the man's self-destruction. This Jon was better. Albion's Jon would be the stuff of legends.

"I'll get people from Brevington to help out," Elias said. "They'll be happy to hear what you've done."

Jon shook his head. "Don't," he said, looking toward a building. "The city, though economically unsound, needs to find its own way. These people have lived in fear for years. They finally have a safe place to live. Elias," he continued, turning to the judge, "they finally have a home."

Elias understood. He knew Jon was not like Wade but in many ways, this would be better. Jon didn't care for popularity or winning the people's vote. Elias knew Jon was necessary for Albion to thrive as a city. And though he didn't know how Jon would do it, Elias imagined he would get a little extra help from above.

"What about the kid?" he asked. "Aren't you going to take him back to Durrington?"

Jon smiled. "No, I don't think I will." He turned to face the judge and pointed at the man's heart. "You should take him with you."

Elias, dumbfounded by the statement, stammered a response. "You... you're the one who saved him, Jon. Let the world know what you've done. There's no shame in that!"

"No," Jon agreed, "but there is pride. I've done enough interviews. I think it's time to focus on the work at hand. And with this," Jon held up the bible, "the city of Albion will receive rightful guidance. It's no longer on me."

Elias laughed. "Was it ever?"

"I suppose not," Jon said, dusting off the item. "Guess that's a bit of a relief."

"I bet it is," Elias said. "If you think it's best, I'll go take him back."

"Good," Jon said, "Oh, and take Lewiston with you."

Elias, not understanding the request, expressed confusion.

"Lewiston?" he asked. "Why would I bring him with me? And what makes you think the smartest of us all doesn't need to be stay and help you?"

Jon waved off the notion. "I have enough help here. Sam knows the city better than anyone, and Lucille will show the people sound infrastructure and goodhearted guidance. Plus, Lewiston thinks too much," Jon joked. "I'm afraid he'll get in his own way if he stays here."

"And you don't think he will in Brevington?" Elias asked.

"I don't," Jon said. "Brevington is a simple place filled with good people who want to do right. He wants to do right, too. This will be best for him because, for once, he'll be working toward bettering others instead of himself."

Elias thought it over. "Maybe," he said. "But what makes you think he'll want to leave?"

Jon laughed. "The city proved to be more than he could take, and I'm afraid the confidence he came with is no longer there. You'll have to show him the way, judge."

Elias didn't know Lewiston's background but from what Sam told him, Elias knew he was the leader of the group. A few mishaps and mistakes, however, led him to doubt his ability. Elias could see that Lewiston was a smart guy. He heard Lewiston's plan to save the city and he believed it might have worked if a greater evil hadn't spoiled it.

"I'll just have to go on faith with that idea," he said.

Elias turned to see Kieran, who was sitting on the ground across the street. Watching others pass by. Grateful, yet unsure of himself. Everything he aspired to gain had ended up hurting him. It had cost him his soul. He was lucky to have it back.

"What about him?" Elias gestured. "Brevington jail or community service?"

Jon looked over. Shaming Kieran was never his plan. And though the man across the street meant him harm, the Brevington savior doubted that man still existed. He believed these past few days had changed Kieran's perspective on power. It most likely changed his perspective on life, too.

"He stays with us," Jon said. "He might have meant us harm in the beginning but I believe that has changed." He turned to face the judge. "Besides, I have a special assignment for him."

# CHAPTER 122

Elias was ready to go but, having no way of getting back, was confused about what to do. Jon wondered the same. He knew his car was long gone. He also knew the chances of finding a functioning vehicle in Albion were slim to none. Not until moments later did a citizen of Albion, who was a little older than Elias, come around the corner in a vehicle very similar to Jon's 2012 Hyundai Sonata.

To Jon's surprise, the vehicle was, in fact, his. As the elderly man put the car in park, Jon walked up to the side. He smiled, still amazed at how God worked.

"Where'd you find her?" Jon asked.

The man pointed. "Farthest spot down Sentry Lane." He opened the door and stepped out, looking at the boy across the street. "Figured someone might need to get him home. I'm sure his parents are worried sick."

Jon shook the man's hand. "I couldn't agree more."

When Monty and Elias loaded into the car, Jon was the last to see them off. Lucille and Sam spoke briefly with the judge, thanking him for what he had done. They praised Wade for his sacrifice and for being the good man they believed he was. Then they spoke with Monty. Lucille, to her surprise, began tearing up, not necessarily wanting to see the boy go but understanding how much his parents must have missed him. She assured him that they missed him and would be more than happy to see that he was alive.

Sam said a few words—mostly advice on how to be a man and what kind of morals he should have. He realized it wasn't much considering his cowardly acts in the beginning, but he knew the boy better now. He didn't want Monty to make similar mistakes.

When Jon came to the passenger side to see Monty off, the boy hopped out of the car. He hugged Jon, who found it hard to let the boy go. Monty was the closest thing to a son for Jon, and the man knew he wouldn't have made it without the boy. He was glad to see Monty return to his parents, yet saddened at how unlikely it was that he would see the boy again. He patted Monty on the head.

"Remember what I told you," Jon said. "Your parents never knew you were alive. Cut them some slack. I'm sure their time grieving has brought more pain than you know."

Monty nodded. He knew Jon spoke the truth. And though he desperately wanted to return to his parents, part of him also wanted to stay. To be there with Jon, helping to rebuild the city. Wanting to see what became of Albion.

"Will I see you again?" asked Monty.

Jon shook his head. "It's unlikely," he said.

As the boy pulled away, Jon could see a tear trailing down Monty's cheek. Jon wiped it away, smiling. Assuring the boy that everything would be okay.

"I have a lot of work to do here," Jon said. "But I suppose the spirit rarely adheres to what I think is important."

Monty looked up. "And if the spirit tells you to come see me?"

Jon grinned. "Then I suppose I'd be a fool not to listen." He helped Monty back into the car. "You and I both know how stubborn the spirit can be. Now go. And remember, the spirit may not lead you where you want to go but it will always take you where you need to be."

Monty nodded, agreeing with Jon. Knowing, more than anything, that the spirit was inside him. As Elias pulled off and entered the highway, Monty whispered a prayer. He didn't know if his request would be answered or even heard. He didn't know if the spirit worked only for adults or at all. But as he nodded off, entering a deep sleep, he saw Jon holding his hands wide for the boy. Greeting him as if he had never left.

Monty woke moments later when Elias entered Durrington. He was happy to see his city again, but more than that, he was happy that his prayer had been answered.

# CHAPTER 123

Sosa washed dishes as Shirley planted new seed in the garden. It was a beautiful showing of nature and she took great pride in what she planted. It was the one constant in her life. And though some plants died, she knew others would sprout. She never grew anything worth consuming but every blossoming plant brought life to her and the rest of the neighborhood. They could tell this was her prized possession.

When Sosa finished drying the last dish, he decided to join her. He didn't care much for gardening, having killed more plants than he'd watched bloom, yet he knew it meant a lot to his wife. He knew she was proud of her work. And after everything he had put her through, he knew she could use the break.

Gardening made her relax. Sent her to a place so serene that life itself seemed to stop. When he joined her, it was as if he had entered her paradise. Her realm of calm and relaxation. He didn't dare ruin the moment.

Whatever she needed, he would tend to, and nothing more. She was glad he was there. For a moment, everything seemed as it should. As if nothing were missing. But the very thought of peace brought Shirley back to Earth. She was missing something. She was missing something she could never get back.

As she set down the last seed, Sosa could tell she was upset. Before he could say anything, a car pulled into their driveway. Sosa, more alert this time, rose to his feet. He never knew the paparazzi to be so bold.

As he approached, he noticed something odd. It wasn't how beat-up the vehicle was, though it had definitely seen better days, and it wasn't the unfamiliar bald man who was in the driver's seat. What he noticed seemed impossible. And yet, it was real.

"Shirley!" Sosa yelled. "Shirley come here!"

He ran to the passenger door, which opened before he arrived. Sosa couldn't believe what he was seeing. He couldn't wipe away the tears fast enough as the boy leaped into his arms. He knew this wasn't a dream. Monty was really alive.

He carried the boy back around the car. Shirley, not believing what she was seeing, held out her arms. Sosa was quick to oblige, letting his son go to her. Elias watched from a distance, tearing up. Thanking God for what he'd done. He turned off the car but didn't get out. He knew an explanation would be in order, but not right now.

They would need some time. It wasn't every day that a family was reunited. Elias knew this was Jon's doing. Jon's last promise to Mr. Barrister. He also knew that though Albion was saved, the spirit would have more in store for him, the Barnett family, the city of Albion, and the city of Brevington. So, he would wait as long as it took. He would wait for the spirit to tell him when the time was right.